In the third book of Heather Heyford's series, set in Oregon's wine country, a returning war hero and his "friend with benefits" discover that some vintages only improve with time . . .

Uncorking the Truth

When the town of Clarkston, Oregon, welcomes Captain Sam Owens home from the service, Sophia "Red" McDonald is first in line. The sassy psychotherapist has known Sam since they were kids, and the grown-up Sam is darned near irresistible. With his abs of steel and those gorgeous hazel eyes, he could have any woman he wanted. Naturally, Red is thrilled when he takes her hand . . .

She's a modern woman, happy to canoodle with the sexy soldier, no strings attached—until her heart changes the rules. Suddenly, after months of casual hookups, Red finds she wants more. She longs to possess Sam body and soul. But his warrior's heart was wounded long before he joined the service. As a therapist, Red has ways of making him talk. Only if Sam opens up and spills his secrets can they finally have everything their hearts desire . . .

Books by Heather Heyford

Intoxicating
The Crush

A Taste of Sake
A Taste of Sauvignon
A Taste of Merlot
A Taste of Chardonnay

Published by Kensington Publishing Corporation

Kisses Sweeter Than Wine

An Oregon Wine Country Romance

Heather Heyford

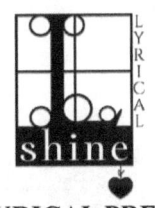

LYRICAL PRESS
Kensington Publishing Corp.
www.kensingtonbooks.com

Lyrical Press books are published by
Kensington Publishing Corp. 119 West 40th Street New York, NY 10018

All Kensington titles, imprints, and distributed lines are available at special quantity discounts for bulk purchases for sales promotion, premiums, fund-raising, and educational or institutional use.

To the extent that the image or images on the cover of this book depict a person or persons, such person or persons are merely models, and are not intended to portray any character or characters featured in the book.

Special book excerpts or customized printings can also be created to fit specific needs. For details, write or phone the office of the Kensington Special Sales Manager:
Kensington Publishing Corp.
119 West 40th Street
New York, NY 10018
Attn. Special Sales Department. Phone: 1-800-221-2647.

First Electronic Edition: August 2017
eISBN-13: 978-1-60183-828-5
eISBN-10: 1-60183-828-X

First Print Edition: August 2017
ISBN-13: 978-1-60183-829-2
ISBN-10: 1-60183-829-8

Printed in the United States of America

Chapter 1

The public display of affection at Poppy's Café was enough to make even a sensible girl like Red McDonald sink her chin in her hand and swoon.

Lost in each other's eyes, the two lovebirds were oblivious to the furtive glances of the breakfast crowd. The man's hands rested lightly on the woman's waist. Her arms extended straight across his shoulders, hands dangling limply from her wrists, her new diamond sparkling brilliantly in the morning sunshine.

"Take a picture," drawled Sam Owens, sitting across from Red, spreading lingonberry jam on his toast. "It'll last longer."

Red's palm fell to the Formica. She cut Sam a pointed look. "That's a cushion cut, one-point-five carat stone in a platinum halo setting, for your information. How can I not stare? Even if it were just a cigar band, can't you see how romantic that is…to have found the one? To have that deep down assurance that never again will you have to face the world alone, as long as you both shall live?"

Up at the register, the man kissed his fiancée's cheek. "See you at home tonight."

Home. Red continued to watch her friends and pictured the sleek, glass and steel structure on the bank of Chehalem Creek where Heath Sinclair and Poppy Springer lived. To her, it was paradise on earth. Not because of the impressive architecture. Red longed for a special place of her own. Not just another apartment or mobile home, but the permanence of four, solid walls surrounding her. A refuge where she could curl up at the end of each day, safe and protected from the outside world.

She sighed audibly while the pent-up force of nature across from her devoured his toast in one bite and, grabbing his mug, washed it down with a slug of Stumptown Hairbender.

The bell above the café door clanged and in walked Juniper Hart, making a beeline for the counter. When she spotted Red and Sam, she cut a detour over to their corner booth.

"Hey, you guys." She turned to Sam. "I just dropped off two cases of pinot at the consortium. Your idea for a monthly wine subscription was genius."

Red gave Sam an inquiring look.

"He didn't mention it to you?" Junie asked. "Sam came up with a plan to let customers sign up for two reds and two whites a month from any local vintner. They can either pick them up at the consortium or have them shipped practically anywhere in the country. Their order comes with information about the wine and the winemaker, plus a recipe written by the chef at The Radish Rose."

Red cocked an admiring brow at Sam. "Well. Aren't you the marketing ninja?"

"It's the cross I bear," replied Sam with an air of nonchalance, folding another toast triangle into his mouth.

Red saw right through Sam's cocky attitude. Beneath those taut pectorals beat the heart of a teddy bear.

"There were the usual naysayers," Junie continued. "The ones who said Sam was crazy. But he turned out to be brilliant. Ask any winemaker. Any grower. None of us know what we did before Sam came along."

"Junie, your order's up," called Poppy from behind the register, setting a paper bag and two lidded cups on the counter.

"That'll be Manolo's sticky buns. I bribed him to come with me to meet up with my mom. Glad I ran into you two. Mom's still waiting for your RSVPs. She needs an exact head count. You two and Keval are the only three still in limbo."

Keval Patel, the Clarkston Wine Consortium's god of I.T. And, like Red, a perennial singleton. Put like that, being single sounded so...sad.

Red pasted on a smile. This was Junie's special time, and she was her sole wedding attendant. There was no time for her own wishful thinking.

"I still can't believe you and Manolo are getting married in two months."

Love was definitely in the air these days. Heath and Poppy were the second couple in Clarkston to announce that they were tying the knot. Of course, everyone had always known they were meant to be.

But this time last summer, Junie was alone and in dire straits. All the smart money was on her losing her vineyard to creditors and moving to Portland with her mother to get a "real" job. And then Sam's Army buddy, Manolo Santos, had come to town and transformed Junie's tasting room into one of the hottest destinations in the Yamhill-Clarkston viticultural area, just in time for the annual fall crush.

"Eight weeks. I know you're both coming. Just do me a favor and pop your replies in the mail so Mom can scratch you off her list, okay? She's making me a little nuts these days." She rolled her eyes. "Even more nuts than usual."

Nothing, not even a prickly mother of the bride, could pop Junie's bubble, Red realized. Her happiness was almost palpable.

She sighed yet again. *How romantic.*

"Bye!" Junie's fingers fluttered in farewell, flaunting her own stone in its antique setting, handed down through Manolo's family.

And then it was just Red and Sam again. *So,* thought Red. *He hasn't responded yet, either.*

A less competent man might simply have forgotten. Not Sam. There was a carefully calculated reason for everything he did, every move he made.

Her cream-colored invitation addressed to Dr. Sophia McDonald and Guest that she carried around in her bag was getting more tattered by the day. Every time she went for her keys or her wallet, there it was, a nagging reminder that she had no partner.

Obviously, Red was going to the wedding. It was the blank line next to, "and Guest" that had made her nibble the edge of a fingernail yesterday, ruining her manicure before it even dried.

"What's your excuse, Owens?"

"It's probably lying in the bottom of my inbox." He studied her lazily, his long, tawny lashes like crescent moons above those shining eyes…eyes that seduced her without even trying.

If only there were a romantic bone beneath those abs of steel, to go with the charisma.

"Besides, you know what they say. Fifty percent of marriages end in divorce, the other fifty end in death."

"Samuel Owens. That's an awful thing to say."

Sam attacked his omelet, oozing cheddar all over the sturdy china plate. "You know the stats."

Oh, she knew. If it weren't for relationship problems, she'd have no practice. But where was Sam's sense of hope? His optimism? She fought the urge to both slap him and kiss him. How could any man be so charming and so infuriating at the same time?

While he was preoccupied with his breakfast, Red studied Sam's perfectly bowed mouth and slightly crooked nose, courtesy of Rory Stillman's mean fastball freshman year. He was charming, all right. Charming almost to the point of arrogance, if you hadn't known him back in the day—before he was Clarkston's favorite son. Sam was that scruffy kid who came to school with uncombed hair, wearing clothes that looked slept in. He had never been gorgeous in the classic sense. And he had more issues than *Vogue*. So lately, why did her heart thump like a rabbit's foot every time she was in his presence?

"Omelet's great. How come you aren't eating?"

"I'm not hungry."

How could she tell him she'd begun losing her appetite whenever he was around? And that while it was nothing for her to strike up an intimate conversation with a pure stranger, she'd begun stumbling over her words to Sam, and conversely, giving *his* words way too much weight?

Sam glanced up from his plate and caught her staring.

Immediately, she averted her eyes.

"Don't tell me you're on a diet."

"No." Not only had Red never been rail-thin, she'd had the humiliating distinction of being the first girl in the seventh grade to need a bra. But that was sixteen years ago. Since then, she'd come to accept—even appreciate— her womanly curves, the same way she was grateful for having inherited her mom's long legs, her grandma's blue eyes, and the thick, auburn hair of her Scots-Irish ancestors.

"Good. I like a woman with something to hold on to," Sam said with wink, smiling around his sticky bun.

Not *one* woman. *A* woman. Meaning, *any* woman.

And that was precisely the problem.

It was all her fault. *She* was the one who had pursued *him*, starting the night of his homecoming celebration, when she'd accidentally-on-purpose spilled her Riesling down the front of his uniform. In hindsight, she didn't know what she'd been thinking. No—she *hadn't* been thinking. It was purely the hormonal response of a healthy, warm-blooded woman at the sight of a hot guy in desert camo.

That is, at first.

For over a year, Red was content to hook up with Sam whenever, wherever. She was a modern woman. When it came to love, she kept her senses. After all, practicality and flexibility were two of the traits that had helped her rise from humble beginnings to the respected professional she was today.

But lately, she felt some deep, seismic shift. An incandescent tingle of joy swirled inside of her at the mere mention of Sam's name. What was worse, she felt like her feelings were written all over her face. It amazed her that no one—not Sam, their many mutual friends, not even Grandma—had a clue.

"I can't blame Junie for the nudge. The replies are due back in a matter of days," Red said, regretting her words as they came out of her mouth. Some modern woman she was. She sounded like an old school marm scolding a student about a late assignment.

Sam spread his palms and let them drop. "Goes without saying that I'm going."

"You still have to mail back the reply card. It's a courtesy to Junie and her mother. A lot goes into planning a wedding reception, you know. There's the food and the cake and the seating plan—"

"They're keeping it simple. I figure all I have to do is remember the rings and judge the number of shots of tequila it'll take to, A, get the lieutenant down the aisle and, B, keep his feet through the recitation of the vows."

"*Sam.*"

"Right. There's the speech. Hope I don't get a last minute case of the jitters."

"You? Stage fright? Not likely. But what about supervising the guest parking—"

"Taken care of. Hired a couple of neighbor boys."

"—and the music?"

"Manny and Junie want to make their own playlist. Already booked the DJ."

"How about organizing the bride and groom's departure from the reception?"

He laughed easily. "Don't worry about me. When did I ever not step up to the plate? What's with you, anyway, Doc? Ever since the fashion show, you're getting as wrapped up with weddings as you are with houses."

They'd worked together on The Brides for a Cause fundraiser earlier that spring, to benefit couples in need. Maybe that was the trigger for all these weird, nesting feelings she'd been having. In the months since the benefit, she'd collected enough ideas on her computer to start a full-fledged bridal blog. And she spent her evenings hoarding even more pictures of rings, her favorite, full-skirted dress styles, and the most painstakingly crafted cakes.

So far, it was an untidy agglomeration. Red was far better at collecting pictures than she was organizing them.

The wedding board might be new, but her assortment of old house pictures had started even before she was old enough to borrow Grandma's car to drive around hunting for them. Last year she'd even rescued a crumbling Victorian from the wrecking ball by bringing it to the attention of the local historical society. Now it sported a fresh coat of Loch Blue with Wild Currant trim, shades from the official Newberg Downtown Coalition Color Palette.

But Red didn't spend her valuable weekends house hunting out of goodwill. She was driven by the concept of home. The very word conjured up a slew of clichés: the smell of warm apple pie in the oven and newly mown grass. She'd sat on the other side of the couch enough times to recognize those as symbolic of an entrenched longing for security that dangled just out of reach of transient kids like her. But that didn't stop her from searching. She was still bound and determined that one of these days, if she just kept looking, she would stumble across the one house that would satisfy her deepest need.

Meantime, she lived with her grandmother, sharing expenses, driving an old clunker. Saving every cent toward the day she finally pinned down her forever home.

Her only indulgence was a regular manicure, though she sometimes forgot to show up for it.

"Maybe you're right. Or maybe it's because I'm maid of honor, and I'm already getting anxious about my responsibilities."

"What do you have to do besides..." He blanked. "What the hell *does* a maid of honor do?"

Astounded by his blissful, male ignorance, Red began counting off the daunting list of tasks that had to be accomplished in the next two months. "Go with the bride to her final fitting so I know how to get her into her gown when the saleswoman isn't around. Check off my own copy of her to-do list to make sure no detail falls through the cracks. And then there's the bachelorette party."

Sam's head came up from his eggs.

"Oh. You haven't heard? We're taking Junie to see The Lumber Jack Hammer Show a couple of weeks before the wedding."

Sam coughed on his gulp of Hairbender.

"You okay?"

His eyes watering, he shook his head and slurped from his water glass. "Toast crumb. Does Manolo know about this?"

She lifted a brow and shrugged. "I think so. It's not a secret."

"Isn't Lumber Jack Hammer a little, I don't know...*racy* for Clarkston girls?"

"What do you mean?" Red huffed, insulted. "Junie and Poppy and I are plenty racy. In case you don't remember, Cool Pain invited me back to his hotel room after that concert at Edgefield. Nothing *happened*, mind you. All we did was drink a little pinot and listen to music. But it could have, if I hadn't had an eight o'clock final in Behavior Modification the next morning."

"I'm sure Cool Pain was impressed with your academic dedication. All I was saying is that, in my humble opinion, Junie doesn't exactly seem like the strip show type."

She peered up through lowered lids. "It's called delegating."

"Ohhh." Sam nodded sagely. "Delegating."

"It was Mona's idea." Mona Cruz was a single mom of two who had spent time in Los Angeles before returning to Clarkston and going to work for Sam. "Letting Mona take the reins of the bachelorette party gives me one less thing to do. Mona says Lumber Jack's the hottest act around for bachelorette parties. He's like six-five and totally ripped. We were lucky to get in." Her eyes grew round. "She said one bride-to-be actually left her fiancé for him."

"So much for the rule against exotic dancers fraternizing with the customers," Sam mumbled.

"I know, right?" She giggled. "Kind of sleazy." More soberly, she added, "But fascinating, from a purely behavioral standpoint."

"Don't worry so much, Doc. It'll all fall into place." Sam wiped his mouth, crossed his arms, and sat back against the padded booth. "Live in the present. Isn't that what all those self-help books say? Speaking of which, what are you doing the next couple hours?"

His eyes glittered with meaning.

"Looking for that house again." *Don't cave.* She might be putty in Sam's hands, but she wouldn't be sidetracked today, on her day off.

He smirked. "Again? You're obsessed."

"Maybe it has something to do with growing up in trailer parks," she said.

Their eyes flirted in a mirror memory of harder times, hers of free school lunches and thrift store clothes, and Sam's of somewhat murkier origin.

"You may be happy to go on living in your old office forever, Owens. But I want a real house. And I'm not stopping till I find it."

"Go on." He cocked his head, humoring her. "Tell me what it is about this one that's got you so fired up."

"I've been doing some research," she said eagerly, "and I think there's a good chance it might be the only surviving saltbox in Yamhill County."

"Saltbox?" Sam's eyes grew guarded.

"A style of architecture that's two stories in the front and one in the back," she said, sketching a rectangle in the air with her finger. "It got its name from the lidded boxes the early New England settlers kept salt in. A few of the original Oregon pioneers built them, but overall, they're scarce. They're easy to spot, though, from the central chimney and the long, low rear roofline."

"How do you know about this place?"

A small part of her took note of Sam's knuckles, white around his balled up napkin. But her fascination with the house eclipsed all else.

"Back when I was living with my mom, she used to drive way out past

Meadowlake Road to one of those U-pick places to pick strawberries. I made her take a picture of it. Still have it. Want to see?" She brought up the photo on her phone and turned it his way. "It was different from all the other houses. It's been stuck in my mind all this time."

He looked at the image and though his fingers barely brushed against hers, his touch reverberated throughout her body.

An untrained observer never would have caught Sam's face falling for that split second. Maybe not even another PhD in Psychology—if she didn't also happen to be attuned to his every nuance.

Red frowned at him. "What's the matter?"

His face returned to normal with a speed that had her not trusting her own eyes. Then his gaze darted around the room and circled back to her. When he leaned in, she fell into their depths, trying for the umpteenth time to put a name on their color. *Hazel. No, Amber. No—*

"Brought the extra helmet and the blanket roll on the back," he said in a whisky-smooth voice. "Weather's perfect. Forget the house. Let me take you for a ride."

An expanse of azure blue filled the front windows of the café. She pictured herself on the back of his Harley, wind whipping through her hair.

She knew what would happen if she said yes…the same thing that always happened when she and Sam went riding.

She bit her lip.

"I've been looking for that saltbox for weeks, and I'm getting close. I can feel it. Maybe we can do something else together later. Like, see a movie or something."

She held her breath. Sam didn't do movies, or romantic dinners for two, or any of the other things official couples did—like go to weddings together.

True to form, he didn't get sucked in. Just gave her that sideways grin that made her insides go gooey. "What's better? Some old, run-down house? Or you and me and a bottle of Montinore 2014 Reserve out on Ribbon Ridge? We'll stop and get some good bread and cheese. Have a picnic."

Under the table, Sam's foot rubbed against hers. She felt like there was an invisible string attached to her core, pulling her toward him. It was all she could do not to slide out of her seat and into his, wrap herself around him, and confess her infatuation for the whole town to hear.

But that would send him running for the hills, not to mention scandalize Poppy's breakfast crowd and jeopardize Red's reputation as a mental health professional.

She shivered. How did he get to her? Make her put aside her priorities for him?

She knew how. As pragmatic as he was in public, the real Sam was the most loving, giving man imaginable. And not just because he'd volunteered space in his new consortium building for her favorite fashion show charity. When they were alone, he knew exactly how to please her. How to coax her along...draw out her pleasure at his own expense until the look of raw need in his eyes alone was almost enough to send her over the edge. Finally, when she was beyond ready, he unleashed a passion that had her moaning, clawing his blanket, and thrashing around in ways that never failed to leave her limp as a noodle, her cheeks burning with the memory.

Sam grabbed both their checks and got to his feet. "Meet you in the usual spot in five."

And Red knew she would be there, back behind her office a few doors down from the café, waiting.

Chapter 2

After his rendezvous with Red, Sam dropped her off in the alley behind her office and waited to make sure she got safely inside.

He should run over to the consortium before it closed. When you had your own business, Saturdays were no different than any other day. There were always a million and one things that needed doing. But ever since Red had opened up that can of worms about the saltbox, he couldn't push it out of his mind.

Instead of going to work, he steered the bike back out of town in the opposite direction from where he had taken Red. Out onto Meadowlake Road.

When he was growing up, Sam thought the only good thing about his house was that it was the last stop on the school bus route. None of the other kids saw him get on or off. That meant he didn't have to worry about any of them coming over unexpectedly, witnessing what passed for normal in his family.

Not that his formative years were all bad. In the summer, he and the O'Brien brothers down the road had the freedom to do anything they wanted. Looking back on those times, he, Jeff, and Derek lived their lives the way boys should live everywhere, in every age. Hunting small game, fishing Walker Creek for cutthroats, camping out in the woods for days. Happily subsisting on a diet of cereal and candy bars and the occasional coho salmon roasted over a campfire.

And there was Sam's dog, Riggley, never far from his side.

All of that was before Mom left and Dad hooked up with that woman from Tualatin. Penny was her name. But Sam and his brother and sister refused to honor her with it. Any woman dumb enough to hook up with Psychodad didn't deserve their respect.

Although Sam could see the O'Brien house from his bedroom window in the winter when the leaves were off the trees, it sat across some invisible line in the McMinnville School District. Instead of Clarkston Elementary, Jeff and Derek went to Memorial.

It was the first of many divisions in Sam's life.

Past the reservoir, Sam hung a left on the lake access road. His body leaned easily into the curves, at one with his bike. He knew where the hairpin turns hid at the bottom of hills, where the stretches of road were that remained in shadow on the brightest July day, marking the distance to his destination.

Twenty minutes later he came to the remnants of the lean-to he'd jerry-rigged out of a couple sheets of corrugated tin scrounged from Dad's junkyard, the summer between fifth and sixth grades. The previous winter they'd gotten slammed with rain. Day after day, Sam had shown up at school soaked. The bus stopped a quarter mile away. But standing in the freezing rain waiting was better than missing it, then having to stay home all day. Dad worked the opposite way from school, in McMinnville. He would never have gone out of his way to drive Sam in.

He hung a right and then a left, expertly centering the bike in the ridge between the ruts, and finally pulled up to the front door of the mud brown house and climbed off his bike.

As always, his eye went first to the little white cross planted in the earth beneath his bedroom window.

He went over and squatted next to it before yanking out the relentless dandelions and snakeweed that would have obscured it by now, if not for his regular attention.

Sam's face softened, remembering the day one of Mom's strawberry customers carried a cardboard box from her car into the yard. She sat it down, tipped it on its side, and onto the grass spilled a white puppy with splotches of black, ears flopping forward in little triangles.

The puppy immediately went exploring, tail wagging double time, making his mother's chickens cluck and dart out of her way.

"She's the runt of the litter. I thought Sam might like to have a dog. Give him some company out here," said the customer, with a glance at Sam's house—the only house for miles.

Sam squatted and the dog trotted straight into his arms. She was stronger than she looked. Sam fell backward and the puppy climbed onto his chest, tickling his stomach.

"She likes you," said the lady with a smile, pleased with herself.

"She's all wriggly." Sam laughed, squinting against the dog's pink tongue licking his face.

From that day on, Sam and Riggley were a pair.

Sam rose from where he knelt and went to the door. He inserted his key in the padlock, released the shank, and let himself in, looking around the kitchen, trying to see it through the eyes of Red McDonald.

The house had to be a hundred years old. The smell of smoke from the recent chimney fire still hung in the air. He looked up at the water-stained ceiling. If he ever wanted to try to sell it, the least it would need was a new roof.

But Sam had no plans to sell.

Dad wasn't quite as ancient, but he was getting up there. There'd been some worrisome incidents. Last spring, a bar owner had repaid a favor and called Sam instead of the cops when Dad had had one too many Hood River Vodkas. Sam walked into the bar to catch Dad moving in on the young wife of a grizzled motorcycle enthusiast flying the colors of a well-known outlaw gang. Sam had had to do some fancy footwork to get them out of that one unscathed.

And in May, a mysteriously torn tire wall on Dad's truck had left him stranded. When Sam arrived less than an hour later, Dad was still shaken up. He didn't even object when Sam took charge of calling AAA to arrange for the tow.

Just last week, Sam left work mid-day on a hunch to check on things. He walked in just as Dad tossed a match to a fresh stack of split wood on top of the gas fireplace "logs."

Sam could still hear Dad giving him hell for saving his hide.

Maybe he was right. Maybe he should've let him be. Everyone would be happier right now. Instead, Dad was cussing and screaming at the nurses over at the assisted living place. Making them miserable the same way he made every person he ever came in contact with miserable, his whole life long.

Sam's thoughts went back to Red and her obsession with old houses. He wandered through the first floor, trying to understand the attraction. But all he saw was conflict in every corner.

All of his problems originated here, in this house.

He trudged upstairs, accurately predicting which steps would creak beneath his feet, and peered into what had been his bedroom.

He looked at the empty space where his narrow brass bed used to be. He'd spent many a winter night shivering in that bed when that corner took the brunt of the northwest winds. Dad had permanently banned Riggley to the back porch. But sometimes, on the very coldest nights, he managed to sneak him onto the bed with him.

There had never been any question of Sam moving back into this place two years ago when he'd come back to Oregon to stay. Instead, he'd hauled the few childhood possessions he still wanted over to his room in the old consortium in Clarkston.

In his whole life, Sam rarely spent time in this house without his dad lurking nearby. Now that Dad was stuck in Woodcrest without the keys to his truck, Sam should feel better about it. More at peace. Yet all he felt was the same old sinking sensation in the pit of his stomach.

He couldn't stop wondering if maybe, when he had saved his dad at the last second, he had interrupted a brilliant plan. *Suicide by fireplace.* Had to give Psychodad credit—it wasn't a bad one. Given his recent spates of bad judgment plus the deteriorating condition of the house, it might easily have been dismissed as an accident.

Sam could never wish his own father dead. But to watch this house and all its painful childhood memories go up in flames? The idea was dangerously tempting.

Chapter 3

Red cast an analytical eye at the couch against the window where twelve-year-old Cassadee Berg slouched with one cleated sneaker tucked under her, nervously fingering the hem of her soccer shirt.

Red insisted that all her patients deposit their cell phones in a basket by the door during session. Out of sight, out of mind. Deprived of their devices, kids were lost as to what to do with their hands.

"Tell me about your mom."

"She's great," said Cassadee in the resigned tone that said she'd rather be anywhere but a therapist's office on a sunny, summer afternoon. Yesterday's showers had tapered off, and the playing fields at Clarkston Middle School were finally drying out. "A saint, almost."

Red smiled sympathetically. "It can't be easy, living with a saint."

Fiery brown eyes looked up from her lap. "It's not like that."

Defensive, Red jotted on her pad.

"Okay. How 'bout your dad?"

"He's great too."

Red summoned patience and tried to ignore her rumbling stomach. At Pat Berg's frantic phone call, she had agreed to fit her daughter in after her full day of clients and a half-eaten apple for lunch. She was going to be late for supper—again. Grandma was going to be fit to be tied.

Note to self: Start setting boundaries. But she already had made that note, more times than she cared to recall.

They'd already gone over Cassadee's school life, siblings, and friends. Something must be awry at home, or the girl wouldn't be plagued with nightmares. She'd have to dig a little deeper.

"Anything make your dad mad?" she asked conspiratorially.

But Cassadee wasn't taking the bait. "No."

"Never?"

"Not really," she replied sullenly.

"Nothing makes him mad. He's always in a good mood," opined Red, challenging her young client to refute her.

Cassadee sighed, sat on her hands, and gave Red a stony look.

Red had been well versed in the theory and techniques of cognitive behavioral therapy at Oregon State. But since opening her own practice, she'd found that sometimes, to speed up the process, it helped to put your personal spin on things. Share something of your own experience in exchange for getting the client to talk.

She turned her head to the side, parting her hair over her right temple. "See this? Scar from the time my stepdad threw a beer bottle at my head for talking back. Four stitches. Well, technically, he was my second stepdad."

For the first time, Cassadee looked interested. "What happened to the first one?"

To tell her that her first stepfather had left after her mother slashed his truck tires for coming home drunk one too many times would be overkill. Save the big guns for later, if needed.

Instead, she just shrugged. "One day he was there; the next, he wasn't."

Cassadee's head jerked up, remembering. "Well. There is something."

Finally.

"Something that makes Dad, really, really mad. So mad, he rants and raves and gets in a bad mood for like a whole week."

Now they were getting somewhere. Red pictured James Berg, down at the gas station and convenience store he owned on 99. James had been pumping Red's gas since she got her first car. He appeared to be well adjusted, but you never knew what went on behind closed doors. Did he have hidden anger issues that he took out on his daughter? Was that what was causing Cassadee's night terrors?

"What's that?" Red cocked her pen above her notepad and leaned in, preparing to write fast.

"Taxes. He hates taxes more than anything."

Red sighed back into her seat again and clicked off her pen. If James's taxes were anywhere near as complicated as hers, no wonder he got mad when April came around.

To a yawning noise from her belly, she clicked her pen back on and scribbled a note as to where they'd left off.

"We'll pick up from here next week."

Cassadee sprang toward the phone basket as if shot from a sling and immediately began trolling for missed messages, while behind her, Red stood and stretched out her lower back muscles, stiff from sitting all day with barely a bathroom break. She took no offense. When it came to adolescents, self-absorption was the norm, not an aberration.

* * * *

Red breezed into the trailer she shared with her grandmother. "Sorry I'm late for dinner, but I got a call about a girl who's been having trouble sleeping and I didn't want to make her wait until next week."

"The baked potatoes have been done an hour. They're all shriveled up by now, but I suppose they'll taste the same."

"Sorry," said Red again, hurriedly washing her hands at the kitchen sink. "But this couple is worn out from lack of sleep. The girl keeps crawling into their bed in the middle of the night."

"I suppose you know what you're doing," said Grandma, setting down two filled plates on the tiny table. "Sit down, why don't you, and I'll say grace."

After the ritual, Red sliced into her soft potato. "The meatloaf smells heavenly. I'm starved."

"Probably didn't take time out for lunch."

How did she know?

"So. Tell me what's going on with this wedding you're helping plan for Junie. You're always running, like a chicken with its head cut off."

"There's not much to plan, actually." After Red's mother disappointed her, Grandma had raised Red with a stricter hand. Now that she was an adult, Red preferred to keep some aspects of her personal life to herself, to avoid Grandma's scrutiny. Most of the time when Grandma thought Red was wedding planning, she was actually with Sam.

"Junie's an only daughter, and her mom is taking charge."

"A blessing in disguise, what with all the hours you put in down at your practice. And I thought I was a hard worker, back when I was working two jobs to make ends meet."

"Actually," said Red, dotting her potato with butter, "I'm a little disappointed. I was kind of looking forward to having more of a hand in it. Not that I begrudge Junie's mom. It's her daughter's wedding. She's entitled to do things her way."

"You always were the first to want to lend a hand."

"That's why I became a therapist in the first place—to help people."

"That's you, a bit of a Pollyanna. Giving people more credit than they deserve."

Red recognized that for what it was—a dig at Red's mom, now residing in one of Portland's less savory neighborhoods with her latest in an endless string of broken men.

"I've told you before, Grandma, it would be healthier for you to let go of your resentment where my upbringing is concerned. I have."

"You're just like your mother. You got too big a heart. That's going to get you into trouble one day."

"I like people, that's all," said Red, scooping up a forkful of meatloaf.

Grandma pointed at Red, her knuckle gnarly from the menial jobs she'd worked over the years to feed and clothe her only grandchild. "Your mama likes people too. Likes fixing them. Likes it so much she put them before her own flesh and blood, before giving you a stable home life. Why do you think you're so stuck on finding the perfect house?"

Red remembered the year she lived at Sunrise Trailer Park—though someone had painted an 'i' over the 'u' to make it look like 'Sinrise'. The park was close enough to the school that she could walk. Half the time it was drizzling. But instead of ducking her head, Red's eyes greedily soaked up every house along Vine Street. There were the cozy, Craftsman-style bungalows with board siding and distinctive, four-over-one double-hung windows. The boxy colonials whose front doors, brightly painted in hues of tomato and Kelly green, tempted Red to reach for their shiny brass door knockers. And the gingerbread-trimmed Victorians, ornate as wedding cakes. That early impression was what had brought her to the defense of one of them just last year, when it was slated to be torn down after the original owners passed and their far-flung heirs neglected it for too long.

The town of Newberry might be architecturally diverse, but in Red's childhood imagination, the interiors of those houses looked exactly the same. Each one had the same plaid couch, wood paneling, and comforting familial chaos of her favorite TV sitcom. Though the day might bring problems and bickering, by bedtime all the family members returned to the fold and whatever troubles had arisen were settled. Just like in the show, the children in those houses went to bed secure in the knowledge that a team of two adults—whose number one priority was their children's wellbeing—slept down the hall.

At the far end of Vine, the sidewalk ended and the smooth pavement dropped off to the gravel road. Barking dogs strained against their ropes as Red shuffled past. Dish TV antennae jutted out with tangles of wires beside portable air conditioners. The older model cars of the residents came to rest at random angles, as if straightening them out wasn't worth the trouble.

Red held her breath on trash day when she walked past the stinking black plastic garbage bags and melting cardboard boxes. Even at that age, she already recognized it as the smell of just getting by.

Here a pair of flowered curtains fluttered in a kitchen window; there some discarded cinderblocks had been repurposed for a flower bed. But unlike the Vine Street houses, you never knew what you might see inside the trailers. Red's only hope was in knowing that they never stayed anywhere for long. And sure enough, by the next year, she and her mother had moved to an apartment and Red rode the bus to school.

"Stop worrying about me, Grandma. I'm fine. I can take care of myself now. Not just me, both of us. I'm making decent money...finally."

"I'm not talking about money. I'm talking about love."

Now was probably not the time to tell Grandma that she'd just signed on as a consultant with the senior living center. The added responsibility might be pushing it, but the extra money would come in handy.

Red sipped from her water glass and tried not to think about "love"—especially not "love" and "Sam Owens".

"All right. I'll stop harpin' on it before I start soundin' like one of your whatchamacallit, meetings, is it? Or sessions?"

"The second one."

"One more thing, and that's all I'll say."

Red sighed, wishing she had a dime for every time Grandma said that was the last time she'd say something.

"Lord knows this world needs all the givers it can get. But there comes a time when you need to start putting yourself first. One of these days you need to realize that some people can't be fixed. And your time's better spent hunting for the right kind of man, the steady type who's looking to settle down, than chasing after houses."

Chapter 4

Once in a while, Red did manage to get an entire hour for lunch. In the middle of the week, she called up Keval to ask if she could bring her salad over.

Truth be told, she had an ulterior motive for stopping by the consortium. That RSVP in her bag was getting more tattered by the day, and she was still trying to figure out a way to get Sam to go with her.

She crossed Main Street, walked down the block past the café, and around the corner. The public area of the building Manolo had built for Sam last summer was bright and uncluttered. Behind tall windows sat tables, dining chairs, some comfy upholstered couches, and a bar where wine aficionados could sample local products. It was nothing like the settlement-era house the consortium had started out in, where Sam still resided. Apparently Sam was blind to the dinginess of the old building.

Then again, not everyone was as preoccupied with houses as Red.

She spotted Keval in his usual seat, behind his computer monitor.

"How are you?" she said, a little out of breath.

"Okay," he replied, in a very "not okay" voice.

"You sure? You sound kind of down." She plopped into the visitors' chair.

"I still don't have a date for Junie's wedding and the RSVPs are due next week," he said.

"What about that new guy in town? The one who bought Curl Up & Dye?"

"Jordan." Keval got a dreamy, faraway look.

"That's right, Jordan. Why don't you invite him?"

"Have you *seen* Jordan Hasselbeck? He's from Seattle. He's way too hip for me."

"Are you kidding me? With those mad sideburns of yours and those"—she peeked under the desk—"er...fitted, jogger pants? Have you looked in a mirror lately? Trust me, Keval Patel, you are plenty hip. Who says he wouldn't go? He's probably lonely. You know how it is when you move to a new town. I bet he'd jump at the chance."

"Maybe." He sighed, unconvinced. "Who are you going with?"

She hadn't seen that coming. "Uh," she hesitated, "no one, yet."

"I know!" Keval brightened. "We should go together. Neither of us has anyone else, right?"

Red envisioned slow dancing with Keval, she in her fitted, salmon-colored dress and ivory wrap, Keval in his mustard-colored pants with the green stripe down the side. They'd look like a hotdog in a bun with relish.

Grandma's words sprang to mind. *You need to put yourself first.*

But Keval was her friend, and he needed her. The last thing she wanted to do was to hurt his feelings. And her hope of going to the wedding with Sam was growing dimmer by the day.

She got a reprieve in the form of an angry voice from down the hall.

"Why do you even list a customer service number if all I get is a recording? Do you think I have all day to sit on hold? I'm trying to run a business here!"

Keval cringed.

"What's going on?" asked Red.

"You know the new wine subscription program? We're having a computer glitch on our sign-up page."

Red rose slowly, gazing in the direction of the yelling.

"I'm paying you for a service, and I expect service."

Keval bit his lip.

Holly Davis, the sales manager, and Mona, Sam's newest employee, popped their heads out of their respective spaces.

Red took off down the hall.

Keval half rose from his seat. "Don't go," Red heard him plead from behind her. "Give him time."

But she kept going until she was standing in the doorway of Sam's office.

The face Sam put on for the outside world was that of a supremely competent businessman with an endless supply of jokes. But Red had gotten a glimpse behind the façade: the fleeting rages, gone almost as soon as they started, using work as an avoidance tactic, and above all, the reluctance to let anyone get too close.

She watched him pace his small office like a caged lion, his attention fixed out the opposite window.

"We're paying a lot of money for this broke-dick service of yours. We've already promoted it and you assured me it'd be up and running yesterday. What's it gonna take to give you a sense of urgency?" Pause.

"Put a manager on the phone. And don't keep me waiting another fifteen minutes, or—what the—hello? Hello? Dammit!"

Something whizzed past Red's ear.

When Sam saw her standing there, he came flying around his desk.

"Doc. You all right?"

"I'm fine." She picked his phone up off the floor, dusted it off on her shirt, and handed it to him. "What's going on? You look upset."

"*Upset?* Damn right I'm upset. My vintners have gone to a lot of trouble and expense to haul cases of their wine over here to ship to subscribers starting today, and now I find out there are problems with the website?"

"Take a deep breath." Red lowered herself into the chair across from Sam. "So what I hear you saying is, you have wine ready to ship, but customers aren't having a positive subscribing experience. Is that right?"

"Right." He kept up his restless pacing. "How am I supposed to fix it? Do I look like a programmer?"

Maybe, if said programmer had smoldering eyes, a nose that listed slightly left, and flat abs.

"What about Keval? Can't he help?"

Sam scraped a hand through his hair, making it stand adorably on end. "If he could get into the system, but he's locked out."

Finally he took his seat, mirroring Red's calm body language.

Worked every time.

"I'm really sorry you're going through this."

He shook his head, his tempest having blown itself out as quickly as it had started. "I'll figure it out," he said in a more rational tone.

He blinked as if seeing her for the first time. "What are you doing here?"

"I had an actual lunch hour, for a change. Thought I'd eat with Keval, al desko."

He began gathering the papers strewn across his desk. "First time for any project is bound to hit a few snags. I'll be here till midnight working it out."

"Have you eaten? I could get you some food." Her next appointment would be at her office in a half hour, but if she only ate a few bites of her salad she could run down to Poppy's and pick up something to go for him.

"I'm meeting a grower around Lafayette in"—he checked his watch—"ten minutes," he said, standing up, patting his pockets. "Where'd I put my keys?"

Red spotted a set on the end table next to where she sat. She dangled them aloft, and he swiped them from her finger on his way out the door.

"Thanks," he said with that grin that made her weak.

When had her happiness become dependent on Sam's moods? It was unwise. But she couldn't help it.

She followed him into the hall. "I hope you get things straightened out," she called to his back.

In his wake lingered a clean, masculine scent. She closed her eyes and sniffed like a dog with its head out the car window.

Sam should have his own candle.

She opened her eyes to see Holly staring at her with a blank expression and back in the reception area, Keval with his fingertips pressed to his lips.

Red breezed past Holly with a casual wave of her fingers. But there was no reply, just the sensation of pitying eyes boring into her back.

When she reached Keval, he said, "Oh. My. Gosh."

Red frowned, glancing over her shoulder at where Holly and now Mona stood, both with shell-shocked expressions.

"What? Why are you all looking at me like that?"

"You got it bad," said Holly gravely.

Red scanned her exposed skin for obvious signs of disease. But freckles weren't contagious.

No. She couldn't have it all over town that she was gaga over Sam Owens.

What if he got wind of it? They had an unspoken agreement to be mature about their arrangement. Modern and unfettered and free.

She waved off Holly's exaggerated pronouncement with a smirk. "I'm the shrink around here. I'll do the analyzing."

But her denial must have looked as phony as it felt.

"You're in love with Sam," Keval stated matter-of-factly.

Red met each pair of eyes in turn.

"No I'm not," she said, trying to convince herself as much as them.

"Yes," said Holly, slowly closing in on her like a zombie. "You are."

In love. From a scientific point of view, she had to admit the evidence deserved serious consideration. She'd been carrying around these mushy feelings for far too long. *Something* was going on.

"Maybe."

Keval took her by the arm and led her back to her chair. Everyone started talking at once.

"Are we the first to find out?"

"That is so exciting! How long have you known?"

"Does Sam know?"

"One at a time, please! Yes, about a month, I think, and no."

"Sit," said Keval, pressing on her shoulder, giving her no choice.

"I'm in love. I'm not an invalid."

In love. There. She'd said it out loud.

Sweet relief flowed through her. She'd been struggling under her burden even longer than she thought. She fanned her face while the three fussed and fluttered around her.

"What can we get you? Some water?" Without waiting for an answer Holly dashed over to the water cooler, opened the spigot and scurried back, sloshing water in her wake.

Keval upended his brown bag and there was the sound of crinkling plastic wrap. "Here."

Red lowered her cup from her lips. "What's this?"

"Vegan sandwich. Hummus and cashew cheese. Clean protein."

What little appetite she'd had disappeared. Gently, she pushed it away. "Thanks, Keval, but that's your lunch. I still have my salad. I'm fine, you guys. Really."

"That's why your cheeks are all pink."

"When aren't my cheeks pink? It's a package deal. Comes with the hair and freckles."

Keval hauled his chair around his desk to directly in front of hers, facing backward. He straddled it and folded his arms across its back. "I want you to tell me everything, starting from the beginning. Go."

The temptation to get it off her chest was overwhelming.

"I—"

What was she doing?

She sealed her lips and sprang to her feet.

She'd made a colossal mistake. She couldn't tell Sam's entire staff that she'd been sleeping with their boss for months on end. It might not violate any HIPAA laws, but it was a gross breach of trust.

"I didn't come here to talk about my love life. I have to get back to my office. I have clients coming...."

Keval glanced at his smart watch. "It's only twelve twenty-five. We have plenty of time."

Red picked up the bag containing her untouched salad.

"It's too late now," crowed Keval. "The cat's out of the bag."

"None of your beeswax."

Maybe she could grab some bites between clients.

"He has no clue, does he?" Keval stood too and rested an elbow in his hand, tapping his lips. "Now that I think about it, you and Sam are perfection together. Who else could handle his ups and downs?"

He turned to his coworkers. "Imagine...a saner, calmer Sam. No more approaching life like it's a battlefield."

"No more pushing things to the edge," said Holly.

"We call him El Capitan behind his back," confided Mona.

Keval and Holly gave Mona a scathing glance.

Then Keval's eyes narrowed. "The wedding," he said to Red. "You're not committed yet?"

"What about Sam?" Mona caught on quick. "Is he?"

"His response card was still in his in-box last time I looked." Keval sprinted back to Sam's office to check.

Within seconds he came flying back, holding Sam's unsent card.

"Still he-re," he sang happily.

Holly said, "You have to get him to go with you."

"It's not that simple."

"What's so hard?" asked Keval. "You just come right out and ask him to go."

"I can't."

"Why not?"

"Because that's not how Sam operates. He only—"

She'd almost said Sam only dates women to whom he had zero attachment, but that would be an admission of sorts. In Sam's eyes, going to the wedding with Red would make a public statement. Set expectations.

"Sam doesn't date friends. Only strangers."

"She's right," said Holly. "Remember the Houser wedding...that pretty brunette? Where was she from—McMinnville? Whatever. We never saw her again. One and done."

"If you don't ask him to take you, I will," said Keval.

"No."

"Yes I will."

"*Keval.*"

"*Sophia.*"

"If you say something to Sam, then I'm going to say something to Jordan Hasselbeck about you, next time I get my nails done."

"You wouldn't!"

"Wouldn't I?"

"Who's Jordan Hasselbeck?" Mona and Holly asked in chorus.

"This is stupid," said Red. "We sound like twelve-year-olds."

"The responses are due back next week. Ask Sam to go to the wedding by Sunday, or I'll ask him for you. I don't care if you do go to Jordan."

Realization washed over Red. "You *want* me to."

Keval shrugged, his lips curving up in a coy smile.

"Who's Jordan?" asked Mona. "I'll go to him."

"I'm out of here," said Red with a roll of her eyes.

"You have until Sunday," Keval called after her as she crossed the threshold. "And if you think I won't know, don't forget—I have access to Sam's desk."

* * * *

Red's nails were soaking in a bowl of soapy water when Jordan Hasselbeck waltzed over and asked how she was. Jordan was conscientious like that, being new at his job. This time, Red took it a step beyond the usual small talk.

"Clarkston must be another world compared with Seattle. How are you adjusting to life in a small town?"

"I love it. I used to have a salon up in Seattle. Then, my parents retired in Tigard. I came down to visit them and some people in Portland and fell in love with the Willamette Valley. I saw a for rent sign on this building, and next thing you know, voila. Here I am."

"Did you come alone?"

"Yes, just me."

"Are you finding it easy to make friends?"

"Oh, sure. I mean, you know. I meet people here at the salon."

Red met Jordan's eyes in the mirror and made a decision. No more tiptoeing around—for Keval *or* her.

"Maybe you know Keval Patel? He gets his hair cut here."

"Keval. Let me think." He tapped his lip. "About five ten? Dark hair cut in a high fade?"

"That's him. He's in charge of social media for the Clarkston Wine Consortium. Keval and I have been friends forever. In fact, we're both invited to the same wedding."

"Really? I love weddings."

"You do? If I think of it, I'll have to mention it to Keval. He might be looking for a date."

"Oh? When is this wedding?"

"August thirty-first."

"Well, if he still doesn't have one by his next appointment, maybe we can talk about it."

The minute Red left the salon, she called Keval to tell him what had transpired.

"Oh my God. Are you serious?"

"That's what he said. I laid the groundwork. If you're still interested, talk to him the next time you go in."

She hung up feeling victorious, already imagining the sight of Keval walking into Junie's wedding with Jordan, thanks to her wise intervention.

Later that evening in her room, with the Keval problem sewn up, she went back to concentrating on Sam in the same, straightforward fashion.

To determine exactly what was working with her and Sam and what wasn't, She used the same questioning technique on herself as she did when counseling a couple.

Propped against her pillows with a tablet, she tapped her lips with the end of her pencil. Studies had shown that sometimes writing in longhand versus typing onto laptops increased conceptual understanding.

What kept Sam and her together? A passion that only grew stronger with time.

What stressed them? For Sam, any suggestion that they were anything more than casual hook ups. For Red, just the opposite. She was ready to take the next step.

What about the nature of your conflicts? Simple. Sam didn't want to talk about anything emotional and Red wanted him to. Period.

What qualities are missing or dysfunctional in your relationship? See above.

An hour later, she had a concise list of suggestions for improving their relationship.

Chapter 5

Before his pulse returned to normal, Sam was already zipping his fly and working his bike helmet over his ears.

"Let's roll," he said, reaching down where she lay sprawled on his blanket to give her a hand up.

She propped herself up on one elbow. There was a different kind of fire in her eyes now.

"Not so fast, Owens."

Whisky Tango Foxtrot. His hand dropped to his side as he felt his grin slip from his face.

Red reached for her discarded shirt to cover her ample breasts.

Since when was she the modest type? Sam looked around. Come to think of it, out here in his friend Hank Friestatt's vineyard in the middle of a sunny Saturday afternoon, anyone—a vineyard worker, a carload of tourists, or even Hank himself—could come along. It was just dumb luck that they hadn't yet.

"What do you think we're doing here?" asked Red.

Confused, he gazed down at her wild mane of copper…the curve of her waist between her hip and shoulder. The mere sight of her lounging there—not to mention the fresh memory of that body beneath his—triggered a renewed response in the vicinity of his groin.

He grinned again. "Same as usual," he said, his voice echoing inside his helmet. "We're scr—"

"No." She held up a hand. "Don't call it that. That might have been what it was when you first came back from the Army, but it's not that anymore. We're beyond that, don't you think?"

Sam felt the color drain from his face. *Thank you, tinted visor.* It wouldn't be good for Red to see the effect her rebuke had on him.

It looked like they wouldn't be going anywhere anytime soon. He sighed as he took off his helmet, tucked it under his arm, and adopted a comfortable stance, hoping this wouldn't take too long.

Red began buttoning her shirt. "Would you mind handing me my jeans?"

He looked around, spotting them where he had chucked them in the heat of passion, draped across a clone of Pinot Noir 943. He lifted them off the fragile cane with the utmost care. "Rather see an orphanage burn than lose one of those grape clusters," he cracked, to the sound of crickets.

Balancing on one foot to slip into her jeans, she gave him a disapproving look, then stumbled on the uneven ground.

Sam's hand shot out to steady her.

When she was decent, he raised his helmet to his head again.

But instead of neatly rolling the blanket and handing it to him to bungee onto the back of the bike like she usually did, she reached into the back pocket of her jeans and pulled out a folded piece of paper.

"What's that?"

"A to-do list," she replied, methodically unfolding it.

"There are apps for that."

Her hand holding the creased paper fell to her side. "Listen up, Owens. I've put a lot of thought into this."

"Can we talk about it later? I've got to get back. I got buyers from Pennsylvania coming at two to talk about a state contract."

She pulled her phone from her pocket. "It's only one fifteen."

He checked his watch, and it occurred to him: after they'd drunk a little wine and eaten some of the bread and cheese, the boom-boom part had only lasted about five minutes.

"Did you need more time?" He yanked the tail of his belt free from its prong with a slapping sound and hastened to close the distance between them. "'Cause we can fix that."

She took a step backward. "Really? You can make time for more sex, but otherwise, you're in a hurry to get going? Sit back down for a minute. Please."

Aw, jeez.

Jeez? When had he started taming his mouth around Red—in his own thoughts?

He had no choice but to hear her out. Small price to pay for having her, no strings attached. Not that he'd even looked at another woman since the first day Doc had put the moves on him. She was all he could handle and then some.

With a sigh of resignation, he lowered himself back to the ground and slung a forearm over a raised knee.

Wearing a serious expression, Red tucked in her shirt and sat down across from him. She flipped her hair over her shoulder. "I've been thinking about this for a while. About us. Now, you know I'm no prude. I've been fine with us having uncommitted sex up till now. Maybe even a little bit smug. I told myself we were different than other people. Smarter. Cooler, keeping things fresh. But it's not working anymore."

Sam pinched the bridge of his nose and tried to scrounge up another excuse why they had to get going—*now*.

"Hear me out…give me the respect I deserve. We can't go on forever like this, pretending what we have is meaningless. Hiding our relationship—"

"Relationship?"

"That's what it's called when two people share their lives over a period of time. A relationship. I'm tired of hiding what we have from our friends and families and the whole town."

"Whose business is it what we do behind closed doors?"

"And in vineyards and on hiking trails? What's wrong with a good old-fashioned bed?"

"You make it sound so *shady*."

"Your words. Hear me out. The past few years, I've been busy setting up my practice, struggling to pay the rent, trying to become known. The same with you and your consortium. We've barely had time to eat and sleep, let alone nurture another person. But now that the craziness is winding down, things have changed. *I've* changed."

Sam looked longingly over his shoulder at his bike resting on its kickstand at the crest of Ribbon Ridge Road.

He scratched his chin. "What's wrong with being spontaneous?"

"What's wrong is sometimes it feels like you're only thinking of yourself, not considering what I want. What I need."

Red and her logical mind. How could you disagree with the way someone felt?

"I feel like I'm ready to take what we have to the next level. And I need to be honest with you about those feelings."

Sam swatted at a fly on his pant leg. If she didn't get to that stupid list pretty soon, they'd be here all afternoon.

He jerked his chin toward the note. "What's it say?"

Red cleared her throat and wiggled her cute butt on the blanket, settling in.

Why couldn't she have been a hairstylist or an obstetrician or something… anything but a psychologist? This was disconcertingly reminiscent of when he got sent to the Freud Squad, shortly before he was informed that it might be a good idea if he were to, in so many words, "retire early" from active duty.

"Don't worry. There are only three items on this list. Number one. I want us to go to Junie and Manolo's wedding together. As a couple."

Relief sluiced through him. This wouldn't be as bad as he'd thought.

He nodded curtly. "We can do that."

"Thank you." She granted him a prim smile. "See how easy this is? That leads to number two. We come out as a couple."

"Why? Why should we care what other people think?"

"Because it makes it real. I care about you, Owens. You're a big part of my life."

"You're a big part of my life, too. Don't we hang out with our friends every chance we get? Didn't I just agree to go to the wedding with you?"

"Being together as part of a group doesn't count when you don't act like my boyfriend. I mean, what are we? Friends? It's more than that. Lovers? Or what?"

"Why the hell do we have to put a label on it?" Sam scrubbed a hand over his jaw, hiding the zing of pain when he forgot and hit the spot where he'd been zip-tied to a chair with a bag over his head, pistol-whipped, and left for dead. Compared to this, those were the good old days.

"I'm proud of being with you," Red was saying earnestly. "Aren't you proud of me?"

He looked her over dispassionately, the way he'd study a human target. *Generous, yet well-proportioned curves. Exuberant laugh that made her fun to be around. Scary-smart, and not afraid to speak her mind.* No wonder Dr. Sophia McDonald had been voted Clarkston's Best Therapist the past two years running.

"Sam."

He'd forgotten that a response was required.

"Hell, yeah. What's not to be proud of? What else do I have to do? Spell it out."

"Go to functions with me instead of just meeting me there. When you walk into a roomful of people and I'm there, kiss me hello. Sit next to me at parties, put your arm around me. When you leave, kiss me good-bye, or take me with you. Do you think you can do all that?"

He lifted a shoulder in assent.

"Third."

Bend over, here it comes again.

"Cuddle with me."

He blinked. "Isn't that what we just did?"

"That was not cuddling, and you know it. That was a straight up act of reproduction."

"You didn't seem to mind it when you were hollering my name to the hills." He threw back his head and howled in a mocking falsetto, "Oh, Sam! Sam! Please don't stop!"

She blushed even harder and did a lousy job of biting back her smile.

A soft-bellied civilian like her would last about one minute outside the wire. But suddenly he realized—he loved that she was so soft...so tender. So *female*.

"You're still missing the point. I want more."

"Tell me if I hear you right. I hold you for a few minutes after we do it, and then everything else can go on being status quo." All this fuss for nothing. And here, he'd been worried.

"I need you to rub my back. Feed me ice cream. Waltz with me in the dark."

"You keep adding things."

"Do you care about me or not?"

"Sure. Fine." *He was getting to be such a wuss.*

"Really?" she said, her voice softening. For the first time since they'd sat down, she lost that offended look.

"Yeah. My legs are getting stiff." He got to his knees. "Can we go now?"

"There's one more little thing."

"You said three. That was more than three already."

"It goes along with the cuddling. Kind of like number three, part two. And after that's done, maybe we can talk about having sex again."

He dropped back down to the blanket. "Did I miss something? Who said anything about not having sex?"

His near-panic didn't seem to affect her a bit. "I need you to show me I mean more to you than just a body."

"That's bullshit, Doc," he said sheepishly, dropping his gaze to hide his emotions. "You know you do." He ripped a handful of grass out of the ground.

"No, I don't. How could I, when mostly what we do is this?" she said, indicating his blanket. "I need you to talk to me. Really *talk* to me."

Sam's sphincter slammed shut. *Cuddle, sure. Buy her the occasional ice cream cone. Maybe even admit that they were in a relationship. But* talk?

"You know what I mean. Stop hiding your emotions behind jokes. Stop holding back and tell me what you're feeling."

She was asking him for nothing less than the antithesis of who he was and what he'd been trained to do. Talking meant exposing feelings, which left you wide open to being hurt. His military training had only strengthened that conviction. Sharing anything more than his name, rank and serial number created vulnerability, endangering both him and his fellow soldiers.

Nobody unmanned Captain Samuel Owens. *Nobody*.

He grabbed his helmet, rose, and headed for his bike. "You said there were three things, and I agreed to three things," he said as he strode off. "Now I've got to get back to work."

Red scrambled to her feet and tailed him, still without the blanket.

"Starting with when you were overseas," she said to his back. "What your job was. The kind of work you did." She took his arm, gently turning him around. "I don't know anything about it. Nobody does. It's not healthy, holding it inside. It's emotional constipation."

A burst of nervous laughter short-circuited the tension building up in him. "When will everybody finally get off my case? I was a supply officer. How many times do I have to say it?" he said, swinging a leg over the saddle.

"I'm no expert, but something tells me not every supply officer gets fêted by the local VFW when he comes home."

His little welcome home shindig. Just because of that, people thought they knew everything.

"Let's roll," he repeated. He revved the engine and a rumble filled the valley, striped with vineyards as far as the eye could see. He raised his voice over the roar. "Look at you. You're getting burned. Get the blanket and let's go."

"We're not through talking," she yelled back, crimson-faced.

"Maybe you're not, but I am. I don't need you to dismiss me."

"*Fine*. I don't need you at *all*." She crossed her arms and planted her booted feet in the dirt in a wide-legged stance.

"Fine with me."

He'd been patient long enough. He gunned the bike to show he meant business. "I mean it. Get the blanket and get on board."

"I'm not finished."

"Stay here, then."

It wasn't like she'd die of exposure out here on this picture postcard day. There were several wineries within walking distance and plenty of shade, if she wasn't too bullheaded to take advantage of it.

"I will." She raised her stubborn little chin.

Sam checked his watch again. "The Pennsylvania people are going to be at the consortium in fifteen minutes and it's a twenty minute drive and I have stuff to get ready."

Red jammed her fists on her hips. "You're hiding behind your work again. That's your typical response to anything that threatens your defense mechanism of shutting people out."

"Those growers and vintners trusted me enough to put me in charge of their livelihoods, you hear me? For some of them, a state contract could mean the difference between folding and scraping through another season. Their future's in my hands. I gave them my word I'd have their backs, and nothing's going to stop me."

With a flick of his wrist, the bike bucked.

One more twist and the rear wheel swung sideways, spraying gravel in a rooster tail.

Red flinched, squinting to keep the dust out of her eyes.

Now Sam was back on the hardball, facing the direction from which they'd come.

Still, she stood there, glowering.

"Goddamn it, Doc..."

They locked eyes in a showdown, her blinking in the harsh light, his eyes disguised behind his visor. The seconds ticked by while the July sun beat down on Red's center-parted hair, and Sam's insides fought a war between caving to her demands in exchange for more vineyard nookie and his responsibility to his winemakers.

Just when he thought he was going to have to forcibly bungee cord her onto his bike, she said, "Set up a date with me, a real date, to show me you're serious. And then I'll go."

"I said I'd go on a date, didn't I?"

"Not the wedding. A separate date, just for us. Like, dinner for two."

"Go ahead," he said, despite the curl of fear that wrapped around his intestines, threatening to strangle him from the inside out. "Pick any place and day you like."

"The Radish Rose. Next Saturday."

"You got it."

With that, Red smiled sweetly, turned, and retrieved the blanket.

Chapter 6

Sam sped along at speeds that would have his ass in a sling if a statie happened to be lurking around a bend in the road. That is, if they could catch him.

Most men might associate the feel of a woman's pillowy breasts pressing against his back, her arms wrapped securely around his core, and her firm inner thighs against his outer ones as a pleasant, even safe sensation. But what was innocuous to some was a threat to others.

It had taken months of riding these roads with Red for Sam to trust that that feeling wouldn't suddenly turn on him. He was almost there. But after the demands she'd just laid down, instead of being comforted, her presence behind him made him feel like he was being chased.

His first tour of duty had turned him into an adrenaline junkie. He'd started to need bigger and bigger thrills to feed his habit.

He gave it more diesel, pushing the bike's speed balls to the walls.

His second tour, while not as physically stressful, made up for it in head games. How had the white coats at the OMS put it in their discharge orders? "Captain Owens no longer trusts his own feelings."

Didn't take a shrink to see that. Sometimes he didn't even know who he was anymore, let alone what his feelings were.

When he finally got back to the states, he'd found it hard to let go. He wasn't a snake that could just shed his skin whenever the powers-that-be said it was time. Almost two years later, he still found himself ducking personal questions, constantly looking over his shoulder.

His siblings were long gone. So was his mother, raising another family that she valued more than him. His dad was no different from what he'd always been, a royal pain in the ass. At least now that Sam was grown he was no longer under his thumb. That made his occasional visits to check on him bearable.

He had a handful of close friends and tons of new acquaintances, thanks to the consortium.

But when it came to the one person he couldn't live without…well, that person was Red. He needed her calm. Her logic. Despite growing up with a succession of shady characters in mobile home parks before her grandmother stepped in, she was remarkably balanced. Without her, he feared he'd go spinning out of control again.

But he couldn't let her fall in love with him. If she insisted on forcing his hand, making demands…

He'd let her believe he would kowtow. Wasn't manipulation his special talent? He was a highly trained professional, adept at setting up relationships—there was that word again—and influencing and controlling others, based on fabrications.

Chapter 7

"Come back again," called Sam to the foursome who'd come all the way from Amarillo to see for themselves what all the fuss was about the Willamette's wines.

"Thank you kindly." The Texan in tooled boots held up a parting hand, then used it to hold the door for Manolo, on his way in.

Manolo saluted. "Lieutenant."

Sam dried his hands before clasping Manolo's. "Appreciate you taking time."

"Least I can do."

Sam had met Manolo in Iraq after dropping out of college in the middle of his freshman year.

Manolo had joined the Army as an alternative to taking over his family restaurant, just outside New York City. Lost and disoriented in a foreign land, the two had bonded instantly.

Despite acting nonchalant about it with Red, Sam took his best man responsibilities seriously. Last time he and Manolo had talked there'd been some confusion as to who on the groom's side was going to show up for the wedding. His mom was having some health problems, and he didn't get along with his dad.

Sam knew all about difficult fathers. The details weren't important. He and Manolo shared their stories on a need-to-know basis. Didn't hurt so much that way.

There was probably still time before the nearest motel sold out of rooms, but he couldn't risk failing at one of his tasks; risk disappointing his friend.

He poured a glass of the good stuff he kept under the counter, slid it over to Manolo, and rested his folded arms on the bar. "Wanted to touch base with you on the rooms. You got a final headcount yet?"

"My sisters still don't know what to do about letting my mom travel by herself since the knee replacement," said Manolo, scratching his head. "She insists she's okay, but they found out she was lying about still using her walker, so they're talking about one of them flying down to Miami first to get her and then flying out here."

"Family. Always got to be some complication."

"Tell me about it." Manolo took a sip of wine.

"That mean your dad's definitely a no-show, then? Can't be because he disapproves of the bride. They don't come any better than Junie Hart."

"Hard to disapprove of someone you've never met. No, it's not her he disapproves of." He looked down at where he cradled his glass. "It's me. Last I heard, he denies even having a son."

"That's rough, man."

There was a heavy pause.

"What about your dad?" asked Manolo. "What was it you used to call him?" He snapped his fingers and grinned. "Psychodad. That's right."

"Until just last week he was still living in the old homestead, out in the middle of nowhere. Seventy-seven years old and still chops his own firewood, even though I had the fireplace converted to gas when I got back from the service. Thought I was doing him a favor. Making it easier on him. But the numbskull won't stop."

"Seventy-seven? Christ! He had to be, what, late forties when you were born?"

"Let's just say I was a surprise, an unpleasant surprise. Luke, my brother, was fourteen, and Cindy was eighteen and on her way out of the house. Anyway, last week Psychodad earned his nickname."

"What'd he do?"

"You're not going to believe it. Piled real kindling on top of the gas fireplace logs."

"Aside from the obvious, it's July," said Manolo, his face screwed up with confusion.

"Musta caught a chill." Sam smiled drolly. "If I hadn't happened to go out there to check on him that day, they'd be finding pieces of that house in Portland. It'd be like Mount St. Helens all over again."

"There're public gas lines out there?"

"The fireplace runs on an above-ground propane tank. The place isn't exactly falling down, but he refuses to part with enough money to keep it properly maintained. And every time I've sent people out to look at the roof or clean the gutters at my own expense, he's sent them packing.

"It's frustrating as hell, man. Sometimes I think all it'd take is one shot from my Winchester into that propane tank, and—" He raised a pretend rifle to his shoulder. *"Peeeerrrr."*

"Right," drawled Manolo. "And what are you going to say when the fire department shows up?"

Sam spread his palms. "Who's gonna call the fire department? It's the only building for miles. The O'Briens moved to Hood River years ago."

"The place must be worth something. Sell it. That's my advice. Take the money and don't look back."

"The O'Brien place is still on the market. Nobody wants it."

"Let's say, for argument's sake, the authorities did come, catch you in the act."

"I'd tell them to let 'er burn."

"I believe there's a word for that."

"It's not arson if it's my own property. It's not like I'd file an insurance claim. And I could still sell the land any time I want. Come to think of it, the land's probably worth more without the house. Anyone who'd want it would only raze it and start over, anyway."

Manolo shifted uncomfortably. "No sense talking about something that's not going to happen, Samuel, my man. What about your Dad? Goes without saying he can't be left unattended after that."

"Roger. He's at the assisted care place being evaluated as we speak."

"So that's it? There he stays?"

Sam shrugged. "You know how bureaucracy is. It'll take a while."

"What about your mom?"

"She left us a long time ago. Who could blame her? Dad cheated on her with half the women in McMinnville. She found a younger guy, got remarried when I was in high school."

"You see her much?"

Sam straightened drink coasters that were already neatly stacked. "Aw, you know how it goes. She went from being a cougar to being all caught up raising her step-grandkids."

"What about your sister and brother? How come you're the one left holding the bag?"

"Luke and Cindy don't want anything to do with him."

"If he's such a pain, why bother? What keeps you hanging on?"

He shrugged. "Don't give me too much credit. All I do is stop in every couple weeks, see that he's got food in the house, keep the weeds down."

Manolo shook his head.

"Before I forget, Junie got all the RSVPs back but yours and Red's. She's not concerned about Red's. Said Red can be a touch scattered. But knowing you, there's a reason. You don't make a move—or, in this case, not make a move—till you've covered every angle."

"Tell her to check tomorrow's mail." Sam couldn't hide his grin. "Doc and I are coming together."

Manolo's face lit up. "No shit. So. The lady finally put her foot down."

"What?" Sam's shoulders went back and his chin disappeared into his neck. "Where'd you get that? No one tells Sam Owens what to do."

"Who are you talking to here?" Manolo tapped his chest with the side of his hand.

Sam slouched. "Okay. There may be an outside chance that maybe Doc might have mentioned something about a rela—a rela—"

"Relationship?"

Sam decided he could use a drink, too. He reached above the bar for another glass.

"Well, it's about time, you old rascal!" Manolo's hand clasped Sam's palm-down, angling, locking thumbs. "I was wondering how long you expected her to wait."

"What's that supposed to mean?"

"You told me you had a thing for Red over a year ago. Remember? It was the same time you warned me to keep my paws off Junie."

Sam traced the wood grain in the bar with a finger. "Not even I can be right one hundred percent of the time."

"In case you didn't notice, I didn't need your permission to date Junie. Back to Red. Did you think nobody else knew about you two? You're losing your touch, Spidey."

Sam wondered when he'd gotten careless about his and Red's comings and goings. If he hadn't wanted them to, no one would know.

"It's not all me. Doc wasn't into the whole going steady thing either. She was cool with the way things are—"

"Were."

"Until last weekend."

"Told you how it is, huh?" Manolo grinned wider, and the still-smoldering fire inside Sam at the idea of being controlled flared momentarily.

"A minor glitch." It would take a special kind of torture not yet invented to get Sam to admit that Red's plan involved putting the brakes on their sex life. Even to his best friend. *Especially* to his best friend.

Anyway, that wouldn't last. With their explosive chemistry? He'd have her hollering out his name in ecstasy again in no time. Maybe as soon as tomorrow night, after their first, real date.

"Hey," said Sam. "What's this about Junie and the girls going to see Lumber Jack Hammer?"

Manolo waved away his query. "I heard about it. Some male revue or something."

"You worried?"

"Me? I'm not worried." Manolo's grin waned. "Why. Are you worried?"

"Do I look worried?"

"Junie has eyes for no one but yours truly."

"At times I forget you're not from around here. Hammer's been known to get, let's say, overly friendly with the women who go to his shows."

Manolo's grin didn't falter. "When a woman's got this," he asked, puffing out his chest, "what need would she have to go elsewhere?"

Sam rolled his eyes. "You say so. Me? I don't know why anybody'd want to get married. It's like enlisting in the service."

"How's that?"

"You'll have to learn how to eat, sleep, shower, and shave all over again."

"Wait till it's your turn."

"That's going to be a long wait. Nah, I kinda like seeing how many days I can go without a vegetable crossing my lips. Falling asleep to *SportsCenter*." Sam clapped his hands. "So. What about the rooms?"

"Book a suite for each of my sisters and their families, and then one for Mom. If Dad comes, he can stay with her. If not, at least she'll have a respite from her grandkids. My extended family can get a little rambunctious."

"I'm picturing a *Star Wars* bar."

Manolo brightened. "You got nieces and nephews too."

"Negative."

He slumped again. "Your siblings never tied the knot?"

Sam shook his head as he took another swig of his drink. "The Owens clan's no good at happy ever after."

Chapter 8

The following Saturday, Sam found himself knocking on the door of Red's trailer clutching a last-minute plant he'd grabbed at the market. Red loved anything having to do with flowers and gardening. Only now did it dawn on him: planting things went hand in hand with her hankering for roots.

Sam shifted his feet on the doormat. In his hand, the cellophane-covered plant crackled. He propped up a wilting daisy. *So, this was dating.*

The flower fell again just as a woman in wire rimmed glasses with wavy silver hair opened the door. "Come on in. Sophia's back there getting ready."

"Thank you, ma'am."

She took the plant from him. "Aren't these pretty? I'll get a saucer to put under it."

The woman toddled over to a cupboard while Sam's feet remained on the rug in front of the door. This was exactly what he'd been dreading. And she hadn't offered him a seat—not that she seemed like the formal type.

A muted clatter came from behind a closed door down the narrow hallway, followed by an ominous crash.

"It's okay," called Red. "Just dropped my shoebox full of nail polish. It'll only take a minute."

Said no woman ever. *C'mon, Red.* Had she actually chosen this time to paint her nails?

"Sophia says you two went to school together. I thought I knew all her friends. My memory must be getting bad," said her grandmother, setting the flowerpot in the center of the kitchen table.

He shoved his hands in his pockets. "I've changed a little since then."

Grandma returned to her easy chair in front of the TV and motioned toward the sofa. "Well, you sure are a clean cut fellow now. Might as well have a seat. I don't know how long she'll be." She picked up the remote and turned down the volume on the show she was watching. "My granddaughter might be smart as a whip and have a heart the size of Texas but she isn't the most organized. Besides that, her dating skills are a little rusty. This is the first time she's had a boy to the house since she graduated college."

Not having gone out with anyone else, it hadn't occurred to him that Red might. He was surprised, then touched.

"Did you play sports or act in any of the school plays or anything like that?"

"A little baseball. That's it."

"Well, I had one girl, Sophia's mama, and then came Sophia. In all my years I couldn't have gone to more than a handful of baseball games." She tapped her lip and frowned. "Come to think of it, I do recall some boy getting hit in the nose with a ball one time. There was no family there to tend to him, and Sophia insisted on us driving him down to the med center in McMinnville. She always was one to look out for the underdog." She shook her head and clicked her tongue. "Ragamuffin, he was. I was half embarrassed to be seen with him in my minivan. Made you want to take him home and give him a bath, then a haircut. Can you believe the way some children are raised? Eventually the receptionist managed to track someone down and told us we could leave."

Sam fidgeted. *Where was Red?*

At the height of his discomfort, a door opened down the hall and a dressier, sexier version of Red appeared, smelling flowery.

He stood. "Wow, Doc. You look great."

"Look what he brought you," said her grandmother. "Gerbera daisies. You can plant them, later."

Tentatively, Red fingered a blossom. "Wet nails." She smiled at him. "Pretty."

"Where are you two off to?"

"Sam's taking me to The Radish Rose."

"Isn't that nice? Well, be good."

On their way to his van, Sam said, "That wasn't awkward."

"What do you mean? Were you uncomfortable?"

"Like a cow on roller skates. Kept expecting she was going to tell me to have you back by ten."

"You'll be happy to know I have a liberal curfew."

"Then again, you are a grown woman with a PhD and her own business."

He put the van into reverse and looked in the rearview, catching a glimpse of her legs on the seat next to him where her skirt had slid up when she got in.

His arm automatically contracted to place his hand on one milky thigh before he remembered the new rules.

"How was your week?"

"Busy," she replied, smoothing her skirt down demurely toward her knees, leaving her hands on her thighs for her nails to dry. "Yours?"

"Same."

A clumsy silence descended. Hard to believe this stiff, wooden couple was the same one who had a penchant for steamy matinées in the great outdoors.

"Hope you're hungry."

"Starved. I worked later than I intended. The only time this one couple could come in was between five thirty and six thirty. They paid their sitter double to stay late."

"Kind of throws a wrench into your day, letting people pick their own hours."

"I know. But they have little kids, and if they're willing to do the work and I can keep their family together…"

"Lucky for them you're so willing to adjust your schedule. Hope it works out."

Was this the kind of dry conversation Red was looking for?

After the van, The Radish Rose hummed with energy and movement. They had just got their breadbasket when the hostess led the Bergs past their table. James owned the gas station across the street from the consortium, and Pat worked at the Albertson's in McMinnville.

"Dr. McDonald," exclaimed Pat, touching Red's shoulder. "Thanks again for seeing Cassadee on such short notice. Those nightmares of hers are keeping the whole house up."

Red smiled tightly. "No problem."

Did Pat not realize the position she was putting Red in? Not to mention clueing in the whole town that her daughter was in therapy.

It was at that moment that Pat noticed that Red wasn't alone.

"Hello, Sam. How's the wine business?"

Sam saluted, silently willing Pat to move along.

"Hold on," Pat said, eyeing Red's fancy top, her hair piled on top of her head. "Are you two on a date?"

Red lifted a questioning brow at Sam, passing the burden of answering on to him.

"Everybody's got to eat," he said, ripping off a chunk of baguette, slathering butter on it and cramming it into his mouth.

Red's brightly painted lips pursed. Then she turned to Pat. "Yes, as a matter of fact, we are."

"Isn't that special?" Pat clasped her hands. "James, did you hear that? Dr. McDonald and Sam Owens are dating."

"The girl's waiting," said her long-suffering husband, pointing with the top of his head to where the hostess stood holding their menus while at the front of the house, a line formed.

"Whole town'll know now," sighed Sam as the Bergs walked away.

Red perused her menu thoughtfully. When Sam didn't open his, she asked, "Do you already know what you're having?"

"Same thing I always have here. Spaghetti."

"Don't you even want to look to see if something else might catch your eye?"

"Why should I? They make great spaghetti."

"Hm. I hear the seared tuna is good. Or I could get the artisanal cheese quiche."

"You could."

"Tonight's special is chicken parm with penne. You know what they say about penne."

"Tell me."

"It's the perfect date pasta."

"There is such a thing?"

"Sure. It's all about the shape of the pasta. Not like spaghetti, where you have to slurp it up and there's a chance you might splash red sauce on your top."

"Who knew? Well, I happen to like spaghetti. I'm willing to live dangerously."

When their food came, Sam dug into his spaghetti and meatballs and continued his story of how the website snafu got cleared up.

"So then I posted the problem on their help forum—"

Red tapped the corner of her mouth discreetly. Sam assumed that meant he was dragging the story out, so he speeded it up.

"—and bam, right away, customer service comes back and—"

She tapped again.

"What?" He waved his fork in the air.

"You got red sauce. Right…" She indicated a spot on her own face.

He wiped at his chin. "Did I get it?"

"No."

He stunk at this dating thing. He wondered if Red was wondering the same thing he was—what they were going to do with themselves after dinner, if sex was off the menu.

Their server, Liz Greenburn, came back around to ask if they wanted dessert. Last winter, Liz and Heath Sinclair's dad, Scott, had stunned all of Clarkston by moving in together. Turned out middle aged people weren't too old for such shenanigans.

"We have homemade peach pie tonight."

Red brightened. "I like pie."

Sam slapped closed the menu and handed it back to Liz. "One slice of pie."

"Am I supposed to feed it to you?" he asked when it arrived.

"You're mixed up. That's ice cream." Red cut through the flaky crust into the sweet filling and deposited a bite into her mouth, closing her lips on the fork and drawing it out slowly.

An erotic feeling stirred in Sam's center.

"Besides," said Red. "That would be out of the correct order of things. Remember? We're backtracking. Doing things sequentially, starting with cuddling." She took another bite, savoring it slowly.

"Yeah," he said, his eyes glued to her mouth. "So how about you fill me in on just what you mean by 'in order'? Sooner we can get started, the sooner we can get back to the good stuff."

"Well," she said, "I want to ask you if you'd be willing to try something called Sensate Focus Technique. It's a process that was designed for couples with sexual dysfunction, although—"

"Keep it down, would you?" Frantically, Sam looked around at the closely packed tables. "You want people to think I have a problem in the sack?"

"Sorry," she whispered loudly. "As I was saying, strictly in general terms, because IN YOUR CASE, SEXUAL DYSFUNCTION IS DEFINITELY NOT—REPEAT, NOT—A PROBLEM."

Heads turned.

"Jesus." He couched his forehead in his hand.

Red continued with her candid description. "SFT is a well-established method to treat things like, oh"—she licked her fork and waved it in the air—"erectile dysfunction, premature ejaculation..." She ticked off the examples as if they were architectural styles or wedding dresses instead of the most emasculating conditions known to mankind.

Sam leaned across the table and hissed, "Do you think maybe we could talk about this someplace else, where there aren't thirty-seven people eavesdropping?"

Out of nowhere, Liz reappeared. "Listen to you two. Sound like an old married couple instead of one on their first date. Will there be anything else?"

"No," he said, running a finger between his neck and collar. "Just the check."

Liz bent over to within a foot of Sam's ear. "Don't worry. When Scott and I first got together, he had a little problem with delayed ejaculation. You know, when men can't reach orgasm? Sometimes they call it inhibited ejaculation. It's not unusual for a man Scott's age. Anyway, I sent him over to Dr. McDonald, here, and now he's as good as—"

"Please." Sam stuck his fingers in his ears. *He'd survived two wars, but don't make him listen to his friend's dad's problems getting it up.* "Stop."

Liz straightened her spine and drew in her chin with a hurt expression. "I was only trying to help. I'd hate for your sexual shortcomings to come between—"

"Just the check," Red repeated cheerfully.

Chapter 9

Sam had never been so relieved to get back to his van.

"About the technique," said Red. "It was developed for people who're having trouble achieving satisfaction. But in our case, we have the opposite goal: to slow things down."

"Sounds to me like practice bleeding. Isn't the whole point to get to where we're already at?"

"I would like us to focus less on the sex act itself, and more on intimacy. You'll see what I mean, once we get started."

Automatically, Sam steered the van in the direction of Ribbon Ridge.

"Where are we going?"

"For a ride."

"You're not going to seduce me."

"Who said anything about seducing you?"

"We both know how it is. You look at me in that certain way, touch me in that certain place, and I'm helpless to resist."

"Fine. We'll play it your way. Just hold hands." Dutifully, he clasped Red's hand between the seats.

"That's done. Now what?"

"It doesn't count while you're driving."

"Why not?"

"You have to be able to relax and focus on the sensation."

* * * *

Only the savviest wine tourists knew about Ribbon Ridge. Traffic was light, even during the daytime. That, plus the view was one of the reasons it had become Sam's favorite place to take Red.

The sounds of civilization tapered off as they left the town behind. Sam thought of turning on the radio to mitigate the silence, but his right hand was entangled in Red's and he had to use the left one to drive.

When they reached the road that ran along the ridge top, he made a U-turn to give Red the superior view, then parked along the side of the road. He cut the engine, slid the windows down and leaned around Red to peer out at black, downward sloping land, across familiar vineyards to swaths of pines and the winking lights of farmhouses.

From Army cots, hovels, and five star hotel rooms all over the world, Sam had dreamed about coming back to this place. Only in leaving it had he realized how much he loved this valley…its lush vineyards, its wildflower meadows, its carefully tended farms. But even more than the geography, he loved its people, grounded in the soil, passionate about living close to the land.

Cicadas hummed and clicked in the night air.

After a minute, Red murmured, "Temperature's perfect."

"Mm."

Their voices sounded different, up here. Like they were in their own, private world.

"I like to imagine what people are doing down there. Finishing up their last tasks of the day. Checking on their animals for the night. Winding down."

"Yeah."

She inhaled audibly.

"Sniff," she ordered him.

"Huh?"

"I said sniff."

After assuring himself that he wasn't being watched—ridiculous, given their location, not to mention that it was pitch black out—he took a tentative whiff out his own window.

"Smell that?"

"The roses?" Roses planted among the vines acted like canaries in coalmines. Any sign of mildew on the petals, and the growers could react before it spread to the grapes. "Smells good." Great. Now *he* was talking about posies.

Red sighed and let her head fall back. "How far would you say we can see from up here?"

His TAC-338A had a range of two thousand feet. That was six hundred ten meters, or 0.379 miles. Multiply that by ten…

"Three point eight miles."

The moonlight silhouetted her head rising from the headrest.

"That's weird."

"What's weird?"

"Why don't you just round it off to four?"

"Because that's not what it is. It's imperative to approximate distance as accurately as possible."

"I was just making conversation. It's not like it's life or death or anything."

"Yes, it—"

Get a grip, Owens.

She let it drop, much to his relief. "I'm glad we came up here," she said, her head falling back again. "It's nice. Peaceful."

Without warning, she loosened herself from their chaste handclasp and began slowly, rhythmically sliding the very tips of her fingers up and down between his.

He'd never noticed how much more sensitive the skin was along the inside of his fingers compared to his palm and the back of his hand. It tickled, in a good way.

He found himself relaxing, being lulled into a state of pleasant lethargy. She could do that forever and he wouldn't mind.

His head fell back in imitation of hers, as his eyes drifted shut.

"Where'd you learn how to do that? On second thought—don't tell me. I don't want to know." He'd have to give the guy a slow, painful death.

She didn't respond in words, just curled her fingertips around the base of his fingers, sliding her middle one up and down along the ridge between his knuckles.

It was incredible how good something so simple could feel. How sensual. The feeling went up his arm and down his spine, triggering his usual, infallible response.

He shifted in his seat, reaching between his legs with his free hand to give himself more room.

At that, her fingers stilled.

"Don't stop," he said thickly.

She resumed stroking the skin between his fingers. He could feel his heart rate increasing, his breathing becoming audible in the still night.

Such a little thing, her fingertips brushing against his hand. How could it have taken over his entire being like this? He opened his eyes to the darkness. No sight, no sound but his breath rushing in and out and the crickets in the background. His entire universe centered on the nerve endings in that slight hollow between the knuckles of his middle and ring fingers and the scent of roses.

Finally, he couldn't take it anymore.

"Doc…" He squeezed her hand, stopping the tantalizing movement of her fingers and lolled his head to the side.

Her head turned toward his in response, lips parted.

He leaned in to kiss her, and she intercepted his aim with a fingertip to his lips. "Nuh uh. No kissing."

"I get it. I passed this part of the test."

"Not yet. We're just getting started. Do you like holding hands with me?"

He tightened his grip. "Have mercy, Doc. You know I do. Now let's stop playing games and get to the real deal."

"Not tonight. It's not part of the plan."

"Then when? How long do we have to pretend we're thirty-year-old virgins?"

"We're not thirty. Not yet."

"The stress is accelerating the aging process. Look." He traced a line along her forehead. "Worry lines."

"It's not going to work."

His head fell against the headrest with a resigned sigh.

Unexpectedly, she reached out and ran her finger along the small scar along his temple. "But I have noticed something there before. What's that from?"

He rolled his head away slightly. "Nothing."

Red dropped her hand. After a pause, she said, "I think now would be a good time for you to take me home."

He thought about that. "Give me a sec."

He got out and strode a few yards behind the van to clear his head. The crunch of gravel under his feet, the cool breeze on his scalp when he ruffled his hair, took the place of a cold shower. He stood there with his hands on his hips and his head bowed and tried to think about things other than Red's hand, her mouth, and her body that responded to his touch like a German sports car. Work problems. What he was going to do about his dad. The house and his lifelong deception. Anything to ease the cramped state of affairs south of the border. He blew out a frustrated breath.

A minute later he climbed back into the van and started the engine.

Halfway back to town, Red said, "There's a romantic comedy at the drive in Friday night. I wouldn't mind seeing it."

At least he wouldn't have to think of things to talk about. And maybe he'd even get to first base.

"I'll drive," she added. "That way you can drink some wine."

Done.

"What time?"

* * * *

"It's supposed to storm," called Grandma to Red out the door of the trailer.

"Can't be too bad," Red called out her car window as she backed out of the driveway the next day. She couldn't pass up a Sunday to look for the saltbox. Summer or winter, storms were rare in this part of Oregon. The Chamber of Commerce touted the misty, cool climate as one of the factors in the success of the local wine industry.

She headed west out Meadowlake Road toward the McGuire Reservoir. She'd been down this road before looking for the house, but even GPS was no help when you didn't know the address you were looking for.

She drove her trusty old Impala up hills and down, across boulder-strewn streams, through desolate stands of towering Douglas fir, and around switch backs so sharp that one minute she was headed straight south and the next, north.

Twenty minutes into her drive, the light changed. The innocuous white puffs of clouds dotting the western horizon had begun to build.

At a vaguely familiar intersection, she frowned, looking for the rickety old lean-to made out of corrugated metal. There it was, collapsed onto itself, half covered with vines.

All at once, the clouds burst.

Red hadn't seen another car in miles. Windshield wipers swishing, she sat in the intersection, debating which way to turn. She was pretty sure that the last time she'd come to this crossroads, she'd taken the left. Now she went right.

The rain stopped as quickly as it had begun. Red splashed at a snail's pace through muddy ruts until she came to a fork.

She idled beneath a dripping canopy of tree branches, biting her lip. It was kind of eerie. Surely, not even her adventurous mom would have driven all the way out here just to pick berries. No one in the world knew where she was. If something happened to her, she might never be found.

That's when she saw the hand-lettered sign that said "Strawberries. U-pick" half hidden in the weeds.

Her heart leapt. Could this be it? She turned down the narrow road, wincing as branches scratched the sides of her car like fingernails. She was debating putting it in reverse when the sun came out. A little farther on, she came to a clearing.

She stopped and peered out the squeaky clean windshield. There sat a wooden frame house with two stories in the front sloping to one in the back with a chimney in the middle.

The earth steamed. Raindrops sparkled like diamonds on every blade of grass.

But this couldn't be her saltbox. Moss grew on the roof shingles and ivy climbed the corners.

She pulled up the picture on her phone, comparing it with what lay before her. There was the hill behind the house and the boardwalk along the side leading to the back, enclosed by the Popsicle stick fence.

The house sagged in the comfortable way that an old lady sits, a little tired, but rooted, immovable. The kind of solidity Red had never had, always craved.

The branches of a once-dainty lilac now scraped against the second story windows. What had been a close-cropped yard inside the fence now looked more like pasture, uneven and dotted with clumps of crabgrass.

She got out and walked slowly toward the house. The invigorating smell of pine oil on dry rocks released by the rain and wind filled her nostrils.

This was it.

This was her dream house.

A wave of emptiness overcame her…homesickness for the home she'd never had.

Up against the house, barely noticeable, a small white cross poked up through the weeds. Kneeling, she saw that it was crudely nailed together from wood scraps, as if made by a child. She straightened the crooked cross bar. *Odd place to bury a pet—assuming that's what it was.*

She rose, dismissing the cross from her thoughts. Much more intriguing was the late-model pickup truck parked out front.

But even that couldn't draw her attention for long from the house she had dreamed of, back when she still believed in happily ever afters.

If it was neglected, maybe that meant it was available.

She struggled with the rusty latch on the gate, then strolled through calf-high wet grass, heedless of her sandals becoming soaked.

From the center of the yard she peered up at the sky. She spun in a circle, gathering in the energy of the place, grounding herself in its center.

A wave of self-consciousness swept over her and she stopped cold. What if someone was watching? She scanned the windows, but all she saw were dark rectangles.

Gingerly she approached the front door—only to find that a padlock had been installed on it.

She tried pulling out the shank, but it was in tight.

If no one lived here, then whose truck was that?

Overhead, a blackbird sailed by.

She abandoned the door for the nearest window. The interior was white with brick-red trim. The cupboards were painted a soft, Colonial blue. There was a chandelier with flame-shaped bulbs above a shabby-chic table that would fetch a pretty penny at an antiques store.

From the look of the charred black surround, the fireplace had been well used. Above the mantel hung an old hunting rifle. The faint smell of wood smoke lingered in the air.

She pressed palms and nose to the glass, conjuring up her fantasy family to go along with her dream house: a dad who never left, a mom who didn't latch on to every man who showed the slightest interest in her.

After a moment, she left the window to search for signs of the strawberry patch. Across the yard she found fruit still growing on untended plants with runners reaching out in spokes like wagon wheels. She bent over and picked a berry, fat and freshly washed in rainwater, and it was as sweet and delicious as she remembered. She went to her car and got a bag to fill with berries. Wouldn't Grandma be surprised.

She got out her phone and began photographing the house from every possible angle. She couldn't wait to bring Sam here. Maybe if he saw this place with his own eyes she could make him see what it was about old houses that she loved so much.

Chapter 10

Red threw open the door to the mobile home.

"Grandma! The house. I found it!"

"What are you going on about?" Grandma looked up from the sink.

"I found the house."

She thrust her phone under Grandma's nose. "Remember? The house where Mom and I picked berries."

"Let me dry my hands off. Hand me my readers."

Red snatched them off the end table next to Grandma's recliner and waited impatiently for her to unfold them and slip them on. Behind the lenses' magnification, Grandma's hazy, cornflower eyes grew huge.

"Only your mother would haul you out in the middle of God's green acre."

"And here," Red dangled a bag under her nose, "strawberries. The old patch is still there, among the weeds."

Grandma picked out a berry that wasn't too smooshed and ate it.

Red waited for her approval.

"Not like the ones you get nowadays from the supermarket."

"I can't tell if anyone lives there or not. There was a pickup parked there, but nobody came to the door."

"You knocked?"

"I was dying to see inside. I looked through the windows. It's mostly original, with a few modern appliances. Not much in the way of furniture. I'm hoping whoever owns this place might want to sell it. By the looks of things it's an older person who doesn't have the means or the energy to keep it up."

"Seems like an awful lot for a single girl to take on all by herself. How far away'd you say it was?"

"About twenty miles."

"You want to live all the way out there in the country like that?"

"It's nothing! Lots of people commute farther than that. You'll love living there. Wait till you see it. We'll revive the old strawberry patch. Maybe even start selling them again. It's so peaceful there you can hear the whoosh of birds' wings."

"Me? What makes you think I'm going anywhere?"

"You're coming with me, of course. You don't think I'd leave you here, do you?"

She shook her head and returned to her sink full of dishes. "You won't get me out there in the sticks where I got to drive forever to get a quart of milk."

"You won't have to," said Red, trailing her to the sink. "I'll take care of you. I'll see that you have everything you need."

"You heard me. I'll come visit—that is, when the roads are clear, and only when it's light out. I don't like driving in the dark any more than I have to."

"Grandma. You have to come. You're my family. The only family that counts." She tipped her head, forcing Grandma to meet her eyes. "I always wanted to live in a real house. But if you won't come…"

Grandma slid a dripping plate into a slot in the dish drainer. "Someday you will live in a real house. You, of all people. But not me."

All Red's excitement fell flat.

Grandma inched her way back to her kitchen chair.

"Don't pout. Come over here, sugar," she said, patting her lap.

"Grandma." Red rolled her eyes. "I'm too old for that. And"—she assessed Grandma's fragile frame—"too big."

"You're never too old to sit on your grandma's lap. Now, get over here."

Reluctantly, Red circled around the table. Grandma was so slender, she made Red's arms register as legs. "You sure?"

"Sure I'm sure."

Gingerly, she began lowering her weight.

Grandma gasped. "Ugh. Good God, Sophia, you're enormous."

Red jumped up and spun around, red-faced. "I told you."

"Now you listen. It's not the house that's important. I'm thankful for growing up the way I did, in that house. All six of us kids were. We had a lot of good times. But things weren't always peaches and cream. The girls at school were jealous of me, with my matching accessories. You know how girls that age can be. My mother threw me a sweet sixteen birthday party and nobody came."

Red lowered her eyes. No matter how many times Grandma repeated that story, the image of her all dressed up in a room hung with twisted crepe paper and a cake in the center of the table, waiting for her schoolmates to arrive, eventually realizing they weren't going to come always made her heart squeeze.

"Thursday and Friday nights when the stores stayed open late Pap didn't come home till after nine. Lots of other nights, too, when he started going to his Rotary and the Masons and every other group in town. Mam was worn out from raising us kids by herself. No such thing as microwaves or dishwashers back then. She made every meal from scratch. I remember nights when she would sit at the dining room table and cry, suspecting that he was stepping out on her. I didn't ask about the particulars. What could I have done about it? It was something that, even though you may not like it, that's just the way things were.

"A house doesn't buy happiness. It's who you share it with. Always remember that."

But things will be different for me, thought Red. Her great-grandmother had gotten pregnant at seventeen and never finished high school. Red was highly educated, earned her own living and lived in a time when women had almost complete control over the number of children they decided to have—or not have.

She was sure that, once she had her dream house, everything else would fall neatly into place around her.

Chapter 11

Red told Sam she'd pick him up at six, well before dark fell and the outdoor movie could start.

He was waiting for her outside when she pulled up to his house in her ancient Chevy.

"Show doesn't start for hours. Where are we going?"

"It's a surprise. Wait till you see."

Red drove west out Meadlowlake Road.

"I know. You're taking me to Gran Moraine. I've been wanting to go back there. They do a nice, sappy Chardonnay."

"Nope."

He gazed wistfully over his shoulder as her car blew past the estate's entrance. Gran Moraine was the only winery he knew of out this way. The vast majority of Willamette tasting rooms hedged a north-south line between the Coast Range and the Cascades.

"Foothills Taxidermy?"

Red looked at him sideways. "Maybe another time."

On they went, through canyons of ash and cedar, leaning first right and then left as they rounded bends in the road.

A bad feeling came over Sam. He told himself to relax.

"You're taking me fishing."

"People fish in the evening?"

"Fishing's excellent that time of day. Water cools off. Fish come up to feed."

"Sorry, but no, that's not where we're going. Anyway, when was the last time you heard of me going fishing?"

"A man can dream."

Despite his calm exterior, his suspicions were growing by the mile. *Regulate. Don't go there yet.* There was any number of things to do out this way. Hiking paths. Wading streams. Maybe Red had reconsidered her new rules. Maybe she was taking him to some scenic new spot to make love.

He had never seriously considered the possibility that she would find the saltbox. His dad had carefully chosen the site for its secluded location, well outside town. Decades later, it was still as backwoods as you could get.

But when Red turned onto the Nestucca Lake Access Road, he couldn't deny it any longer.

He strategized on the fly. *Fake a sudden bout of gastritis? An important meeting he'd forgotten about?*

Why was he so bent out of shape? This little predicament was nothing compared with the high-threat assignments he'd handled. He had the training, experience, and ability to think on his feet. He was a pro at leading a double life, deceiving people, forming false relationships based on half-truths and manipulations. So why was he sweating bullets over a house?

The difference was that those relationships were with despicable thugs. The baddest of bad guys, not sweet-yet-exasperating, innocent yet sexy-as-all-get-out Red.

He needed to figure out how to react in a way that would serve his purposes, both right now and in the future. And he needed to figure it out now.

Dammit! Why hadn't he taken her seriously? Thought this out before he found himself minutes away from arriving in that clearing, sitting next to her where she could read his face? She was a therapist. She read people for a living.

They came to the intersection where his bus used to stop. He avoided looking at the corrugated metal in the brush, so as to not draw attention to it and spark a conversation that would only lead to more lies.

Why had he gone and lied to Red to begin with? Now, if he admitted the house was his, she would demand to know why he hadn't told her earlier. And that would open up a Pandora's box of questions.

He took a long, slow breath through his nose, filling his lower lungs, then his upper lungs, holding to the count of three, the way he'd been taught. He exhaled slowly through slightly parted lips while relaxing the muscles in his face, jaw, shoulders, and stomach.

But inside, his heart still banged against his chest wall. His pulse still raced.

There was the fork in the road. The vehicle bounced from side to side. Roads like this weren't meant for low-slung cars like Red's.

Estimated time of arrival, one minute.

How deep would she dig? She had gotten houses put on the historical register or whatever it was called. It would be child's play for her to research the deed, find out that it belonged to one George Owens.

Up ahead was the clearing.

Ten seconds...

The only thing he could do was to tell himself she didn't matter to him. That way, it wouldn't matter if he hurt her.

"Ta da! Do you recognize it from my picture? The saltbox!"

"You found it."

"At first I wasn't sure it was the right one. It's kind of run down since I was a girl, and the trees are a lot taller and of course no one comes back here to pick strawberries anymore. But I compared it to the photo, and this is definitely it."

Sam sat glued to the seat of her car, looking out the windshield at the house he had been in only days ago. The house where he'd grown up.

Red's hand was on the door handle. "What are you sitting there for? Don't you want to get out and take a closer look?"

"Hold it," he said, pointing to his dad's pickup. "Somebody lives here."

"No they don't. That truck hasn't moved since last Sunday. And there's a padlock on the door."

"It's still private property. You can't just—" he said to the sound of her slamming door.

He had no choice but to get out. As he watched her practically skip down the boardwalk his dad built to keep from tracking mud into the house, his thoughts raced.

He had to treat this like any other covert operation.

"See over there?" Red pointed to the garden. "That's where Mom and I used to pick berries. Let me go get you one."

"I hate strawberries." In his mind's eye Sam saw his own mom bent over, weeding her precious berry patch, back during one of those Arcadian summers spent hanging with Jeff and Derek. Once when he slipped into the pantry to grab some Cheerios to take back to their fort, he'd caught her depositing the day's take in an old cider jug. Sometime after she left, Sam checked and found that it was empty. That strawberry patch had been her means of escape.

Red frowned. "No one hates strawberries."

She flitted from one corner of the yard to another, plucking yellow dandelions and purple violets while Sam stood in the center of the boardwalk and watched. She looked almost like a teenager in her white sundress that draped and billowed around her curves when she walked. He couldn't bear the thought of robbing her of her youthful enthusiasm...her fondest dream.

She looked up from her tiny bouquet. "Isn't this exciting? Don't you love it?"

Like a Bagram POW camp.

She ducked beneath the clothesline and ran over to the cistern.

"Look at this. It's for catching rainwater. In the old days, girls used to wash their hair in it."

Girls like Cindy and his mother.

"Now, watering your plants with rainwater is the height of chic." She laughed. "It's like chickens. There used to be chickens running around here, and now the hipsters in Portland are showing off their designer hen houses in their front yards. Everything old is new again."

Little did she know.

She eyed the shiny white, hundred-gallon gas tank up and down critically. "What's this? It looks out of place."

"Propane tank."

"A blight on the property if you ask me. Kind of ruins the whole rustic effect, don't you think?"

Sam looked around, suddenly anxious that someone might show up and blow his cover, unlikely as that was.

"No utilities this far out. If you want gas for a fireplace or a stove or something, you got to bring it in."

"At least it's somewhat hidden, here in the back."

She went up to the door, knocked, and rattled the knob despite the padlock.

"We're trespassing. Someone could come down the road any minute."

Not exactly a lie.

"I told you," she said without a care. "No one lives here. It may even be abandoned. I'll find out for sure as soon as I get a break in my schedule long enough to run down to the courthouse."

Sam pointed to his watch. "Let's pop smoke. I'd like to stop and get some decent snacks to go with the wine so we don't have to settle for Sweetarts and popcorn from the concession stand."

She turned from where her nose was pressed to a windowpane and frowned. "I like popcorn. You didn't say anything about wanting to stop for food before."

"I was waiting to see where you were taking me. For all I knew, we were going out to eat. Didn't want to ruin it."

Subdued, she left the window and followed him back toward the car.

"What are you planning to do when you find out who owns this? Put it on some historical listing?" Anything was better than her taking up residence here, in his childhood hell.

"Haven't you been listening? I want to buy it," she said, her eyes filled with hope. "To live in. This is my dream house."

"You can't live here." He couldn't imagine coming here to visit her, eating in the same kitchen, making love to her in his boyhood bedroom.

Her face fell, just as he had known it would.

"Why not?" she said, scampering to keep up with his long strides. "I probably have enough money saved for a down payment."

"It's way too much house for you," he said, feeling like his heart was full of dirty socks.

"I know it needs work, but as long as it's livable, what's the hurry? Part of the fun will be in fixing it up."

"It's too far out, for one thing. You don't want to be a woman alone all the way out there, far away from the police and the fire department."

She snorted. "What's gotten into you all of a sudden? You sound like Grandma."

"You should listen to your elders."

"How'd you get so bossy, Owens?"

"Not bossing you. Just telling you the way it is."

"I'm not scared." She raised her chin. "This is what I want. I've wanted it for a long time, and no one's going to talk me out of it."

Chapter 12

A couple hours later at the drive-in, Sam glanced at Red, engrossed in the film.

Even before the house incident, he had had zero hopes of being able to get lost in a chick flick. He'd agreed to come here purely to comply with Red's "terms."

His dad's mental status was still being evaluated. So far, Sam had stayed on the periphery of things, figuring if anything important happened, the facility would let him know. But it might be time for him to get more involved.

A burst of laughter came from the driver's side and he glanced over at Red munching popcorn, unaware of the fact that the man next to her was not the hometown hero she thought he was, but a dirty, rotten liar whose heart was an empty, black hole.

He would talk to Dad's doctor, see what he could extract from him. If Dad was as far gone as he thought, the next step was a lawyer. The only lawyer he knew was the one who had helped him establish the consortium. Gary Russo.

He exhaled. Now that he had the beginnings of a plan, he could set this evening's house incident on one of the many shelves he'd constructed in his brain in order to maintain his sanity.

He glanced out the windshield at the big screen, automatically reckoning the distance at twenty-four yards, which was seventy-two feet or 21.946 meters.

That done, he was able to relax into the plot a little. The lead actress wasn't hard to look at. And he picked up a couple of decent jokes to add to his repertoire.

Halfway through the movie came the first bedroom scene. Stealthily, he reached for Red's thigh, but she blocked him with an arm.

His head fell back. The woman frustrated him like a one-legged man in an ass-kicking contest.

In the movie, the hero who had brought the heroine a bouquet that made

Sam's limp daisies pale in comparison was now grilling her a five-course meal. And doing it in an apron that showed off his ripped obliques.

Sam took Red's hand, hoping she might do that tickly thing she did last week up on Ribbon Ridge. *Hey, beggars and guys who brought grocery store daisies couldn't be choosy.*

Let the magic begin.

But Red's fingers didn't budge. In fact, she seemed to be so taken with the actor, she'd forgotten there was a real, live guy right beside her.

Sam studied the hero pouring wine for the heroine. What was so great about him? In real life, he was probably one of those guys who actually wore the safety harness when he jogged on the treadmill.

* * * *

"Awwwww." Red sighed with satisfaction.

Sam's eyes opened to the credits rolling.

"You fell asleep."

"No I didn't. Just resting my eyes."

"Yes, you did. You didn't like it?"

"No, it was awesome. Let's come back and see it again tomorrow night."

Red pursed her lips, while in the field surrounding them, cars rumbled to life and maneuvered into the line snaking toward the drive-in's exit. If Sam were behind the wheel, he'd be doing the same, but it was Red tonight, and she was apparently in no hurry.

"If you were watching, then you know what Matthew's job was."

"Who's Matthew?"

"The guy in the film. What did he do for a living?"

"He was a—" *A cheesedick.* "A whaddayacallit. Guy who owns a flower shop."

Red smirked. "No, not a florist."

"A chef."

"Wrong again. He was a professor."

"That's what I said. A professor who's into flowers and nude grilling."

"Humph. That's about the extent of what I know about your old job."

"What's that supposed to mean?" His heart squeezed. Couldn't she see the obvious—that his soul was filled with spiders?

"Don't act like you don't know. You promised to tell me more about what you did in the service."

"Nothing as sexy as the nudist, grilling professor. Like I said, I analyzed the demand for supplies, forecasted future needs, negotiated bids."

"That sounds like a script you memorized out of some recruiter's catalog."
How'd she know? "I can't help it. It is what it is."

"What was that big, shiny medal on your chest the night of your homecoming?"

"What medal?"

"The star-shaped one hanging from the red, white, and blue ribbon."

He looked away. "It's like kids' sports nowadays. Everybody's a winner."

"Come on, Sam. Tell me something."

"There's nothing to tell."

"How about why you came home before your commitment was up?"

His head whipped around. "It was only a couple of weeks shy."

"Three weeks. I looked up when you left and then I counted backward."

She was an aggravating little minx and she wasn't going to stop. He scrubbed his chin. Time for a diversionary tactic.

"I put a Kawasaki Z750 through the front window of the Hotel Sofitel in Luxembourg."

Inside the Impala, all was quiet. The occasional bursts of conversation from open windows of other cars, the kids running pell-mell toward the snack bar clenching dollar bills in grubby fists were gone now. Only a few other cars remained in their slots by the speakers facing the dark screen, waiting for the line of red taillights to dissipate.

"Why?"

"Why's anyone ride their bike through a plate glass window? I was drunk out of my mind."

She considered that. "I've never once seen you get drunk. Even though you're around wine all day."

"I don't make a habit of it."

"So why then? What stressed you out so badly that you felt like you had to get that hammered? And what did that have to do with ending your career?"

His mouth clamped shut. He'd already said too much.

"Were you hurt?"

He laughed. "Ironic thing is, the booze probably protected me. Kept me from stiffening up on impact."

Red trailed her finger across the scar on his forehead. "Is that where this came from?"

"It's a scratch. A few stitches. That's all."

"Why wouldn't you tell me how you got it when I asked before?"

"I said, it's nothing. Forgot all about it."

"Did they arrest you?"

He gazed out at the night sky and nodded. "That's what usually happens."

"Handcuffs and all?"

He shifted his weight, uncomfortable with being questioned.

"I can't imagine what sitting in the back of a cop car with my wrists bound would feel like," she murmured.

There are a lot of things you can't imagine.

"So it was enough to get you sent home, but your discharge must've been an honorable one or Senator Hollins wouldn't have been there taking advantage of the photo op."

"I told you more than I've told anyone else. Can't you just take that and be happy with it?"

"The Army let you go because the pressure was too much. You were a good soldier, so they cut you a break, but you'd had as much as you could take."

I snapped, all right? "That's right. You figured it out. Congratulations, Doc. Happy now?"

It was Red's turn to be silent.

After a moment, he looked over at her. "So," he said, back in control of his voice, "you done?" She'd dredged up a lot of old dirt. All he wanted was to get going, to be alone until it settled again.

"No. Not yet."

Out of the blue, she reached over and put her arms around his neck until her face was inches from his. "I'm sorry for the pain you went through."

And then her mouth was on his, soft and consoling.

He wasn't ready for it. Was still wallowing in his past. He was stiff in her arms.

Red's tongue prodded and probed, urging him to not just passively accept her empathy but to embrace it, to immerse himself in her compassion…her unquestioning belief in him as something whole, something good.

He began to relax.

Like the tide washing broken shells out to sea, her kisses washed away fragments of his past. It had been weeks since they'd made love, weeks of learning to live with the frustration of having her whenever he wanted and then, suddenly, not having her.

His need for her overwhelmed him. He craved her mouth, her hair, every inch of her skin, the entire measure of her. He wanted to take refuge inside her, to merge completely until there was no more him and her, only them.

"Doc."

Had he said that out loud? Usually, she was the vocal one.

It didn't matter. Nothing mattered except having her. He scooped up handfuls of her bottom and slid it toward him, blessing the guy who had designed the Impala's bench front seat.

"We're never trading this in," he rasped.

"We?"

Immediately, he reverted to form. "You, I meant. *You're* never trading it in."

She gazed unsmiling into his eyes, her breath coming in gasps, her lips wet in the moonlight. They shared a look that transcended time and space…a look he wouldn't forget if he lived another hundred years. But his hunger was a raging river and she'd let him get this far. He ruched her lower until he was lying fully across her. But when he parted her legs, she went limp.

"Tonight's just for kissing," she panted.

Sam looked down at her intact clothes, shocked to realize that kissing was all they had accomplished. He hadn't once fingered the silken skin that lay beneath her shirt.

Slowly, reluctantly, he sat up, freeing her to do the same.

But instead of getting back behind the wheel, she turned and burrowed her back up to his chest, drawing her knees up under her chin.

Sam reached out to pet her calf on top of her jeans before he realized that might be breaking one of her arbitrary rules, and instead settled for simply cupping her elbow.

"Thank you for sharing that story with me," she said. "I'm not doing this to hurt you. Just the opposite. I want to help you get free of whatever it is that's haunting you."

He stroked the crease in her elbow with his thumb. It wasn't as if he had bought into her plan lock, stock, and barrel. He was biding his time until he came up with a solution to this dilemma of his own making, without losing the best thing that had ever happened to him.

Chapter 13

Sam dropped off Red, drove to the first stop sign, and pulled out his phone, even though it was pushing midnight.

"Woodcrest Assisted Living and Memory Care."

"This is Sam Owens. I'm calling to see where things stand with my father. George Owens."

"George Owens?"

Sam forced himself to be patient. If he wanted to get information, he needed to stay in the nursing staff's good graces. "That's right," he said in a level voice.

"Let me see...."

Seconds ticked by with maddening slowness.

"Are you on record as someone we can talk to?"

"I should be." *I'm the only one stupid enough to care.* "He was admitted last week for evaluation. Was acting a little strange."

"And this is the first you're checking on him?"

Until tonight, there was no pressure to hide the house.

"I've been tied up at work. Figured if there was news, you'd get ahold of me."

"What was your name again?"

"First name Sam. Sierra Alpha Mike. Last name Owens."

"I'm sorry, Mr. Sierra, but I don't see your name here on the chart."

Jesu— He bit his tongue. "It's Owens, same as him. I should be on there. I'm the one who brought him in in the first place." *Should have just let him blow himself up like he wanted.*

"I'm sorry, Owens." There was another pause. "I don't see that on here, either."

Sam gritted his teeth. "Is the night manager there?"

"She is, but she's with a resident and I'm not sure how long she'll be.

Can I have the director call you tomorrow?"

"Could you? Here's my number." He punched end and tossed the phone onto the passenger seat. He could call the doctor, but the office wouldn't be open until Monday.

* * * *

Sam was seated in his office late Sunday morning when his phone rang. It was the director from Woodcrest. Sam grabbed it and leaped to his feet.

Following the preliminaries, she said, "We're still waiting to hear from his doctor. If Mr. Owens is deemed unable to take care of himself, the doctor has the power to declare a 302, meaning he requires professional care. At that point, your father can fill out the forms to apply for formal admission with Medicare paying for the first—"

"My father can't even fill out a freaking grocery list." He should know. He'd given him a pre-printed pad months ago. All Dad had to do was check off what he needed, milk, bread, whatever, and Sam would pick it up and bring it on his weekly visits to check on him. Yet he never filled it out once.

There was a pause. "Obviously, I was speaking rhetorically," she said coolly. "The patient doesn't have to fill out the forms himself. He can do it with the assistance of you or another authorized signatory."

"But what you're saying is that we're not anywhere near there yet."

"Correct."

"How long does it usually take to get a definitive answer?"

"It's different in every case."

"Can you at least give me an estimate so I know what we're dealing with here?"

"It can take up to several weeks."

"Several weeks?"

"As I said. Every case is different."

Simultaneously he sucked in a breath and drew back his fist. The faint odor of fresh paint stopped his fist as it made contact with the wall. The drywall was less than a year old. He didn't want to have to explain a hole in it.

Bursting with frustration, all he could do was pace his small office, scrub a hand over his hair, and try to reconcile himself to waiting.

* * * *

First thing Monday morning, Sam rifled his desk drawer for the welcoming folder Woodcrest had given him the day of Dad's admission until he found the number of the doctor.

"I'm sorry. Dr. Mowbray is out until Friday."

"Who's taking care of his case load?"

"Dr. Stephan is on-call for emergencies. Do you have an emergency?"

If Red found out that house was his, he was dead. Did that count?

"Can you check my father's record and see if they've come up with a diagnosis for him yet?"

"I'm sorry, only the doctor is authorized to give out that information. Can I leave a message for Dr. Mowbray to call you when he gets back?"

"Yes. When will that be? Will he just see the message Friday, or will he actually call me back then?" His voice control was impressive, if he said so himself. Maybe he still had it, after all. Or maybe it was the pressure. He'd always worked best under pressure—until he didn't.

"I can't answer that. All I can do is leave him the message and you'll have to wait."

Sam hung up and looked unseeing out his office window. He was only twenty-nine. He'd thought he had time before he had to start thinking about the future. Time to get up each morning in a free country and be grateful for no longer being under Psychodad's thumb. For old friends and the opportunity to work hard at a meaningful job. To take his sweet time getting to know a woman before the realities of—he couldn't even say the word to himself. What came beyond that was too scary to think about, because if he were anything like his father, he would wind up hurting the very people he cared most about.

But as scary as the thought of committing to Red was, the thought of losing her was scarier.

And yet, he couldn't let her get hold of that saltbox.

If ever there was a case of being up the creek without the proverbial paddle, this was it. What was he supposed to do?

If he wanted to keep Red, he had to take away her fondest dream.

Chapter 14

Thursday night, the consortium stayed open late. Heath brought in Poppy after her shift at the café, joining a half dozen tourists who were already there. They were followed by Rory Stillman and Mona.

Then, around six, there was movement outside the tall windows and Sam's friends' banter came to an abrupt halt as Red rounded the corner from the parking lot.

Poppy raised her glass. "Here comes your girlfriend," she teased over the rim.

Sam's bar rag stilled. "Say again?"

"Red? You two are going to the wedding together."

Junie's eyes danced. "Got your RSVPs."

"What?" Poppy looked wide-eyed from Junie to Sam and back, while Heath and Manolo sported smug grins that translated as, *welcome-to-the-club, sucker.*

Remembering the new rules, Sam dried his hands and went out from behind the bar to meet Red halfway.

Her flush when he took her hands in his and kissed her cheek made all the teasing worth it.

They walked back to the bar together. Heath immediately gave up his prime location nearest to the register and the women took turns embracing Red.

Then Sam beat a retreat back to his comfort zone behind the bar and poured Red a glass of her favorite Riesling.

"So what's new?" asked Poppy pointedly.

So much for subtlety, thought Sam. But to his surprise, instead of launching into the details of their new relationship, Red brought up her perennially favorite topic. "You remember the house I was looking for? The rare saltbox? I found it."

No. Sam tensed. *Not here, in front of all our friends.*

Junie laughed. "You're always house hunting. Which one is this?"

"This one's different. It feels like I've been looking for it all my life. I want this house. I *need* to have it."

"You're really excited about this. Where is this place?"

"To the west of here, off the Nestucca Lake Access Road, past the McGuire Reservoir."

Junie and Poppy exchanged glances. "That's a ways," said Poppy.

"I've always dreamed of a little patch of land of my own, out in the country where I can have a garden."

Manolo frowned. "Hey, Sam. Didn't you tell me your old house was somewhere out in the boonies?"

All heads turned toward Sam.

"It's a big country. Clarkston's surrounded by woods."

"Not to the north and east," said Rory thoughtfully. "North is Gaston, and east is Highway 99."

Behind the bar, Sam was intent on rearranging a display of bottles and glassware.

"Have you made an offer on it?" asked Poppy.

"I don't even know if it's for sale. But I'm hopeful, because no one lives there. I looked in the window. It still has its original paint. The colors are right off of the Newberg Downtown Coalition Color Palette. And there's a big fireplace. The white surround is really sooty, but I'm hoping it's just cosmetic damage."

Sam could feel Manolo's suspicious gaze burning a hole through his back. Manolo had been raised in the restaurant business. He wasn't fooled by Sam's busywork. But he'd deal with Manolo later. Right now he had to listen carefully to find out exactly how much Red had learned about the house's ownership.

"What are you waiting for?" asked Junie.

"I've had a full slate this week, plus I just accepted a part-time consulting gig every other Friday at the assisted living facility in Newberg. All I've had time to do is look around online for who owns the house, but I haven't come up with a name yet. The county is still in the process of uploading their old records, and The Recorder of Deeds Office isn't open on Saturdays. It looks like I'll have to sneak out early some weekday and drive down to the courthouse and do some research."

The courthouse was in McMinnville. Lucky for Sam that Red's services were in high demand. Plus, she had a hard time with the word "no." It could be days—weeks—before she had a block of time big enough to make the drive worthwhile.

"What's this about you two going to Junie's wedding as a couple?" asked Poppy.

Red lit up and looked at Junie. "I take it you got the RSVPs."

"Yesterday. Now we can seat you next to each other at Poppy and Heath's table. Won't that be great?"

"You guys are officially dating?" asked Poppy.

Red smiled prettily at Sam.

"How long has this been going on?" Poppy complained. "Am I the last one to know?"

"I knew something was up as far back as Sam's homecoming," said Junie, eyeing Red knowingly. "Remember? Red spilled her drink on him?"

"That was an accident," insisted Red.

Junie smirked. "Go ahead. Keep telling yourself that."

"I'm so happy for you guys!" exclaimed Poppy.

All this feminine fuss, thought Sam. They were going to a wedding together. Not getting hitched themselves.

An hour or so later, it was closing time. Tabs were settled, women slinging purses over their shoulders.

Manolo tossed an arm around his fiancée. "Anyone who can, come out to our place Saturday night. The DJ wants a playlist. We're going to be listening to music, making our picks."

And then everyone was gone and quiet descended.

"Wait up and I'll walk you to your car," Sam told Red.

From her perch at the bar, she watched him methodically close out the register and turn down the lights. Then he came around and stood between her legs and dipped his chin. "I think I like being known as your girlfriend."

He kissed her.

"You know what good girlfriends do, don't you?"

"Hm." She grinned lazily. "Nice try, Owens."

That familiar, irresistible need to possess her, body and soul, overcame him. He gave her a mock offended look. "What? I'm just saying. A man has needs."

"And I'm saying, we still have a ways to go."

"You never did tell me exactly what the steps are."

"I didn't?"

He nuzzled her neck and slipped his hands up under her shirt in the back. "First was holding hands."

He ran his hands down her arms, intertwining his fingers with hers. "Then kissing."

He kissed her until they were both breathing hard.

"I think we're officially kissing experts," he said in her ear.

"We could give kissing lessons." She giggled.

"Write a book: *Everything You've Ever Wanted to Know about Kissing*."

"Hm. I'm dying to know what's next."

"I think you're going to like it."

"Don't keep me in suspense."

"We sleep together."

"Yes." He pumped his fist. "About time."

"Don't get too excited. I said sleep. Without touching."

He held her at arm's length. "Come back?"

"Sleep. Just sleep. In the same bed. And talk, and kiss, if you want."

"How is that even possible?"

"That's the plan."

"I guaran-damn-tee you, no man came up with this plan."

She chuckled. "Actually, it was a man-woman team. Masters and Johnson. Ever hear of them?"

"Were they masochists?"

She tipped her head back and laughed. "No, only the most respected sex researchers in the world."

"Well, if Masters—or Johnson, whichever one was the dude—had ever met you, he would've known that his plan counted as torture under the Geneva Convention."

"That's very sweet—I think."

"When do we do this?" A sense of urgency that had nothing to do with desire propelled Sam. He knew what it was but he didn't want to look it in the eye.

"When do you want to do it?"

"How about right now. Tonight."

"I don't have my stuff."

"What stuff?"

"My toothbrush."

"You can use mine."

"You don't have any makeup I can borrow. And I need my pajamas."

"You don't need pajamas."

"Yes I do. Did you think we were going to be naked?"

Sam rolled his eyes. "Sorry, lady, but nothing comes between me and my sheets, except maybe a feisty redhead. You're just going to have to deal with it."

"Technically, we're both supposed to be in pajamas. How about tomorrow night?"

He nuzzled her again. "I don't know if I can wait twenty-four hours. You are just too damn sexy."

"My first client's at eight thirty tomorrow morning," she said, lifting her chin so he could graze his lips beneath it.

"So's mine," he mumbled against her neck.

"Tomorrow's Friday. That'll work better. That way I won't have to set my alarm."

Sam stroked a lock of Red's hair back behind her ear. "You make me crazier than a caffeine addict locked out of Starbucks, you know that?"

"Now you're getting the point of our little exercise."

"To make me suffer?"

"That there's more to being intimate than wham, bam, thank you ma'am."

Shame welled up in him.

"Doc. I never..." He struggled for words. "I always thought we were on the same page."

"We were, until..." It was her turn to be tongue-tied.

Sam tipped her chin up. "I never wanted to take advantage."

"I know. I just need you to see how much better we can be, with a little conscious effort."

"Tomorrow, then."

"Where?"

Sam thought of his own, bleak room with its single bed. "How about dinner out? After that I'll find us a nice room somewhere. See if that B&B outside Newberg you're always talking about has anything. I'll bring champagne."

Red's face glowed. "That would be lovely."

Chapter 15

Red's heart expanded with happiness as Sam locked the consortium door and they walked out into the twilit summer night, hand in hand.

They were halfway to her car when a white puppy toddled out into the road at the same time a sports car rounded the corner from Main Street, gathering speed on its way out of town. The dog was the picture of innocence, wagging from tongue to tail, blissfully unaware of the four thousand pound vehicle bearing down on it.

Suddenly Sam was tearing straight into the car's path. From the center stripe down Highway 47 he raised a halting hand. Brakes screeched as sheer momentum propelled locked tires forward, leaving long, black skid marks on the asphalt.

While the car bounced on its springs, sending dust motes dancing in the evening sun, Sam scooped up the errant dog and jogged back to where Red stood rooted with her hand clapped over her mouth.

As the car zoomed away, a woman loped up with a leash looped around her hand. "Sparkle? Sparkle! Thank God. I've been chasing him for blocks."

Sam transferred the squirming bundle into his mistress's arms.

"Thank you so much," she said.

She looked at Sam for a response, but he hadn't uttered a word since the rescue. Hands on hips, he turned and walked several yards into the parking lot.

"You're welcome." Red dismissed the woman with a smile and a wave. Then she went to Sam, curled her arm around his shoulder, and guided him back toward the building.

He stopped when he saw the direction she was headed. "Thought you were going home."

Her hand ran down his arm, her fingertips pressing stealthily into his inner wrist. "How are you feeling?"

"I'm fine."

"You're pale, your skin is clammy, and your pulse is racing. Are you sure you're—"

Before she could finish, Sam made a dash for the bushes.

By the time he turned back to her, his usual front was back in place. "Last time I order the lunch special at Casey's."

"Sam. You've been traumatized."

"It's nothing."

"You love dogs that much?"

He scowled at her like she was the crazy one. "What else would it be? I couldn't stand there and watch a—" His voice caught. "An animal get killed."

"If I knew, I wouldn't have asked. I was thinking maybe it was your overdeveloped sense of powerlessness and injustice."

"What kind of talk is that?"

"You risked your life for a dog. It was heroic. But seriously, Sam, you could have been killed."

"I said it's nothing. Forget it. I'm fine."

"You're a little green. Why don't we go back inside and you can lie down for a bit. I'll put a cool cloth on your head and take your pulse again after you've rested."

"I said I'm good. Let's go."

She let him turn her around and walk her to the parking lot, where he opened her car door. She slid in, still concerned for his health.

"You know that book on kissing we're going to write?" he asked. "Remind me to include a chapter about when not to kiss. Like after you hurl."

"Owens. It's not funny. I'm worried about you."

He stood with one hand on the hood of her car and the other on his hip. "Told you, it was the lunch special."

"Have you ever thought about adopting a dog of your own?"

His grin evaporated. He slammed the car door.

Red expected him to stomp off, but instead he just stood there, dazed, like a lost little boy.

Red's heart went out to him. She cranked down the Impala's window.

"What did I say to upset you?"

"Already had the best dog there ever was. Riggley. There'll never be another one like her."

Red smiled softly. "Riggley. That's a nice name."

Sam lifted a hand and turned to go. "I'll call you about dinner."

Red sat there in her car and watched him stalk away until he disappeared around the corner of the consortium.

It wasn't something Sam had eaten that had made him retch, she thought. It was something eating Sam.

Chapter16

Sam sat down on his narrow bed, rested his forearms on his thighs, and relived his asinine act of an hour ago. *Throwing his life away for a dog he didn't even know?* What the hell was wrong with him? And Red, a psychologist. What must she be thinking? He sighed and scraped his hand through his hair.

And then there was his childhood home. That was a close call tonight. How had he gotten himself backed into this corner?

He was fated to be a liar, that's how. Lying was the best weapon he knew to handle Psychodad's sick manipulation: denying that it happened. Sticking it away in a box on a back shelf of his mind. If no one else could see it, he could pretend it didn't exist.

Luke and Cindy had their own way of dealing. They hightailed it out of town the minute they could and never looked back, leaving Sam to endure the constant friction between his parents.

Until one day when Sam was eight, his mom took him out to Dad's truck and pointed to the lipstick-stained cigarette butts in the ashtray as proof of Dad's infidelity. Then Mom packed some clothes and left.

Sam reached under the bed and pulled out the newer of the two duffel bags that he'd slung there on the day he'd moved in.

He loosened the Miller's Knot, pulled out its contents and laid them across the top of his dresser, his blood rushing through his veins like Walker Creek in the spring floods.

First, his digies, still neatly rolled. Night vision camera. Binoculars, various disguises.

And then, inside his old mess kit with a misshapen tube of toothpaste and a plastic razor, he found The Silver Star.

Sam tossed the medal onto the dresser as if it were nothing more valuable than a quarter. He had never set out wanting to lie to Red. He just wanted to be economical with the truth…keep a half-wall up between them to protect her from the bullshit.

If she would have let things go on the way they were, everything would be fine. That's not how Red operated, though. All those degrees and her obsessive house hunting were proof of that. When Red wanted something, she didn't stop until she got it.

Now she had her sights set on him. His fear was that once she caught him, she'd be repulsed with what she had found.

* * * *

Sam shot up in bed, still wearing his street clothes. His body was hot, but his hands were freezing. He fell back on his pillow with a forearm slung across his eyes, trying to remember the night terror. Something about a dog. But the dream merely changed shape and then disintegrated. Sam drew his hand down his face, distorting his features. That's how all his dreams ended, unresolved.

Light from the morning sky filtered in from his open window. A car shushed by on the street. Sam checked his watch. His meeting at the Wine Press commenced in twenty-two minutes.

In boot camp he had seventeen seconds to be out of his room before the end of reveille. Those seventeen seconds had taught him how to be ready for any situation. That with every new day comes responsibility and living the core values of honor, respect, and devotion to duty.

He raced to the shower, cranked the knob, and braced himself for the lash of icy needles on his face.

There was a certain, cold comfort in being uncomfortable. Pain forced him to be in the present.

Briskly, Sam lathered himself from head to toe, the day's priorities unfolding in his brain. He'd been waiting for this day all week. It was the day Dad's doctor was supposed to be back. He had the Wine Press meeting to attend to first. Then, another phone call to get the update on Dad's medical situation.

The consortium was going to be hopping. Today was the first day they were shipping wine for the new wine club. Sam had hired extra hands to come in and help, but it was up to him to supervise.

Finally, after all that was done, he had tonight with Red to look forward to.

As he did every morning, he flicked on the TV to listen to the forecast while he dressed. The weather played a significant role in the annual grape crop. Today was going to be a hot one. There was something about a tropical storm over Hawaii that might bear watching.

One hand pressed the electric razor to his face while the other tugged on a fresh pair of jeans. Then he was out the door, keys in hand, the contents of his duffel still strewn, forgotten, across the dresser.

Chapter 17

Sam's meeting with the Wine Press ate up his entire Friday morning, but it had been worth it. He walked out of there more than satisfied with the group advertising rate he'd negotiated for his people.

He took his phone off silent to find a number of missed calls and messages. But before he checked any of them, he had to get hold of Dad's doctor. He punched in the number as he jumped into his van. Following an interminable hold he finally got Dr. Mowbray's medical assistant.

"Has he seen my message yet?"

"I'm sorry, but he's not back yet."

Sam felt his blood pressure ratcheting up.

"I've been waiting all week. Look, it's important."

"If he's not back today, it should be tomorrow," she blurted. "His flight's been delayed by weather."

Something Sam had heard earlier that morning came back to him. "A tropical storm?"

The assistant paused.

Sam sensed weakness in her hesitation.

"How'd you know that?"

"He's in Hawaii?"

"I didn't say that."

"You didn't have to."

Sam tossed his phone onto the seat of the van and cursed. While his very future hinged on knowing what was wrong, Dad's doctor was lounging around some pool on Waikiki sucking down Mai Tais.

He could find a new doctor. But that wouldn't get him the information he needed any faster.

His hands were tied—and there was nothing Sam hated more than not being in control.

He pulled into the back of the consortium where the dock was. What fresh hell was this? From the van, he could see there were problems. Big problems.

Keval was supposed to be in the front of the house manning his computer monitor and welcoming guests. Instead, he was standing on the dock, dwarfed by a circle of burly men.

He slammed the van door and marched over, their irritated expressions ratcheting up his concern.

"What's going on?"

"Thank heavens you're back." Keval's brow was etched with worry. "The good news is, the computer glitch's fixed," he said in a rush. "The bad news is, we got a backlog of orders coming out the wazzoodle—most of them from out of town—and not enough stock to fill them, let alone get them shipped out by the promised date. These guys filled what they could in the first hour. But since then, they've been standing around with nothing to do. One of them already left."

"Why the hell didn't you call me?"

"Check your phone. I must've called five times."

Everyone was looking at Sam for answers.

"Pull up the unfilled orders," he told Keval.

He turned to the extras. "How many vehicles do you have among you?"

"Three," said a whippet-thin man with sage black eyes in a weathered face. "Couple of us rode together."

"With my van that makes four. We're going to have to go get more wine ourselves. I'll print out a map and divide the area into sections. Some of you are going to have to make multiple trips, but it is what it is. I'll keep you as close to the bulls-eye as I can. My van holds the most, so I'll hit the outliers on the perimeter."

"You'll pay for our gas?" asked the leader suspiciously.

Sam nodded curtly as he headed for his computer. "I'll take care of you. You have my word."

Sam had started his day already looking forward to the night. Dinner with Red and then champagne and watching the sunset from their balcony at the B&B. After that, their first, whole night together. Even if she had assigned them to sexual purgatory, there was no one else he'd rather be with.

But duty before pleasure.

He kept his spirits up around his men. Then, alone on his first run, he added up the miles between wineries. Factoring in the necessary small talk with vintners and the loading and unloading, there was no way he could be showered, dressed, and ready for dinner at seven.

With a sinking feeling, he realized had no choice but to call Red and cancel.

Red took the news like a trooper. "I understand. You do what you have to do. And don't worry about canceling dinner and the B&B, I'll take care of it."

"You're a gem, you know that, Doc?"

"I know what it's like to have your own business. We'll have plenty of chances to go on dates."

No, they wouldn't. Not after Red found out about the house. She was bound to never want to see him again.

* * * *

The sun was setting when Sam returned from his final run. His van was heavily laden with cases of wine. Both he and it were covered in a reddish coat of dust from the Jory soil that lent Willamette pinot noir its characteristic earthy taste.

Hungry, hot, and sweaty, he prayed there were still men around to help him unload the van. His biceps were already screaming. But they had all put in way more hours this day than they'd bargained for.

Relief flooded him when he saw the scrappy crew on the dock waiting for him to arrive.

The men formed a human chain from the van to the loading dock. As Sam hefted yet another case down the line, he was surprised to see Red walk out of the building carrying a large tray. Behind her came Keval with a case of bottled water.

Sam straightened and saw the sandwich rolls. She'd brought chow. By the looks of it, enough chow to feed a small army.

The men's eyes followed where Sam looked. One by one, strained faces melted.

Red threw back her head and laughed at something Keval said. Sam caught her eye and her laugh softened into a warm smile, making him want to drop his case of wine and go over there and lift her off her feet in a bear hug.

Chapter 18

There was nothing left of the sandwiches but the crumbs, and the last laborer had been paid and his hand shaken.

"Sorry again about tonight," Sam said to Red. "I'll make it up to you."

"No apology needed. These things happen. As long as you don't let work take precedence over your personal life too often."

Sam halted. "This isn't just work. It's my life. I'm dedicated to bring this community together for a common good."

"Why are you yelling? It's not a contest of wills."

"I'm not yelling!"

Red raised an eyebrow.

"Look, Doc," he said, continuing on his way. "In case you haven't noticed, I'm on a mission."

"To do what? What's so urgent that it drives you day and night? You've built your new consortium. You're positioning yourself as a leader of the wine community. What else do you want?"

What he wanted was nothing less than to discover his true identity.

He'd been a sniper, a student, and then a Special Ops agent. It had taken all of that to bring him to the conclusion that the only way he could be the man he wanted to be was by stamping out his childhood once and for all. Only then would he be ready for a real relationship with the woman he had come to love.

Red took his elbow and laid her head on his shoulder as they walked. "Whatever happened to make you see the world as such a contentious place?" she asked guilelessly, peering up at him.

He wasn't about to get into that now.

His arm snaked around her waist. "What do you want to do?"

She shrugged. "I'm happy to just hang out. If you're not too tired, that is."

"Give me a shower and I'm good to go."

They strolled arm in arm the short distance to his place.

Red stopped inside the threshold. "I almost forgot what this looked like. This is the first I've been back here since the new consortium was built."

Sam had converted the old house's parlor to a reception area when he started the original consortium. It had worked well enough until the business grew big enough to warrant its own building. With the colorful Red standing in it, it looked drabber than ever.

"The only thing I do here is sleep and shower. I eat practically every meal out. You remember what the kitchen looks like."

Red smiled ruefully. "Avocado appliances. Linoleum floor."

At least it was clean. He stooped to pick a piece of lint from the carpet. "What do I need a kitchen for? I don't cook."

Red gave him a gentle shove. "Go, shower. I'll find something to do."

Amazing what a cake of pine tar soap and some half-decent water pressure could do. Sam took longer than usual to wash off his day.

By the time he strode from the bathroom to his bedroom with a towel cinched around his waist, he was whistling—until he saw The Silver Star dangling from Red's fingertips.

"I promise I wasn't snooping. There wasn't anything to do in the living room."

She was generous, referring to the reception area that way. There were no magazines, no TV. Just a motley collection of mismatched office furniture. Who wouldn't be bored?

As for his stuff lying openly on the dresser, he had no one to blame but himself.

He forced his feet forward to confront the inevitable.

"I remember this," she said, fingering the medal. "It was on your uniform at your homecoming. Tell me what it's for."

"The Silver Star."

"I can see that."

He swallowed. "Awarded by order of the Secretary of Homeland Security for 'gallantry while in action against an enemy.'"

"What does that mean, exactly?" she asked cautiously.

He lowered himself to the edge of the bed, propped his elbows on his spread knees, and hung his head, thinking of how much he could tell her.

Red sat down beside him and rested her hand on the towel covering his thigh. "Sam, I'm a doctor. Nothing you could say is going to have me clutching my pearls."

He snorted. If she knew half the things he'd done, she'd do more than that. Pearls would be flying off in all directions of the compass.

"Whatever it was, it's over now. You don't have to carry it around anymore."

Some things were impossible to forget.

In the service of his country, nothing was more important than maintaining his cover. Even if it had left his heart shriveled up and pockmarked like an old potato.

"Trust me, Doc, you don't want me. You don't want anything to do with me. I've done a lot of bad things, most of which I wouldn't tell you, even if I could."

"Can you tell me why you crashed your motorcycle into a window?"

He had mentioned that, hadn't he?

The room started closing in. He couldn't breathe. He got up and opened the window.

"Sam," she pleaded to his back. "Talk to me."

She wanted him to talk?

He'd talk.

He spun around. "Do you know what it's like to sit in the same room day after day, month after month with the personification of evil, and pretend to share their values?" he bellowed, spittle flying. "That no matter how revolted I was with myself for playing along, my life—the lives of thousands of my fellow citizens—depended on convincing them that I was one of them?"

Rapidly he strode across the small room, unable to bear her inevitable disgust. He slung a forearm along the dresser top and hid his face in it.

"They wouldn't stop watching."

He heard her approaching footsteps, felt her comforting hand on his back.

"Watching what?" she asked softly.

"The carnage. Over and over again. Innocent people, begging for mercy. They never got tired of it. Clapping and cheering."

There was a long pause.

"And then what?" prodded Red. "How did it end?"

Sam returned to the window and gazed unseeing at the distant mountains. "There was a glitch. They heard a rumor I wasn't who I said I was."

Another long pause.

"What made you do it?"

He sniffed derisively. "Do you know how many times I've asked myself that very question?"

"And how do you answer it?"

He turned and faced her. "I learned early on that things aren't right in this world. And that it would take people like me, who'd been wronged, to make it right."

"My God," she whispered. "I thought all the talk about spying was just that—talk."

"I learned to further my cause any way I could. Stringing people along. Blackmail. Bribery. Whatever it took."

Red was at his side. "Shhhhh. It's all right. You're safe now. I'm here with you."

"I never caved under interrogation. They never knew for sure. But..." He cleared his throat. Quietly, he said, "Let's just say they weren't happy with me."

He swiped a forearm across his cheek.

She tugged on his other arm. "Come sit next to me."

"It was two days till the good guys found me in that slum outside Firebase Lilley. Alive—but barely. Guess you could say I was a little gorked out after that." He chuckled ironically. "Spent a few weeks at Landstuhl."

"Landstuhl?"

"Germany. Biggest American hospital outside of the states. That's when the bike took a wrong turn into the Sofitel."

"I thought you said that was Luxembourg."

"That's where everyone goes to unwind, soak up the culture. Europe's not like the states—especially the western states. Everything's closer together."

"You wrecked your bike because of post-traumatic stress." She shook her head. "Bastards."

"The Army? Don't blame them. They were just doing their job. Exploiting their personnel's highest potential to defend our country. I was a mess long before the Army got ahold of me. All they're guilty of is making the most of raw material.

"No. I wrecked my bike because of two liters of vin rouge and a half a bottle of vanilla absinthe." He grinned in self-deprecation, despite the painful memory.

Red squeezed his hand and looked him in the eye. "Thank you for trusting me enough to share. I'm very sorry you had to go through that." She brushed his hair off his forehead. "Take a deep breath. You'll feel better."

Closing his eyes, he did as she said.

To his surprise, the hard ball in his chest where a heart should be softened a little. From out the window he heard the steady rumble of a distant tractor...smelled the green sweetness of new-mown hay.

When he opened his eyes, it was as if a cloud had been lifted. He felt a tightening as his pupils contracted in the slanted rays of the setting sun, gilding Red's translucent skin.

Her eyes were a siren song he couldn't resist, drawing him in.

He leaned in to kiss her, lips slipping over satin lips.

Gradually she leaned back, taking him with her. The bed could barely accommodate Sam alone. The screech of springs stretched to their limit was accompanied by the scent of Red's perfume. She smelled like hope and consolation.

He'd lost his towel somewhere. Naked and vulnerable, he raised himself up on his elbows and gazed down reverently at Red, fully dressed. There had always been heat between them. But now there was so much more. His chest swelled with a feeling too big to contain.

Red's hips shifted until they were beneath his.

His entire body throbbed with pent up need. He was hers now. He knew it with the certainty that the Earth spun around the sun. She made the rules. He was simply a player in her game.

The instant he accepted that fact, he felt exhilarated. The truth really did set you free.

Their chests rose and fell in ragged breaths. Red's cheeks grew rosy, her pupils expanded to black disks, entreating him to lose himself in their depths.

Sam was almost rabid with desire. His hands itched to touch her. He searched her face for answers. "You said we can't. You said not tonight."

Her brow furrowed with her own clashing needs.

He swallowed hard. "Tell me now," he growled, his hand sliding up her ribcage. "Tell me to stop. If you don't…"

* * * *

Red fought to keep a clear head. This was what she had wanted all along, wasn't it? For Sam to open up to her? She'd just never dreamed it would happen like this—in a twin bed atop an old Army blanket. Until this moment they'd never shared a bed of any size. Isn't that what she wanted, too? To stop having sex along the side of the road and move it into the bedroom, where it belonged? Or at least, where it would be more comfortable?

But far from solving anything, Sam's admissions had only complicated matters.

She needed to set her emotions aside and think like a scientist. What were the facts?

She wanted him. Oh, she wanted him. Their chemistry was the one thing that had never been in doubt.

This exercise in chastity had been no picnic for her, either. She wanted him inside her. She needed his touch to send her soaring as only he could.

His eyes pleaded. He was waiting for her to go back on her rules, to give her the green light.

Sam had had a breakthrough of sorts, telling her things he'd kept buried for years.

But there was still so much left unsaid.

She had to decide—now. But how could she make a rational decision when his warm, naked body smelling of piney soap lay atop hers, the force of his need fully apparent through her skirt?

Sam cupped her breast, his thumbing brushing lightly across her erect nipple. His eyes glazed with desire. "You want me as much as I want you."

Her tongue darted out to lick dry lips.

"Say something," he ground out, tightening his grip.

She was molten hot. It took all the strength she had not to arch against him. Their breaths filled the space between them as seconds ticked by.

Sam's jaw tensed. "You're killing me, Doc," he rasped breathlessly. "Say yes or no, but say something."

"Yes," she said helplessly.

"You sure?"

"Yes."

Moments later, a deep, thumping wave of pleasure rolled through Red.

No doubt the farmer cutting hay in the distance heard her call Sam's name over the rumble of his tractor.

Chapter 19

Red and Sam spent the rest of Friday night entangled in each other's arms. The bed left them no choice. He had to admit though, even a twin mattress was better on his lumbar region than the ground.

Saturday morning, they breakfasted at Poppy's. Red hadn't brought up his past again, and no way was he going to stir the pot, not when he had just gotten her back again.

And then it was back to work for Sam for the remainder of the weekend, filling the backlog of wine orders.

Monday morning, he finally got through to Dad's doctor.

"I've given him a complete physical, including medication review and lab tests, and a preliminary cognitive exam. He didn't seem depressed. No treatable abnormalities were found."

"Something's not right," said Sam. "He's as confused as a fart in a fan factory."

"Dementia is a hard condition to accurately diagnose. He might just be experiencing a normal, cognitive decline. It would help if he had been seen regularly over the years, but I'm scrolling through his records and I can't find much history here."

Sam pinched the bridge of his nose. "He never was one for doctors. I don't recall him ever being sick."

"That's all well and good, but not having a baseline makes it difficult for me to ascertain any significant changes. Has your father been having noticeable memory lapses?"

"Not that I recall. Tell you the truth, I don't spend any more time around him than I have to."

"Trouble communicating, then?"

"You kidding? Only way I got him to the initial consult was telling him we were making a run to McDonald's for a hamburger. We went in and he asked the nurse at the counter for a Big Mac and a large fry."

"Sometimes dementia can masquerade as a psychiatric disorder. Has your father had a personality change recently?"

"You mean, is it normal for him to go around jumping curbs with his truck, setting house fires, and hitting on married women half his age?"

Sam sniffed. No. He's always been crazy.

"That last one's pretty typical."

"Flirtation, when excessive, is a documented cause for concern. Unfortunately, it's still very subjective. We can only confidently say a patient has dementia in about half the cases that present."

"I need answers. A lot's riding on your conclusion. He almost burned down his own house. I can't let him go back there unless I know he's not going to do it again. Isn't there some kind of test?"

"There is one…"

"What are we waiting for? Let's get it scheduled."

"It's never an easy thing to hear, but the only way to confirm dementia is after the patient passes... by autopsy."

A beat of silence filled the phone.

"That's it? That's all you've got?"

The doctor sighed. "My recommendation is to either recheck in six months—"

"I don't have six months. I don't even have six days."

"—or refer him to a specialist. Woodcrest has a couple of contractors. Your father wouldn't even have to leave the premises. Do you want to see to it, or have us set it up?"

Between his temperamental wine subscription service, his new "relationship" and the house thing hanging over his head, he didn't need another headache.

"Could you schedule it? That'd take a load off. And would you let me know as soon as you get the results?"

"Of course. And sorry about the delay, earlier."

Sam's next call was to his lawyer to find out what his options were.

Chapter 20

On Saturday night, Sam and Red went to Junie's place to help Junie and Manolo pick out wedding songs for their reception, along with Poppy, Heath, Mona and Rory.

"Should we start?" asked Junie, curled up in a chair with a pad and pencil.

"I thought Keval was coming," replied Poppy.

"Keval is in Portland," said Red.

"Keval's been going to Portland a lot lately," Poppy replied.

"Let's do this," said Red as she distributed sheets of paper from the stack in her arm. "I've compiled a list of the most popular wedding reception songs from the last twenty-five years. I even printed copies so that we could all be on the same page. No pun intended."

Without commenting, Junie looked at her pad, then across the patio at Manolo.

"Now. What do we think of Stevie Wonder?" asked Red.

"Absolutely. Little Stevie, Big Stevie. The more Stevie, the better," replied Poppy.

"Really?" Mona made a face. "That's not very contemporary."

"It's a wedding," argued Rory. "You need stuff that everybody knows, from your great aunt on down. Now's not the time to be showing off how hip your taste in music is."

"How about Michael Jackson?" asked Red. "He's number five on the list."

Rory raised his wineglass in agreement. "Now you're talking. Got to have some Michael in there to get people dancing."

"Is *I'm Too Sexy* on here?" frowned Heath from where he sat on a stone wall in his "Quantum Mechanic" T-shirt flipping through his pages.

Poppy leaned into him, smiled fondly and gave him a one-armed squeeze.

"It doesn't have to be exclusively retro," said Red. "The more contemporary numbers start on page—"

"Um, Red," said Junie.

"Hm?" asked Red, licking her finger to make shuffling through the papers easier.

"Manny and I... we made up our own song list. We just wanted your help in narrowing it down."

"Huh?" Red looked up, her fingers stilling as she saw Junie hold up her pad.

There was a pause. Around the patio, eyes fell in an effort to spare her humiliation. Poppy suddenly found a new fascination with Manolo's intricate stonework and Heath, well Heath was just Heath, no doubt thinking deep thoughts about such things as the origins of the stars and all the lyrics to "*I'm Too Sexy*."

Red swallowed. "Oh."

"I appreciate you going to all this trouble. Really, I do. But if you'd just asked... we want to pick out our own songs."

Red's face grew hot.

"I'm sorry. I just thought..."

"It's okay." Junie got up, went to Red and laid a hand on her arm. "We'll check this out after we've exhausted our list, won't we, Manny?"

"Definitely."

"Maybe there's something here that we hadn't thought of. In fact," she said, flipping through the thick pile, "I'll bet you anything that there is."

* * * *

"I'm going in to get some more wine," Manolo told Sam. "Want to give me a hand?"

"Sorry about that," said Sam, when it was just the two of them. "Red means well."

"Oh, hey. No apology needed, man."

"She just wants everything to be the best it can be for your wedding. Sometimes she goes a little overboard."

"I get it. Junie definitely picked the right person to be her maid of honor. From the moment Junie asked her, Red's been right there in the trenches with her. To the point of even second-guessing Junie's color scheme."

Sam winced. "You didn't grow up around here. You didn't see what we saw. Red growing up in a home like a revolving door. When it came to men, well... her mom didn't discriminate. Red was helpless to make it better. I think that's why she became a therapist. She's still trying to fix things."

"How's that square with this house Red's so set on buying?"

"What do you mean?" Sam asked cautiously.

"I could tell you were bothered by it the other night at the consortium."

"I wasn't bothered."

Manolo thumped his chest. "This is me, Manny, you're talking to."

Sam steeled himself. "The house is between me and Red."

Manolo leaned on the bar. "You can talk to me about anything, man. Don't you know that? When did I not have your back?"

Sam looked over his shoulder at the patio where the others were arguing animatedly for their song choices.

It would do him a world of good to get the house dilemma off his chest.

He sighed, his shoulders slumping. "The house Red wants is the house I grew up in."

"I knew it." Manolo stood to his full height, letting his hand fall on the bar with a smack. "Does she know?"

"No." Sam rubbed his hand over his face.

"Why not? Why haven't you told her?"

"I don't know."

"What do you mean, you don't know? What are you hiding?"

"I don't want her to have it."

"You said you weren't attached to it."

"I'm not. I want to get rid of it. I want it gone. The sooner, the better."

"Why so defensive? What exactly's wrong with it?"

"Don't make me explain. If no one important to me knows about it, then it can't come between us. It doesn't intrude on the good parts of my life."

"A house is a house is a house."

"Not this one."

Manolo glanced furtively around Sam to the patio. "Keep it down. What is it about this place? It haunted or what?"

"You could say that. I was never happy there. Because of that, I kept it separate from the rest of my life. I didn't plan to. It just kind of evolved that way, being that it's so far away from town, from school, from my friends."

"Well, it's a moot point, isn't it, being that belongs to your dad."

"If he can't go back to it, I can take control."

"And what? You don't want it. Sell it. Sell it to Red. Make her happy."

"Except..."

Manolo's face lit up as he pieced it together.

"Then you'd have to keep going there."

"I won't sell. Especially not to Red."

"Then what? Just let it sit there and rot?"

"I don't know yet. I keep thinking about how Dad almost burned it down.

I half wish I hadn't come along when I did."

All his problems, up in smoke. He'd never have to go back in there again, to be faced with them.

"Well, you didn't."

Sam heard footsteps, and then the lively discussion on the patio grew louder as the door opened.

Red's gaze traveled over a somber Manolo and Sam. Normally, they would be bantering, cutting each other up. "Thought you were bringing some more wine," she said cautiously.

"Looking for a certain bottle," said Manolo in his usual, devil-may-care voice, opening a cupboard.

She put her arm around Sam, sitting at the bar. "Hey," she said, eyeing him up and down. "You okay?"

It didn't take a therapist to see that something was off.

"Yeah. You?" In his empathy over her overstepping by bringing her own playlist, he found himself touching the small of her back in consolation.

"Sure." As if to prove it to him, she managed a small smile.

"Go on back out. I'll be out in a minute."

Red regarded Manolo and him with suspicion, but left without saying anything more.

Sam watched her return to the patio and the noise.

"So. What's your next move?" asked Manolo.

"I wish I knew," Sam replied.

"Whatever it is, you got to come clean with her. It's the honorable thing to do. If the situation were reversed, it's what you'd be telling me, man."

"Don't you think I know that?"

That made it even worse.

But this wasn't some minor hang up, some problem that could be solved over beers with the guys. What Sam was dealing with had been his whole life. Now it was coming to a head.

Chapter 21

"Oh!" Red fanned her warm face with both hands. "I…it's… I can't."

Jutting out her chest, Junie turned sideways in the giant three-way mirrors. "Are you sure?" She jammed her thumbs into the boned bodice and yanked upward. "It's not too low-cut? I don't want people to think I'm trying to flaunt my assets."

Red adjusted a wrinkle in Junie's train, propped her hands on her waist, and scrutinized Junie's scant A-cups. "It's perfect. When Manolo sees you walking down that aisle, you're going to take his breath away. What did your mom say?"

"She likes it."

"Well, then. That's half the battle." Red and Junie had been dress shopping for months. Maybe, God help her, maybe she had finally made a decision.

Junie slumped inside her dress, which didn't budge an inch. "I'm not one hundred percent sure." She turned her back to Red. "Unbutton me? I just want to try the blush one on one more time."

Red came face to face with the same fifty-four tiny satin buttons she had just forced into their too-tight loops minutes earlier. She glanced at her chipped manicure, then scraped her hair back and looped it through the elastic band on her wrist.

But it wasn't about her.

"Did you hear about Keval?" asked Junie while Red struggled with her task.

"What about him?"

"He's become friends with Jordan Hasselbeck."

"Really?"

"I saw them at the café the other day. What about you and Sam?"

"Making progress. We're more than just friends."

There was a sharp intake of breath. Junie twisted inside her ivory cage.

"Really? It's about time."

Red was so happy she couldn't even be annoyed that Junie's quick movement had made the button she had almost wrestled from its loop slide right back in. "I spent the night at his place last Friday."

"Next year this time, maybe you'll be the one trying on dresses."

Wedding fever was contagious. And Red was still riding high from the weekend. "I shouldn't jinx myself. But I think I may have already found The Dress."

"You have?"

Given the extent of her digital scrapbook plus thirteen hours shopping in real life with Junie, who wouldn't have? Just thinking about it made her wish she was planning her wedding, too.

The rational side of her knew that the biological clock phenomenon was just a pop culture theory. An excuse for formerly sane women who overnight started going gaga over baby booties and onesies.

But watching her friends pair off had ignited some latent spark in Red. The creamy gown, the towering cake, a home of her own to decorate as she pleased. Suddenly, without warning, she wanted it all, the whole, clichéd ball of wax.

The final button undone, Red spread the heavily boned strapless away from ribs you could play a xylophone on.

"It's fitted through the bodice with long sleeves and a V-neck and—"

"You know what?" Junie interrupted her, modestly pulling the gown back up against her chest. "Speaking of long sleeves, I think instead of the blush, I'd like to try the long-sleeved lace one again. Would you mind tracking it down for me?"

Feeling chastened, Red went off to find the saleswoman.

She and Sam had a lot to work out before they'd be anywhere near talking marriage, assuming they ever were. Sure, making love in a bed had been a huge first step. But there were still nagging questions that couldn't be ignored.

What had Sam meant about being a mess even before he'd joined the Army?

She could gently urge him to open up more over time, but she knew from experience that you couldn't make someone talk before he was ready.

Chapter 22

A few days later, Sam met Gary Russo at the door to his law office. "I know this isn't easy. If it makes you feel any better," he said, taking his seat behind his desk, "with all the boomers getting up in age and their parents reaching their golden years, you're in the same boat with a lot of other people."

Sam sat spread-legged, arms resting on his thighs, fingers intertwined. "I'm no boomer. I'm still a few months shy of thirty."

"Maybe not you, but your dad falls into the golden age category. Sounds like you're really worried about him."

Sam rubbed his jaw. "All I can say is thank God for Woodcrest." It had taken the drastic step of committing him—pending review—to make Sam realize the constant tension he'd been under the past year, waiting for the next bartender to call asking him to come get his Dad, waiting to hear about the next "accident."

"You've taken a commendable first step, which is to make sure your dad's in a safe environment. He's getting good care. Now," he said, folding his hands atop his desk. "What can I do to help?"

Sam couldn't say help me figure out how to wipe the name Owens off the deed of to my house ASAP without sounding as loony as his old man. Instead, he said, "My father almost set himself and his house on fire. He obviously can't take care of his property anymore. When the civil commitment hearing comes, I'd like to get control of his assets."

"How close are you and your dad? Have you tried simply talking to him about yielding control of his finances and getting him to sign over power of attorney?"

"You've never met George Owens, or you wouldn't be asking. Let's just say he makes hornets look cuddly."

"It can be hard for people who've been in charge all their lives to give up their independence. If he won't talk to you, is there someone else in the family who could intervene?"

Sam shook his head. "My mom, my brother and sister, even Penny, his common-law wife, were smart enough to cut bait."

"I have to ask. Are any of them going to fight you on this?"

Sam huffed. "You kidding? They're glad to be rid of him. I'm pretty much the only one he has left. I'm in line to get the house, anyway. I was trying to scare up important papers when I came across Dad's will in a drawer of the china cupboard."

Gary sat back in his chair and clasped his hands behind his head. "I'll want to have a look at that, when you get a chance. And you say his physical is so far inconclusive?"

"According to his GP. He's calling in a specialist to do a psychological evaluation."

"Sounds like it's all going to hinge on what the specialist says. If it's determined that he's a risk to himself or others, we can petition the court to appoint you to assume responsibility for his affairs."

"Then I can do anything I want with the house, right?"

Gary nodded. "I assume you're contemplating selling the house. Places like Woodcrest can drain assets quickly."

"I don't think it's that valuable. It's out in the middle of nowhere. There are no public utilities, and the land's not conducive to grape growing.

"Money shouldn't be a problem, anyway. Dad started buying and selling scrap metal before I was born. Bought copper and aluminum and stainless steel, held it when prices were low and sold when they went up. You might have heard of Willamette Scrap and Metal outside McMinnville?"

"Who hasn't?"

"A big corporation bought him out a few years back. Tight as he is, I imagine he still has every cent. About the house. I was thinking more along the lines of razing it."

"Oh. I see. Your taste runs more minimalist," he said with a complicit smile. "You want to rebuild. Something with clerestory windows, curvilinear design elements."

Sam forced up the corners of his mouth. Whatever curvilinear meant. "Meantime, say I wanted to take the property out of the name Owens, make it anonymous?"

Gary nodded sagely. "You have every reason to be concerned. Concealing assets is a common tactic of the wealthy. The more money you have, the bigger a target for lawsuits. We can put the house in an anonymous trust."

It was no use trying to explain to Gary that he had never given a thought to family money. Sam had always considered himself a separate entity. Even as a child, he had taken care of himself.

Gary spread his hands. "Once you've been awarded control, what you do with the property is your business. As soon as the psych eval comes back we can file for legal guardianship, giving you the power to oversee your father's health and well-being. We'll also ask for you to be appointed conservator of his financial affairs. The judge will also want to hear evidence of his incompetence. From what you've told me, I think you have plenty of material to work with."

Chapter 23

Red's final session ran late, leaving her checking her e-mail on the fly before dashing off to Woodcrest.

There was the biweekly letter from Woodcrest summarizing her cases. Today, in addition to her regular patients, the director was requesting a consult on a newly admitted gentleman who presented symptoms of dementia.

She snapped her laptop shut, shoved it into her crammed work bag, no doubt creasing the important documents that were in there, and raced out the back door to her car, figuring she'd review his history once she got there.

Her first two appointments over, she finally got to the attachment.

George Owens.

Red's fingers paused on her keyboard. She may have met Sam's father once, briefly, at Sam's homecoming party. But that night she was completely smitten with Sam's erect bearing, his aura of accomplishment. Everything else was just background noise.

Her fingers flew, searching for George's age. Seventy-seven. Maybe Sam's grandfather? Surely Sam would have said something. Then again, estrangement of extended family wasn't at all uncommon.

Growing up, all Red knew of Sam was what she glimpsed from across the classroom and on the playground.

He showed up every September with a shaved head, his scalp and nape pale and vulnerable in contrast to his sun-kissed body. By June, his nut-brown curls were scraping his shoulders once again. But in between, he seemed to be on his own. No one showed up at ballgames, holiday pageants, and the other events family normally came to.

There had always been a haunted look in Sam's eyes. Yet there was also a stubbornness that dared you to feel sorry for him.

He could be defiant with teachers, and there had been some fistfights during high school, but never any serious trouble. And Red knew for a fact that one of those fights was Sam taking on a bully who had picked on a weaker kid for years.

When Sam returned to Clarkston a decade later, he was barely recognizable. Exactly what had happened to him was a never-ending subject of speculation in Clarkston's tasting rooms, bars, and cafés.

Back to the chart. She skimmed through the patient's CBC, urinalysis, electrolytes—but before she got to chronic conditions there was a knock and the door to the office opened to a man hunched over a cane, an assistant cupping his elbow.

"Leave me alone!" The man slapped at the woman's hand. "Goddamn people won't even let me walk by myself around here."

Red leaped up and stood by cautiously while he limped the short distance to an armchair and dropped into it, his head falling to his chest.

She dismissed the attendant with a smile and a wave. The woman rolled her eyes, mouthed the words "good luck," and the door closed with a soft click.

Red introduced herself. "And who are you?"

The man lifted his head. Anger-filled eyes the color of amber—or was it hazel?—burned into her. "They didn't tell you?"

She smiled with as much patience as she could muster. "I wanted to hear it from you."

"George Owens," he growled, looking down again.

Red sat down across from him. "Tell me how it is that you came to be at Woodcrest."

"I'm not staying, you hear me?" he lashed out. "My son brought me in last—I don't know when it was. Last week or something."

His son. Could he be referring to Sam's father?

"What happened that your son thought it would be a good idea to bring you here?"

Irritably, George waved away the question. "Why don't you ask him?"

"It's just us right now, and besides, I'd like to hear it from your point of view."

"I don't want to talk about it."

That was nothing she hadn't dealt with before. She would simply come back to it later.

She pointed to a vase filled with artificial flowers on the bookshelf.

"Can you tell me what that is?"

He looked up. "That's a…a thing."

"What kind of thing?"

"An it."

"How about that?" she asked, pointing to a lamp.

"Lamp."

"That's right. Now I'm going to ask you to do a little acting."

"I'm not much good at acting."

She'd take it. At least he wasn't yelling at her.

"I'll bet you know how to hammer a nail."

He scowled. "What kind of a man gets to be my age and can't hammer a nail? Why, that's ridiculous."

"Then I bet you can show me the hand motion that you use to do that."

"What kind of asinine questions are these?" He jerked his head toward the door. "When's Judy coming back?"

"I'm trying to get to know you better, Mr. Owens. That's all. Can you show me how you hammer?"

In spite of his exasperation, he pretended to grip a hammer and made a pounding motion.

"Nice. Now, just a couple more things. What if I asked you to list some different animals? Could you do that for me?

Following a pause, he said, "Bear. Goat. Dog. Banana. Orange. Cucumber."

"Okay."

Red handed him a piece of paper. "Now what I'd like you to do is fold this piece of paper in half and then place it on the floor."

"Why do you want me to do that? What is this, some kind of test?"

"Yes, it is. I'm trying to see how well you can remember a sequence of tasks."

With a trembling hand, George folded the paper off center, creased it, and stared at it.

"Do you remember what I asked you to do with it?"

He looked at her face, and it seemed as though he gazed straight through her. Seconds ticked by. "Put it on the floor," he said.

She nodded. "That's right. Please follow the instructions."

He leaned forward and dropped it near his feet.

Red smiled. "Good enough."

She went back to her original query. "What brings you here today?"

"My son brought me, that's who, and left me here to rot. I don't like jigsaw puzzles and I'll be damned if I'm going to do ceramics. It's time for me to go home. I want to go home." He clutched the chair arms and struggled to get up.

Red started, until she saw that he wasn't going to be able to rise on his own. "I'm afraid you're stuck with me until Miss Judy gets back. Mr. Owens, just a couple more questions, and then we'll be finished. Where is home?"

"McMinnville. Post Office Box 249. 97128."

"What is your street address?" she asked, fighting to remain calm despite her accelerating heart.

"The post office doesn't deliver out past the reservoir. We're on septic. Get our water from a well. You ever taste well water?"

Red swallowed. "I'm not sure." Water sounded good right now.

"Should try it if you get the chance."

"Describe your house to me."

"Wood frame, two stories in the front and one in the back."

Her heart slammed into her ribs, squeezing out her breath with each beat.

"And do you own a vehicle?"

"F-150," he said proudly.

This couldn't be happening. It had to be some kind of horrible nightmare.

"Mr. Owens." She licked lips drier than dust. "What is your son's name?"

"Two sons." He held up wrinkled fingers. "Luke. He's in California. And the younger one. Sam." He perked up. "Captain in the Army, over in Iraq. Earned a silver star."

Following a warning knock, the door cracked and a head poked around it asking, "All set?"

"That's Judy," said George.

"Yes," Red called with relief. She bared her teeth, praying it resembled some faint facsimile of a smile.

Thankfully, helping George out of his chair kept Judy from noticing Red's heated face, her shaking hands.

She followed them to the door, anxious for them to leave so that she could give in to her full-blown panic attack.

"Now can I go home?" George asked Judy. "I don't belong here."

The attendant looked back and saw Red's pallor.

"Didn't I tell you?" she mouthed with a complicit smile.

Chapter 24

Sam drove back to the consortium from his attorney's office, his head swimming with the events of the past few weeks. Voices filled his motorcycle helmet: Psychodad's, Dr. Mowbray's, Gary's, and, of course, Red's.

He heard again Dad's doctor offering to set up an appointment for Dad with a specialist at Woodcrest.

His lawyer, telling him in so many words that his very future hinged on that specialist's report.

Sam parked and entered the consortium through the front door, the public entrance that led to the bar. For some reason, his eye went straight to the barstool where Red had been perched just last week when she'd told Junie that she had just accepted a consulting gig every other Friday in Newberg.

He stopped in his tracks.

Today just happened to be a Friday.

And Woodcrest was in Newberg.

What were the chances? At this very moment, Red might be evaluating George Owens, figuring out that he was really none other than Sam's infamous Psychodad.

He whirled around, thinking to hightail it back to his bike, to race to Newberg and confront Red.

Halfway down the sidewalk he turned and walked back, scrubbing a hand through his hair.

Think. *Think!* What was he going to say to her? His head spun. Too many lies.

Red was probably evaluating Psychodad this very minute. If she found out the saltbox was his, at least that was one thing he wouldn't have to hide any longer.

But after the upbeat meeting with Gary, the idea of wresting control of the house sooner rather than later had started to grow on him. Maybe, after he'd successfully launched his plan, he could recover enough to give himself wholly to Red, the way she deserved.

Once, as a child, he had failed to protect the thing he loved best…the only creature that had ever loved him in return. He'd made it his life's mission never to fail a loved one again. Wasn't that why he kept Red at arm's length—for her own safety?

How could this be happening? How could everything be blowing up in his face when he thought he had it planned so neatly?

He leaped back onto his bike, oblivious to the storm clouds bounding in from the coast.

At this very moment, Red could be discovering that he was a fraud—a skunk. A psycho, just like his dad. She'd never get that he'd only been trying to protect her from himself, just as he had protected his country.

* * * *

Sam's bike roared into the parking lot at Woodcrest just as Red opened the back door to her old bomb.

He drove straight to where she was placing her workbag on the back seat.

"Doc," he called over his engine and a steady rain.

She slammed her back door and glanced up, her face as hard as stone.

And he knew that she knew.

Ignoring him, she opened the driver's door to get in.

He parked in front of her, blocking her exit.

"Let me explain."

"There's nothing you could say that I'd want to hear." She put one foot into the car.

He was at her side in a flash, his hand digging into her arm. "Wait! It's all in your hands. You have to declare Dad incompetent. He can't go back to that house."

Her face was mottled red and white. "Are you telling me how to do my job, now?"

"You said you wanted a relationship. That's the only way it's ever going to happen."

"What's one got to do with the other? You're being irrational."

"Just trust me, will you? He can't go back there."

"I was such a fool to fall for you."

"Red—"

She slid into the seat and reached for the door handle.

Sam stepped between her and the door.

"Move," she said tightly, blue eyes blazing.

"Listen to me," he said, leaning down to eye level, one hand on the roof. "I was trying to protect you."

"From what? You're crazy, Sam Owens. You're brash and arrogant and repressed. You have no clue how to be in a relationship. And if that weren't enough, you're a bald-faced liar."

He stood up and thrust out his chest. "I'm proactive. I don't back down."

"You treat life like it's a battlefield."

"You haven't seen what I've seen," he barked. "It's a tough world out there."

"It's not your job to make it safe for everyone."

"I stand up for what I believe in."

"Instead of relating to people, you try to control them."

"I strive to protect what's mine."

"I'm not yours! I never will be. Anything we could have been, you've ruined." The rain came down in earnest, splotching the front of her shirt. "I'll tell you one thing—from now on, my life will be divided. Before today and after today. Now move."

Sam staggered backward.

Red's car lurched forward a foot, knocking over his bike with a sickening clatter of metal. Seemingly without a care, she rammed the gearshift into reverse and backed out of her space.

He stood there in the rain, his hands hanging uselessly at his sides, and watched the Impala's taillights glow red in the rain.

Chapter 25

Red was so furious she could hardly drive.

How dare Sam treat her this way.

Oh, he might look like he had his act together. He was doing an amazing job running the wine consortium. But she knew better. Beneath that effortlessly seductive exterior, that square jaw softened by the requisite, lumbersexual stubble was an arrogant narcissist who didn't know the first thing about how to love.

Every callous thing he had ever done came back to her. Like how he considered what they had simply a means to satisfy their basic, physical needs. How in the company of their friends he treated her no better than any other, random woman.

He was the last man on earth she should want as a partner.

To think of all the nights' sleep she'd lost over him, going back to when they were just kids. Sam was one of the characters that had led her to go into psychology in the first place. To this day, she still couldn't fathom how he'd willed himself not to cry that time he fell off the monkey bars and the bone was sticking out of his forearm. Or the time when he was at bat and that fastball broke his nose.

Red had yet to diagnosis George. He might have dementia, and then again, he might not. But after Sam's outburst, she was inclined to do the opposite of what he wanted, professionalism be damned. It would serve him right.

* * * *

When Red got home, Grandma stood at the table, emptying Albertson's grocery bags.

"I remembered who he is."

"Who whom is?" asked Red with foreboding, rising wearily from picking up a wet leaf Grandma had tracked in.

"Sam Owens. He's that boy who got his nose broke back when you were in ninth grade. The one you made me take to the hospital."

Red hadn't forgotten that incident. But from the way Grandma had acted—as if Sam weren't good enough for her—she hadn't been anxious to remind her.

"So?"

"You wouldn't believe what I found out about him today," said Grandma, closing the cupboard on a large box of Lipton Tea Bags.

Red didn't know if she could take anymore bad news today. Her head was still pounding from her confrontation in the Woodcrest parking lot.

"I talked to your mama today. Wanted to tell her about that house you found."

Red sighed. "If I had wanted to get Mom involved, I could have asked her months ago."

Ignoring her, Grandma plowed ahead. "She gave me an earful. Did you know Sam has a sister by the name of Cindy about the same age as her? Cindy and your mama went to school together in McMinnville. Stayed friends even after they got out of school, until Cindy moved to Arizona."

"How did you two figure this out?"

"I told her you were seeing this boy named Sam and then about that saltbox house you're so excited about. But it was the strawberries that did it. She remembered the place. The chickens and everything."

"This Cindy always talked about this way littler brother of hers. She felt guilty not taking him in when her mom left, but she couldn't stand to be around their dad. Psychodad, she called him. That's how she left home... the mom, that is. The strawberry money."

Red's handbag fell to the floor with a thump.

No wonder Sam hated strawberries. She pressed her fingertips to her temples.

Grandma yammered on. "Haven't you learned? Some men are beyond fixing. If you keep on being Suzy Sunshine, you're going to end up going down the same road as your mama, and look where it got her: throwing away her life on one broke down man after another... Sophia. Look at you." She frowned. "You're soaking wet. Why, you're shivering."

"I'm going to go get out of these clothes," Red said through chattering teeth. As cold and miserable as she felt, she was grateful for an excuse to get away.

* * * *

Red peeled off her clothes, wrapped her head in a towel and donned a bathrobe. Then she walked sedately over to her bedroom window, threw up the sash, and opened her mouth to scream.

Just in time, she snapped her mouth closed.

The worst part of being a shrink was not being able to vent in public. She couldn't afford to scare away her clients.

She had to settle for a sigh.

She lowered herself to the edge of her bed.

Poor Sam.

Poor Sam? Where had that thought come from?

But in spite of her anger, her concern for him wouldn't let go. She knew firsthand what it was like to lose your mother. At least she had had Grandma, however shortsighted she was. Sam had been stuck with a cold, uncaring father. No wonder he had issues.

Numb, she lowered herself to the edge of her bed, trying to make some sense of everything she'd learned. She should hate Sam, not feel compassion for him.

Maybe Grandma was right. Maybe she was attracted to fixing broken men, just like her mom.

Sam boded nothing but trouble. She should run from him as fast as she could. He was like a lion—proud, imposing, but ultimately, treacherous.

She fell back on her bed.

But he made her laugh with his stupid jokes. And that wasn't all. She bit her lip. Whether in bed, a deserted vineyard, or anywhere else they happened to make love, in their most intimate he made her feel cherished. If she lost him, she'd spend the rest of her life making comparisons.

What was more, Sam wasn't the only one who'd behaved badly. She'd used professional techniques to her advantage to get him to open up about his issues.

He'd given her no choice.

No. There was always a choice.

It wasn't as if she'd tried to dupe him behind his back. She had asked for and received his permission.

But she was a psychologist; he wasn't. And she'd used her professional knowledge to manipulate him for her benefit. She'd bartered sex for secrets.

He might be repressed, but she was unethical. Instead of acting like a professional, she had screamed at him. Called him crazy. A therapist never told anyone he was "crazy." Psych 101.

She put her face in her pillow and screamed. Crazy was exactly what Sam Owens made her. Crazy with a capital C.

And now she was tasked with diagnosing his father. No matter what she concluded, her decision would have a far-reaching effect on Sam's life.

A vision of Sam standing in the rain, yelling at her, came back to her.

"'It's all in your hands,'" he'd said. "'You can't let him go back there.'"

Or what? What was so important that he had to rush over to Woodcrest in the pouring rain to tell her?

She had lashed out at him, called him irrational. But he wasn't always irrational. He was a natural leader who didn't make a move that wasn't well thought out. Despite his shadowy past, in two short years his dedication had inspired the respect of every grower and winemaker in the county.

There was something about that house. Something so painful it made him resort to outright lying...to her, of all people.

She'd been spending all her time trying to get others to talk. Now she was in desperate need of someone to talk to.

Chapter 26

The landscape surrounding Broken Hart Vineyards swept out before Red in the evening light like a painting, the house and outbuildings as much a part of the hillside as if they had grown out of the soil, just like the towering Douglas firs and the white oaks hung with mistletoe. Fertile vines dripped with fat, purple clusters. Everything was settled and orderly.

The bucolic sight should have calmed Red. Instead, it only served as a reminder of what she was missing. What her life had always missed.

A movement in the distance caught her eye, and she saw Junie putt putting along a row of vines atop her little orange tractor.

Red parked and found Manolo on the patio of the tasting room, sweeping beneath the tables and chairs.

"Junie's out spraying. Probably be out there till dark."

"She waved to me on my way in."

"Beautiful evening. You're welcome to wait. Something to drink?"

"No thanks. I came to see you, actually."

"Me?" Manolo leaned on his broom handle and grinned. "Sorry, but I'm taken."

"It's about Sam."

"Ah." He went back to work. "Sounds serious."

"You know that house I've been talking about?"

"The one you call the saltbox."

"Did you know that's the same house that Sam grew up in?"

He picked up a windblown branch too big for the dustpan and tossed it into a pile. "I'm from back east. Didn't meet Sam till the service."

She peered across the vineyard at the tractor. "I wonder if Junie knew," she murmured.

"She didn't say anything to me."

She sighed. So she couldn't find out anything about the house. There must be something Manny could tell her. "What was Sam like when you met him? What was his job?"

Manolo dumped the contents of the dustpan into a trashcan and propped the broom in a corner.

"Let's go in." He held the tasting room door open and followed her inside. "You know you're the best thing that ever happened to Sam."

Hearing that only worsened her growing guilt.

"Why do I have to hear that from you? Why doesn't he tell me himself?"

"Sure you don't want something to drink?"

"No, thanks."

"You won't mind if I do."

Red expected Manolo to reach for a wine bottle. But instead, he poured himself a whisky, neat. He took a sip and set his glass on the bar with a tick. "What's Sam told you about his time overseas?"

"Not much. That's why I'm here. I was hoping maybe you could fill me in."

"Not really my place."

"Manny," pleaded Red, leaning over the live edge slab of oak that was the centerpiece of the bar. "I'm at my wit's end. I thought Sam and I were finally going somewhere. He was starting to open up to me. And then, this afternoon, I found out he lied to me about something so basic as the house he grew up in."

She filled Manolo in about consulting with Sam's dad. "Why would he do that? He knew how much that house means to me."

"Tell me something," said Manolo. "What makes someone decide to be a psychologist?"

Red shrugged and took a breath. "No one survives childhood without some bruises, do they? In my case, my parents loved me, but they had issues. They couldn't keep it together enough to raise a child," she said matter-of-factly. "My dad left early on. Mom brought home so many men I started losing track of them all. Finally, my grandmother intervened. I've been with her since I was nine."

"And studying psychology helped you come to terms with that?"

"When I was little, I took all the blame on myself. I thought if I could just get better grades, help more around the house, I could make my parents happier, keep them together. A teacher noticed I was struggling and referred me to the school psychologist. That was my introduction to talk therapy. I got some more help after I went to college. Saw a series of therapists. From them I learned it's better to be honest and open. It's not what happened that causes people grief so much as how they process it."

"You make it sound so easy."

"I never said it was easy. I said it was healthy."

"You knew you were loved. And you had your grandmother. There are some people whose wounds have been buried for so long they don't even remember where to find them."

"Who are we talking about here?" Red said.

"I got a wedding coming up, and I don't know if my own father is going to come."

"I'm sorry."

"He's still hung up on me not following him into the family business."

"That must be hard for you. Is that why you didn't go back to New Jersey after the Army?"

Manolo folded his arms on the bar. "Like I said, sometimes talking just doesn't cut it."

"Did you *try* talking about it?"

Manolo huffed. "Trust me. I got three sisters. All they do is talk, talk, talk. Growing up, they took my side with my old man time and time again. All it did was make him dig in his heels."

"So you distanced yourself," she said without judging. "Put a whole continent between you and your problem."

"Well," he said with a grin, "there *was* Junie. I'd have gone to the moon for her."

"But from what Junie told me, you'd already been living like a nomad for some time before you met her."

"Alls I'm saying is, sometimes talk's not enough. Sometimes a person's got to take action." He lifted a case of wine from beneath the counter and started unloading it, lining up the bottles on the counter.

"Like that list of songs you came up with the other night."

"I might have over-stepped. I was only trying to be helpful."

"I'm just saying. Years of talk therapy and you still can't get over wanting to make everything all right."

Red's face began to burn all over again. Her lips thinned.

"Isn't there anything you can tell me that would help me understand where Sam's coming from?"

Manolo's hand paused on a bottle of Junie's pinot noir. He thought for a moment, then spoke in measured words. "You're a shrink. You know there's a limit to how much a man can take. Sam had the kind of assignment that can mess with a man's head even when it's short-term. Problem with war is, you can't clock out at five PM. You got to stay as long as it takes. That's what Sam did, because that's the kind of soldier he was, the kind of individual he still is: fully committed to the people and principles he cares about."

"I still feel like if I could just get him to open up..."

"The way you opened up just now when I brought up your need to fix everything from my play list to Sam's psyche?"

A bud of realization unfurled.

Manolo let it sink in for a moment before going on.

"You want my advice? Here it is." He leaned on the bar and met her eyes straight on. "Hang in. Sam'll open up when he's ready."

Humbled, she looked away.

"Or—"

She looked up again.

"—he won't. Only you can decide if that's a gamble you're willing to take. For both of your sakes, I hope you are."

Chapter 27

When Sam woke up, he knew without looking at the calendar what day it was.

Still, he went to work like it was any other day.

Later that afternoon, he headed out to Broken Hart Vineyards, knowing that like him, Manolo would be on his own.

On his way in he saw a handful of customers milling around the patio, admiring the view while they sipped wine.

He found Manolo behind the bar, taking inventory.

Sam slung his camouflage messenger bag onto the barstool next to him. "Got any beer back there?"

"This is a wine tasting room, buddy," replied Manolo, recognizing Sam's voice without having to look up from his electronic tablet. "Can't you read the sign?"

"I'm not in the mood."

Manolo took one look at him and said, "One beer, coming right up."

He popped the top off a Deschutes IPA and the cap clattered to the counter. "Nice man bag, by the way."

"Didn't ask you." Sam took a long pull on his bottle.

"So," said Manolo, putting aside his tablet for the moment. "You gonna tell me what's crawled up your ass? Or do I have to guess?"

"Not a damn thing."

"Your choice." He paused. Then he said, "Might as well tell you. Red was out here last night."

Sam averted his eyes. "She tell you she's the specialist they called in to diagnose my dad, too?"

"Yep."

"My own damn fault." He picked at the label with his thumbnail.

Manolo leaned his folded arms on the bar and cocked his head at Sam. "Why'd you lie to her about your house? Talk about your old man—are you nuts, too?"

"Insanity doesn't run through my family. It gallops."

"Look, man. I'm probably going to regret sticking my nose in, but from where I stand, you're starting to look like a chip off the old block."

"Now, that stings."

"You say he didn't let anyone in. Where'd that get him? Lost everyone who meant anything to him, that's where. Except you. Who knows why you keep putting up with him, when all you get for your trouble is grief and more grief. And now, you're perpetuating the cycle."

Having said his piece, Manolo stood back up to his full height.

Sam lifted a corner of his lips. "Causing people grief is an Owens family trait."

"Doesn't have to be."

It was almost closing time. The four customers came inside, set their empty glasses on the counter, bought a couple of bottles of pinot noir and left.

In what he hoped was a casual voice, Sam said, "The girls ought to be rolling into Portland by now. Probably dressed to the nines."

"Yeah." Manolo grinned with pride. "You could smell Junie's perfume coming down the steps. She looked great."

Sam managed half a grin. He had no doubt that Red looked and smelled gorgeous, too. But it hardly mattered anymore. Whatever they had was over. He'd blown it.

Tears welled up in the back of his eyes, to his mortification. He hid them behind a loud sniff and another slug of beer. "Tell me something. What do you really think of this little soirée of theirs?"

"What do you mean?"

"Them going to a male revue. You down with that?"

"I already told you. Girls gonna be girls. Let 'em have their fun. That's what I say. Why? You got a problem with it?"

"Do I look like I have a problem with it? Trust me, even if I had a say— which I don't—I'd have no problem. Whatever melts their butter. Last minute bit of fun before getting hitched, that's all. Doesn't hurt a damn thing."

There was a pause.

Sam looked up at Manolo, who was lost in thought. "You ever been to one of those shows?"

"Why should I?" Manolo grabbed his crotch. "I want to see a perfect male specimen, I can just go look in the mirror."

Manolo could always make Sam grin. He'd never admit it to his face—his ego was already too big—but he was eternally grateful for the unlikely scenario of his old buddy ending up here, with him, in Clarkston.

"Well," Manolo picked up his tablet, "see if I can finish this inventory. Only got one shelf left."

"Ever wonder what goes on at those things, though?" Sam couldn't seem to let it go.

"Don't know, don't care," said Manolo.

He counted the bottles on the shelf, put away the tablet, and transferred the day's receipts into a bank bag before slamming the register shut with the heel of his palm.

"Probably strut out there on the stage and shake their packages all over the place."

"Yeah," said Manolo. "Then they rip their pants off in one fell swoop, without any zippers or buttons. How's that work, anyway? I always wondered."

"Beats me. Velcro?" Sam finished his beer and thumped the bottle down.

"After that, I see 'em prancing their way over to the tables, to give the ladies a close up."

"Bending over so they can stick dollar bills in their ass cracks."

The men laughed in derision. But there was something forced about their laughter.

Sam bent his neck from side to side, to work out the kinks. "Hear Lumber Jack Hammer's quite the stud."

Manolo went over and locked the patio door, giving it a rattle to make sure it was secure. "How so?"

"He's a legend in these parts. They say women have gone so far as to get tattoos of him."

"Junie would never do that," called Manolo from back in the office where the safe was kept.

"No. Neither would Red." Sam contemplated his empty bottle. "Although there was that time she went home with a rock star after a concert."

"What?"

"You heard of Cool Pain? He handed her a note from the stage with his room number on it. Handed what she thought were identical notes to a bunch of other people, too. Naturally, when she went back to his room, she assumed she was going to a party. But turned out he was the only one there. Those other 'notes' were guitar picks."

"Holy shit."

"Nothing happened."

Manolo smirked. "Because if it had, I'm sure Red would have told you every last, juicy detail." He picked up Sam's bottle. "Done with this?"

"Yeah." He thought for a minute. "Then again, you know how it is. Plenty of guys go to strip joints, do whatever, and no one ever finds out."

"What's good for the goose," said Manolo philosophically.

Sam looked up in sudden realization. "Is that a hint? You want me to set something up for us guys?" That Manolo would want to go out carousing one last time before biting the bullet hadn't occurred to Sam. If that were the case, he'd better start looking for venues. All his late-night partying had taken place when he was still overseas.

"Get wasted and sleep with some nameless hooker?" He huffed a dry laugh. "I never paid for it when I was single. Not about to start now."

"That's a relief. Ever since I came back to Clarkston, I'm usually in bed watching ESPN by midnight. Besides, I doubt there's anything around here to compare with Amsterdam."

But his relief was short lived when he started thinking about Red again. "That Hammer's quite the stud."

Manolo spread his arms, looked down at his trim, six-foot plus physique, and grinned. "Better than this?"

Sam scrolled through his phone. "Here. Judge for yourself."

Manolo came out from behind the bar and grabbed Sam's phone. "Christ. That's him? That's Lumber Jack Hammer? That guy looks like he's made of stretched tiger meat over twisted blue steel."

The men locked eyes for a long moment.

Then they both moved at once.

Sam slung his bag over his shoulder and they bolted to the door.

"I'll drive," said Manolo.

"I've got the GPS," said Sam.

Manolo jammed his boot on the accelerator, oblivious to the dust billowing up, marring his truck's mirror finish.

Sam checked his watch. "They got an hour's lead time. Show starts at twenty-one hundred hours." Ignoring the truck's pitching over the bumps in the road, he started pulling the tools of his former trade out of his bag.

"What the hell?" asked Manolo, a grin overspreading his face. "Coyote-brown binos? I haven't seen a pair of those since the Sandbox."

His eyes grew even wider when he saw Sam thumb through a stack of one dollar bills.

"Think you brought enough money?"

"When were you ever sorry you had too much cash?"

"Point taken. What else you got in there?"

"Off-the-grid chargers. Night vision camera. And this." He dangled what looked like a dead animal.

"You expect me to wear a wig?"

"Are we going to waste time arguing or are you going to take orders?"

"You keep forgetting: we're not in the service anymore. You don't outrank me. No way am I wearing one of those things."

"Suit yourself," said Sam. He flipped down the sun visor and started applying a faux mustache in the small mirror.

"What's the plan?" asked Manolo, turning onto the highway.

"We go in after the show starts and leave before it ends. Hug the wall in the back of the room until our eyes adjust to the light, then find the girls. Sit where we can see them, but they can't see us."

"What happens if they do?"

"It's imperative that they don't. Unless you want to hear about the time you were caught ogling male strippers for the rest of your life."

"Hey," said Manolo, as Sam pulled on his own wig. "How come you get the brown one?"

"It's called warm mocha. Goes better with my skin tone."

"Bullshit. I look better in brown than you do. I'm Ital—"

"Not brown, warm mocha. Put these on too. Won't affect your driving."

"What don't you have in there?" Manolo asked, sliding on the dark-rimmed glasses Sam gave him.

"I don't have any duct tape for your mouth."

It was dark when they got to Portland. They parked a half block away from the venue. Sam clutched the door handle, ready to hop out. "What about the wig?"

"Do I have to?"

"You want to start out your marriage with your bride believing you don't trust her? Be my guest."

Reluctantly, Manolo pulled the auburn wig onto his head and adjusted it in the rearview mirror. "Next time, I get the brown one."

* * * *

A soul-shaking beat greeted the men at the entrance to the club. The interior walls were draped in black curtains and lit with flashing white, purple, and blue. The atmosphere was charged with anticipation. Up on the stage, the opening act of men in trench coats went to work agitating the gaggle of chattering women, some of whom were mom-dancing from their seats.

Sam elbowed Manolo and pointed with his chin. "I got a visual."

On a white couch front and center, auburn mane glinting in the lights, sat Red. She had on that bright lipstick again, his favorite. The one that always made him want to kiss it off. She didn't look like a woman who'd just been deceived by her lover. On the contrary. She appeared to be having the time of her life, tossing her curls, sipping something pink through a straw.

Next to her wearing a sparkling crown and banner was Junie, the bride-to-be. Then came Poppy. Together, the three made an eye-catching trio.

The only unoccupied seat in the joint was a nearby loveseat.

The two men sized each other up.

"Gonna be a tight fit," said Sam.

"We could stand," said Manolo hopefully.

"Too risky. They turn around, we're exposed."

Resigned, they approached the loveseat from opposite sides. Once seated, they tried to look as macho as possible, squeezed in next to each other.

"What'll it be, boys?"

"Whatever's on special," Sam yelled back, craning his neck around the short-skirted server to keep Red in his sights.

On stage, the dancers had doffed their coats and a strobe light revealed them shirtless in low-slung jeans, their muscular chests oiled to a high shine.

The server returned a minute later with Cosmos pimped out with paper umbrellas. Sam peeled some bills off his wad and shoved it back in his pocket.

"Too bad you two cuties didn't get here sooner so you could have sat closer to the stage," she yelled over the music with a nod to Sam's man bag. "You might have caught the eye of GQ."

"GQ?" asked Sam.

She appeared taken aback for a moment. Then a sly smile overcame her frown. "No need to pretend. Only one reason guys pay to see this show." She winked and sashayed away.

"Did you hear that?" yelled Manolo over the din thumping his chest. "She thinks we're gay! Me—Manolo Santos from Hoboken, New Jersey."

But there was no time to reply. The dancers were filing down off the stage, accompanied to lyrics layered with double entendres. And, just as Sam had predicted back at the tasting room, they were targeting clusters of seats. The spotlights followed them so their antics could be seen from anywhere in the room.

While Sam and Manolo watched, the men straddled women with their knees, clasped their hands behind their necks and undulated their hips.

Then, the spotlight swung toward the loveseat where he and Manolo sat. Sam closed his eyes in the glare for a second. When he opened them, he saw a barrel-chested man striding right for them.

"Dear Lord," cried Manolo, "tell me that guy's not coming over here."

But the man didn't slow his pace until they could clearly make out his initials inked on a bulging pectoral in a Gothic-style font.

"He's coming here," muttered Sam. "Get ready. T-minus seven seconds."

Now they were the center of attention, surrounded by women's eyes glaring at them like wild animals beyond the safety of a campfire.

Sam threw his arms around Manolo. "Kiss me."

"Wha—?"' Manolo struggled, but Sam held him fast. "It'll hide our faces. Do it, or be the brunt of every joke at every party for the rest of your life," he yelled over the pounding music into his ear.

Sam clamped his lips together and aimed for Manolo's cheek. But Manolo jerked at the last second and the corners of their lips touched.

Repelled like opposite ends of a magnet, they immediately switched nose positions, only to commit the same foul on the other side.

The strobes flashed orange on the insides of Sam's eyelids. He stiffened against Manolo's wiry beard scraping his cheek. Held his breath to keep from choking on his cologne.

Then the blinding light was gone.

Sam peeked out from behind Manolo's head to see GQ stalking off in search of victims who were into him instead of each other.

Sam grinned. "Was it as good for you as it was for me?"

"Go hump a land mine," replied Manolo.

There was a drum roll and the room went black. From out of the darkness came an amplified voice. "Ladies! I want to thank everybody for coming out this evening. Don't forget about our five dollar marshmallow vodka Jell-O shots, ten dollar cosmos and, of course, our twelve dollar hot 'n' spicy wings. And now, get those dollar bills ready because up next we have the one. The only. *Lumber. Jack. Hammerrr!*"

The spotlight came on to a giant of a man in ripped jeans, work boots, and plaid shirt. He strode to the front and center, hands clenched, mouth tight. He was broader than a barn, his massive chest tapering into a V-shaped torso.

The women screamed their approval.

He laid down his axe, took hold of the sides of his shirt, and ripped it off from back to front, to even louder screams. Then he stood sideways with his fingers locked behind his head and proceeded to ripple his torso.

Even Manolo was clapping.

Sam looked at him like he'd lost his mind.

"Gotta give the guy props," Manolo said with a shrug.

Jack stepped down off the stage before roaming the crowd like a hungry animal, head swinging back and forth on his thick neck.

Hands waved. Voices pleaded, "Pick me! Pick me!"

He searched restlessly for just the right mark.

And then he stopped, right in front of Junie.

Until then, Sam thought the women couldn't scream any louder. But somehow, they did.

Solemnly, Lumber Jack offered Junie his palm.

Manolo stopped clapping and half rose before Sam clamped a hand on his shoulder, pressing him back into his seat. "Easy. It's just a show."

Junie laughed and shook her head no, making her crown wobble. She reached up and pulled it off, replacing it on the head of none other than Red.

Lumber Jack eyed this new prey.

Red leaned back against the sofa, a bit daunted yet still laughing. Her hands fluttered to her cheeks.

The stripper leaned forward from his ankles, catching himself straight-armed on the cushions on either side of her head. Inches above hers, his hips began to ripple.

Sam couldn't bear to watch what came next, yet he couldn't tear his eyes away.

Effortlessly, Lumber Jack seized Red, scooping her voluptuous body into his arms as if she weighed nothing, sweeping her off to do God knew what with her.

Sam had endured some painful things in his life, but nothing—nothing compared to this. He swallowed, the sides of his throat scraping together like sandpaper.

The beast laid his beauty on the floor in the center of the stage.

No. *No.* But Sam's hands were tied. There was nothing he could do but sit there and watch.

To the silky strains of "Let's Get it On"—a song hot enough to get a woman pregnant all by itself—Jack straddled Red. He fell to his knees, then his hands, placed on either side of her head.

And then he proceeded to consume her without ever touching her. His body rippled and swelled. He dipped. He dived. His head disappeared between her thighs.

At least she had pants on tonight, and not a skirt.

If Sam thought the women were crazy before, now they went berserk.

He ground his jaw and clenched his fists.

"It's like watching a Cirque porno," yelled Manolo from behind his hand.

For Sam, every second was pure agony.

Finally, the act came to a climax when Jack did a forearm stand between Red's legs, his lower body straight up in the air, knees bent, heavy legs dangling backward over her body.

If he hurt so much as a hair on her head...

Luckily for him, Lumber Jack did not topple over. He got gracefully to his feet, sweeping Red up with him.

The tempo switched to three quarter time with the accent on the first beat. With exquisite tenderness, Jack gathered her into his powerful arms. And then, as if nothing in the world could be more important than that woman in that moment, he waltzed with her in slow, sensual circles.

The room quieted. Where had the crazy mob gone? Sam tore his attention away from Red long enough to register a sea of rapt, female faces. Here and there, a tear crawled down a flushed cheek.

I need you to rub my back. Feed me ice cream. Waltz with me in the dark.

He had brushed Red's words off without a second thought. It had taken a male stripper to make him listen.

The song over, Lumber Jack lowered his lips to Red's hand, thanking her, and led her back through the crowd like a bride to a smattering of polite applause and wet cheeks. All the way, hundreds of envious eyes remained glued to her.

Sam blinked. How long had Manolo been shaking his arm?

"They're about to turn up the houselights. We gotta get out of here."

Chapter 28

Back in Clarkston, Sam licked his wounds. Trying to sort out his emotions was like untangling skeins of Christmas lights without breaking any bulbs.

First, *lust*. Lumber Jack's axe handle had nothing on him after seeing what that epitome of manhood had done with his woman, even if it was all pantomime.

Shame. If he really cared for Red, he should have been revolted by those erotic acts, not aroused. Yet more proof of how undeserving he was of her.

Jealousy. No explanation needed.

Finally, *anger* at himself for ruining their good thing. It had taken losing Red to realize—they almost had it all.

The next few days passed in a haze of remorse and self-loathing. He holed up in his office, speaking only when spoken to.

He missed Red. He thought of her buoyant personality. Her lush body, once his personal playground. Her logic, often the only thing that kept him grounded.

He would never have that again. Red wasn't the sort of woman who would be trampled on. She'd made that clear.

He couldn't sleep. He knew he should eat, but he wasn't hungry. He stared into his kitchen cupboards looking for something that piqued his appetite. Turned over random jars and packages, searching for expiration dates, then, one by one, put them back, even one that had expired before he moved in.

Finally, sheer loneliness forced him back to the light and warmth of Poppy's Café. He ventured in at an odd hour between breakfast and lunch, when he knew Red would be at work.

Poppy set a mug in front of him and poured him a coffee. "Where you been, stranger? Was getting ready to send out the National Guard."

He had almost forgotten that the women didn't know they had been spied on.

"The usual. Work."

Poppy rested her pot on the Formica. Lowering her voice so the few other patrons wouldn't overhear them, she tipped her head and said, "Sorry about things with you and Red."

She knew that he'd lied by omission about the saltbox. He couldn't bear to meet her eyes, to see the judgment in them.

"Bad news travels fast."

"If it makes you feel any better, she's as torn up over it as you are."

His eyes on the scratched tabletop, he sipped the hot liquid carefully. "Who says I'm torn up?"

"Tell me the last meal you ate."

He thought back. "Half a canister of peanut butter-filled pretzels and a vending machine burrito?"

Poppy slid into the padded bench across from him. "Why don't you talk to her? Red's one of the easiest persons there is to talk to. It's what she does."

He looked up at Poppy's perfectly symmetrical face, her imploring blue eyes, recalling when she was a knobby-kneed kid with pale eyelashes coming in from the playground with leaves tangled in her cottony blond hair. Only in rare moments like these did it occur to him how she must appear to someone seeing her now, for the first time.

Stunningly good looks aside, how could she, of all people, know what it was like to be him? She was born into a loving, two-parent family, a family who cherished her and ultimately handed her this established business on a platter. Not a *silver* platter, but still. From where he sat, Poppy had it all.

"I know what you're thinking," she said, still gripping the coffeepot that by now had become like a natural extension of her arm.

No sense in refuting her. She knew him, too. Or parts of him.

"Now, you're marrying a smart, successful brewer." Heath. A noble man, unlike himself.

"I've had my share of problems."

Of course. Caught up in his own ego, he had forgotten about the times the sadistic Ms. Baker made Poppy stand up at the whiteboard and struggle to parse sentences till she was in tears, and their classmates were shifting in their seats. If Poppy had truly had it all, that woman wouldn't have been allowed within a mile of a classroom.

"You're a decent person, Poppy. I'm lucky to have you for a friend."

She smiled kindly. "I know what you need. How about a nice roast beef sandwich?"

His frozen insides thawed a bit. "Is that what I smell back there?"

Poppy slid out of her booth. "I marinated it in rosemary, thyme, and garlic. It's been slow cooking since last night. Should be nice and tender. If you want, I'll give you the end piece." She lifted a brow.

His mouth watered. "It does smell pretty good."

* * * *

Sam stepped out of Poppy's Café onto Main Street, his stomach pleasantly full. The three cups of coffee he'd downed helped cut through the fog. That, and a kind word from an old friend made him feel almost human again.

In the window of The Radish Rose, he spotted one of the many signs plastered around town heralding Dr. Sophia McDonald as Clarkston's Best Therapist.

Though he'd seen it a hundred times, he stopped to stare.

The first chuckle in days escaped his throat, and he found himself smiling. How many therapists did a town the size of Clarkston have, anyway? Five, at most.

Still. Even if there were a thousand, he bet Doc would still be the best.

It dawned on him, standing there in the middle of Main Street, what he had to do if he were ever to get back in her good graces…to salvage some remnant of what she had optimistically called their "relationship."

Talk.

It sounded so simple. But it would be one of the hardest things he'd ever had to do.

Chapter 29

Sam stepped into Red's tiny receiving room. She didn't employ an assistant, so there was no desk, just two second-hand slipper chairs atop a wrinkled throw rug with a round table wedged between them, issues of *Wine Spectator* scattered among some self-help brochures. Clearly, her fans weren't deterred by a little untidiness.

An "in session" sign hung askew on the door to her inner sanctum.

It was a few minutes until the top of the hour. Sam took the time to straighten the rug and separate the brochures from the magazines.

He rose when the door opened. A middle-aged woman concluded her business, and then it was only he and Red.

Red's face was arranged in a careful blank. "If this is about your father, I haven't made a decision yet."

His heart clenched at the sight of her red-rimmed eyes. He scratched the back of his head. "It's not about him. I got some things to get off my chest. Hear you're a good listener." He shoved his hands in the pockets of his jeans and waited.

She hesitated. Then, with a resigned sigh, stepped aside and gestured toward her office.

Sam perched on the edge of a purple couch. Therapist or not, here on her turf she had the advantage. He looked around at potted plants and shelves full of hardbound volumes with titles like *Games People Play* and *Emotional Blackmail*.

Red took a seat directly across from him.

Sure felt like therapy to him.

Both started talking at once.

"Sam, I—"

"Not really sure—"

"Go ahead," said Red. "You have the floor."

He rubbed damp palms down his thighs. Now that he was here, what the hell was he supposed to say?

"Hard to know where to start."

"Try the beginning."

He huffed a humorless laugh. "How much time do you have?"

"My next appointment's in a half hour. If you don't want to start from the beginning, start wherever you feel comfortable."

The walls started closing in. His pulse thrummed. He stood up and took a step toward the door. "This was a mistake."

Red stood too. Her fingers on his wrist were warm and soft. "Just say what's in your heart."

Reluctantly, he sat down again.

"Maybe it would help if I told you what I already know, so you can fill in the blanks," said Red. "I know you left Clarkston right after high school. After that, it gets kind of fuzzy."

Sam thought. "I'd been waiting for years until I could finally leave home. I was shocked when Dad agreed to fork out the tuition. I'll never forget the train ride up to Seattle. UW was a chance at a new life."

The past came back in a haze of burnt orange leaves skittering across the quad.

"Come Thanksgiving, I took the train back home. I was standing outside on the platform in Portland waiting for Dad and decided to light a cigarette. I knew I was taking a risk. Ever since Mom found cigarette butts with lipstick on them in his ashtray, Dad hated smoking." He laughed drily. "Probably one of the reasons I took it up. But I was eighteen and out to break the rules.

"So there I am, puffing away, keeping an eye on the road leading from my house. Next thing I know, someone's tapping me on the opposite shoulder. I spin around, and it's him."

"Uh oh."

"To this day, I don't know what happened to that cigarette. I might have thrown it. I might have eaten it. I have no idea."

The corner of Red's lips went up.

"Thanksgiving came and went. I figured I'd gotten away with it. Forgot all about it. Until Sunday, when he drove me back to the train station. He knew spring tuition was due. I'd waited all weekend for him to give me a check. On top of that, I had no money for train fare. We got closer and closer to the station, and he still hadn't given it to me. It was hard enough asking the first time. I hated to ask again."

"What happened?"

"We got to the station. He stopped the truck, and I finally got up the nerve to ask him about my tuition. And he said, "If you think I'm going to give my hard-earned money to a cigarette smoker, you got another think coming."

Red didn't blink.

"I'm like, 'What do you mean?' I had straight As. I'd already filled out my course selection for spring.

"'Guess you better figure out a way to pay for it yourself,' he said."

Red's smile disappeared. "What about your fare back to school?"

"I wasn't going to wait for him to tell me I had to get that myself, too. I grabbed my bag and got out of that truck. Dad drove off without so much as a backward glance."

"But how did you get back to finish the fall semester?"

"Hoofed it across the Broadway Bridge to I-5. From there, I hitched a ride north."

Red released a breath.

"That Christmas, I finagled an invite to my roommate's house so I wouldn't have to go home. By early January, I was in Fort Benning."

"You enlisted."

He nodded. "Sixteen weeks later, I was a scout in Iraq."

"That must have been quite an adjustment."

"You could say that. I went from writing term papers to—"

"To what?"

"Forget it." Only those who had not seen war talked about it. Those who had, never did.

"It's okay. I don't think you came here today to talk about the war. But I thought you had to have a degree to be an officer."

He sniffed. "You do. Wasn't until I was twenty-two that I served my first tour and was able to go back and finish my poli sci degree, this time on Uncle Sam's dime.

"I still had no taste for coming back to Clarkston. The Army was as much my home as anywhere. I re-upped, this time as an officer. They took one look at my aptitude tests and shipped me straight to intelligence school." He looked up at her. "If that doesn't prove I'm crazy…"

"I don't understand."

"I told you before. It's the military's job to figure out how best to use its personnel. One they're damn good at."

"That's when you became a spy."

He shook his head. "Nobody calls it that."

"Then, what?"

"CTPT. Counter-terrorism Pursuit Team, tasked with dealing with high threat covert ops. We didn't wear uniforms or carry anything on us that, if captured, would associate us with the United States government."

"Sounds awfully exotic," she said, a touch of awe in her voice.

"Most days, it's anything but. It's about getting into the head and guts of your source. Most days, it's anything but exotic."

"What makes a good spy? Sorry—CTPT officer?"

"Self-discipline. An analytical mind." He shrugged. "A knack for languages doesn't hurt. The ideal candidate is someone who's morally upright, but able to suspend his morals for a cause." He badly wanted to make her understand. It would be so freeing to share the specifics of the burden he could never set down. But he was bound by honor to settle for abstractions. "Someone who's able to separate his values from his actions." He searched her face. Surely, this was enough to make her realize that any relationship with him was doomed from the start.

But no. Her eyes lit in recognition. "It's called compartmentalizing. People isolate threats in their mind as a way of defending themselves against them." She thought for a moment. "Actually, it makes perfect sense. When you recognize that your emotions aren't relevant to your decisions, you're able to take bigger risks. Being able to compartmentalize to some extent is considered a sign of high emotional intelligence."

Leave it to Red to put a positive spin on a major character defect.

"Was your dad always passive abusive?"

"Passive-what?" He laughed and before she could answer he said, "If you're asking if I never knew where I stood with him, that'd be a big, fat yes."

"You didn't feel like he valued you or your feelings."

"Valued?" Sam sniffed a dry laugh. "Mostly he just ignored me. By the time I came along he was in his forties. He was done raising kids. He didn't care to know anything about me, and when I acted out to get him to listen, I got the message loud and clear that I wasn't worth listening to. So I just stopped trying. Put my feelings on the shelf."

"And yet, he was willing to pay for your college, until you, in his opinion, messed up."

"Don't get the wrong impression. We might have had some backward ways, living out where we did, but we weren't complete yokels. Dad had a decent head for business. And I have to admit, he used to brag to his friends and customers about my grades and later on, getting into a decent school and my military honors." He smiled wistfully. "It made him look good."

"But he never praised you directly." Red sat back. "That explains why you buried that entire aspect of your life."

"Just easier. Wasn't hurting anyone by not talking about it."

"Until I came along and showed an interest in your house."

"You don't want that place," he said, shaking his head slowly from side to side.

"Why do you say that?"

"Trust me, you don't. That place is a world of hurt."

Red re-crossed her legs. "You took away bad memories from your home. But Sam, don't you understand? Whatever those feelings are, they exist inside of you. You can project them onto the house, but in the end, it's still just a building made from bricks and beams."

Shaking his head, Sam rose from his seat and turned toward the slatted blinds that limited the interior view of Main Street passersby. "No."

"Sam."

He looked down at Red's freckled hand on his forearm.

"I have the answer. Let me buy the house."

He whirled around. "No!"

Enough psychobabble. He headed to the door. No one, not even Red, was going to keep him from finally getting to the root of his pain and obliterating it.

Red was close behind him. "Why not? I want it. You want to be rid of it. It's perfect."

"You don't get it. I want to fix it so that I never have to see that house again. Is that what you want? To live in a house I'll never visit you in? Never set foot in?"

Their eyes met while the meaning of his words registered.

"You never visit me now," said Red softly.

"Because I didn't want your grandmother to recognize me," he said, palms outspread. "Who my old man is."

"Because you'd worked so hard to separate yourself from him."

"I wasn't ready to go there yet, to lay it all out for you." The edge had crept back into his voice. "God knows, there's nobody else who could get me to do this. If it wasn't for you badgering me..."

"Does that mean that you *would* visit me if I had my own house somewhere else?"

"Of course I would," he scowled, as if she were blind not to have seen that already. "I want us to live together."

He couldn't believe he'd said that.

Red's forehead creased in confusion. "But..."

"I want us to be together. I've known that since you were the only one who ran to home plate when my nose got in the way of Stillman's fastball."

None of his family was at the game. Red and her grandmother had taken him to the hospital in their beat-up minivan.

"Then why—?"

"Because it's my job to protect you, you get it?" he said, louder than he'd intended.

"Protect me? From what?"

"From me."

From the other side of the door came the sound of someone entering the vestibule.

"That's my appointment," Red said slowly.

Sam rubbed the back of his neck. "Right."

He felt her palm in the center of his back. "Are you going to be okay?"

"Don't worry about me."

"I do worry about you. Let's talk about this some more. Tonight?"

Sam nodded, his usual bravado nowhere to be found. "I'll give you a call after work."

* * * *

After work, Red grabbed a coffee and sat down to study George Owens's chart.

Alzheimer's was a cruel disease that affected not only the patient's life but the lives of those around him. It was notoriously difficult to pin down. Symptoms varied wildly among patients. Some presented with simple, mild cognitive impairment—memory and olfactory problems that never progressed any further and sometimes, even resolved. Others experienced problems with word-finding skills, vision, and impaired reasoning or judgment.

However, diagnosis was always a bit up in the air, as the plaques and tangles in the brain that were proof of the disease process were only discernible after death, during autopsy.

Hope was on the horizon in the form of biomarkers that could detect early changes in cerebrospinal fluid and blood, but they were a long way from being part of the typical GP's bag of tricks.

In the meantime, physicians conducted tests to rule out underlying medical conditions responsible for the mental symptoms. So hard was it to pinpoint that the diagnosis was split into two categories: "possible Alzheimer's dementia," when dementia may be due to another medical condition, and, when no other cause can be found, "probable Alzheimer's dementia."

In George's case, all they had to fall back on was subjective analysis like interviewing people close to him and batteries of psychological tests.

That's where Red came in.

She had been putting off George's diagnosis until she calmed down. Now she clicked on George's chart and began reading where she'd left off, before their initial appointment.

The chart acted as a trigger that brought her anger flooding back.

If only Sam had confided in her about the incident that had instigated him carting his father off to Woodcrest, maybe she could have helped them both sooner.

But that wasn't what she and Sam were about then. Up until that day on Ribbon Ridge when she first made her demands, all they had was sex. Sam never talked about his family.

To be fair, she didn't, either. Not because she was hiding old wounds. Just the opposite. Whatever her childhood wounds were, she'd told herself they were healed. They weren't wounds at all any more at all, just scars that faded more with every passing year.

But Manolo confronting her about the play list reminded her of Grandma's scoldings for putting clients ahead of meals.

Maybe the real reason she couldn't turn away a client was because that would deprive her of yet another chance to fix something, and she so wanted to fix *everything*.

Her thoughts went back to that day she took Sam to the saltbox. The charred fireplace surround. The big, ugly propane tank. By then she had laid out her demands. He knew she wanted more. She had even asked Sam specifically what that tank was for. There couldn't have been a better opportunity for him to open up.

Her heart softened. Manolo was right. Sam just wasn't ready.

She sighed and went back to the chart, but all she could see was Sam standing in the Woodcrest parking lot.

"*It's all in your hands*," he'd said. "*You can't let him go back there*."

Whatever Sam's demands, they were irrelevant when it came to making a diagnosis. The same went for any personal feelings she had for Sam or the house. Her first obligation was to her patient.

After carefully weighing her findings, she consulted with Dr. Mowbray by phone.

Only then did she begin typing her opinion into the record. The minute she sealed George's fate with her electronic signature, Sam called.

"Still want to go out?"

She felt like a weight had been lifted from her.

"Do I ever."

Chapter 30

Red snapped her laptop shut with a click, eased out of her flats, and hopped up to answer Sam's knock, still wedging a foot into the heels she kept under her desk.

"My reception area looks nice. A little elf must have tidied up in here when I wasn't looking."

"Had to. You're about as organized as three chickens in a shoebox."

Sam sounded like his normal self. She smiled. "I'm glad you're feeling better."

"All set?"

"All set. Where are we going?"

"Thought we might run down to Serendipity."

"I would love that." They stepped out into the warm August evening arm in arm, to the envious glance of a woman walking alone on the other side of the street.

Red snuggled into Sam's side. Earlier that afternoon, he'd said he wanted them to be together. That he'd always wanted that. Whatever their problems, that was topmost in her mind. For now, it felt good enough just to be with him. To be in the present.

They held hands all the way to McMinnville.

"Serendipity donates a percentage of sales to a local non-profit every Tuesday."

"Underneath all that sarcasm, you are a nice man, Captain Owens."

"You wanted ice cream. Figured it's about time."

A little while later, Red carried her bowl of vanilla bean outside to a tiny sidewalk table on the corner of Third and Evans.

"I don't want to ruin the mood. But I'm sure you're anxious to know what's going to happen with your dad. Do you want me to tell you?"

"Nope," Sam replied, folding his arms on the table, watching her dig in. "I want one more night knowing he's secure at Woodcrest. Don't know how many more nights like that I'll have."

"We won't talk about him, then. But I do have something to get off my chest."

"Shoot."

"I haven't been very empathetic with you."

"What do you mean?"

"Expecting you to open up on demand about all the things you've been holding back for so long."

"Yeah. Well. I guess I needed a nudge in the right direction."

"What I gave you was more than a nudge. It was more like a decree."

"And something else. The Sensate Focus Technique. I'm not your therapist. It was wrong of me to go there."

"I'm the one who owes you an apology. I didn't realize I was taking advantage of you."

"You weren't. I used sex as a tool."

"Hey, I'm not picky. I'll take it any way I can get it."

"Stop kidding. I'm serious. Say you'll forgive me."

Sam tilted his head, his steady gaze on her mouth. "Forgive what? I can't concentrate when you do that thing with your spoon."

"What thing?"

He took her utensil from her. "This thing." He deposited a small mountain of ice cream into his mouth, withdrawing a smooth lump half the size of the original.

Red felt her trademark flush climbing her neck. "It's just ice cream." All around them, people were eating it.

"Your turn," he said. He scooped up another bite and aimed for her mouth.

He was finally feeding her ice cream, and now she was overcome with self-consciousness.

By rights, the spoon belonged to her. She reached for it, but he was faster. "Uh uh. Put your hand down."

Lowering her hand to the table, she glanced around McMinnville's busiest street corner at the other tables crowding the sidewalk. "Sam. People are watching."

"Watching, are they? You didn't seem to mind that when—"

"When what?"

"Never mind. You wanted to be fed. Now open up."

Her lips parted a little.

"Wider."

She did as she was told, bracing a palm against the table's edge.

"Hands in your lap. That's better. Now. Look at me."

The metal was cold on her tongue. Under Sam's scrutiny, she closed her mouth on it, melting the mound until it slipped easily off the spoon's bowl. The cold cream contrasted with the warmth growing in her lower belly.

"If I'd known how much fun this was, I'd have started spoon feeding you a long time ago," Sam teased, lazily swirling the dessert. "Maybe there's something to that sensate focus thing after all."

Red blushed even harder. How could something as simple as eating ice cream make her feel so dirty?

He held out another spoonful, and Red took it in her mouth, silently cursing herself for having ever mentioned SFT.

He held out the biggest bite yet.

She laughed. "That's too big."

"I'll be the judge of that."

He prompted her lips with the spoon.

The crush had already started at some vineyards. A couple of field hands in muddy boots, hoodies, and backward facing ball caps rounded the corner, brushing close by Red's chair just as Sam withdrew the spoon from her mouth.

She heard one of the men mutter something in passing, followed by coarse laughter.

"Jealous," translated Sam, wiping her face with a scratchy paper napkin.

Cheeks burning, she ducked her chin.

"Chin up. Last bite."

He seared her with his eyes as she closed her mouth on the spoon again. "Your lips conform to the shape of whatever I put between them," he mused. "Did you know that?"

She struggled to come up with something witty to say to prove she wasn't aroused to distraction, that is, if he gave her the chance. But just as the spoon clattered unceremoniously into the empty bowl, he sat back with easy grace. "If you don't like being in public, Doc, then we should think of somewhere private to go."

He was maddening. How could he be so cool? So controlled?

"My place is out. Grandma's binge-watching a *Dancing with the Stars* marathon."

"Wouldn't want to interrupt her TV program with a granddaughter who makes enough noise to wake the whole trailer park." He grinned.

"There's your place," she said wantonly.

"Eh. Too dismal."

"Really? I thought you didn't see how…"

"What? How dreary it is in there?"

"Not dreary..."

"No need to humor me. That place is gloomier than a back alley in Seattle on a January night."

"I thought you didn't notice. Or didn't care."

"Got bigger problems to worry about than décor."

"So you're not wedded to the idea of living there."

"Hell, no." He perked up. "I got an idea. Let's see if we can get into that B&B."

"Chehalem Ridge?"

Sam was already looking up the number.

He hung up a moment later. "We got the High Desert Suite. King-sized bed, private balcony overlooking the vineyard. Annnnd...ready for this?" He lifted a brow. "Two-person Jacuzzi." He made like he was surfing with his upper body.

Red felt a slow smile blossom. One thing about Sam—he never failed to entertain.

She hadn't forgotten about her dream house, in spite of the boulder-sized roadblocks that had been thrown in her way. But maybe Sam was right about living in the present. Tonight, she wanted to bask in being that woman who had just been fed ice cream by a handsome, amber-eyed man.

"I just hope those walls are sound-proof. Word reaches Clarkston that Dr. Sophia McDonald got kicked out of a B&B, who knows what effect a bombshell like that'd have on next year's race for best therapist?"

"Sam."

* * * *

The morning sun flooded the windows of the High Desert Suite.

Red was snuggled into Sam's shoulder, snoring softly.

The previous night played through his head. They had taken full advantage of the Jacuzzi. And compared with what they were used to, the king-sized bed they lay in was: like making love on a cloud.

Red stretched her arms above her head on a yawn.

Sam stroked her cheek with his knuckles. "Hey. You awake?"

"Mm."

"I'm ready."

She flipped away from him onto her stomach. "Not again. Not yet."

"Not that." He rolled her back over. "To hear what you decided about my Dad."

She rubbed her eyes and gathered her thoughts. After a minute she said,

"I consulted with Dr. Mowbray about your father's responses to the battery of psychological tests."

"And?" He lay still, holding his breath.

"Based on the available data, we agree: your father likely has a progressive dementia."

Her head rolled toward him, gauging his reaction.

"Maybe it's Alzheimer's, maybe it isn't. Regardless, we concur that it would be best for him and those around him if he had round the clock supervision."

Sam's eyes closed on an exhale.

"What are you thinking?"

"That this was exactly what I wanted."

"I didn't do it to pacify you."

"I know. I'm also... sad."

"You're bound to be. No one would wish this diagnosis on anybody, let alone his own father."

After a pause, she asked, "Now what?"

Along with the confusing blend of relief and sadness came a sense of freedom. Instead of keeping his thoughts to himself the way he used to, he opened up.

"He's in a safe place. Now that he's going to be a permanent resident of Woodcrest I'm thinking the next step is to get a power of attorney. After that, if you still want to buy the house..." But the staccato pounding of his heart wouldn't let him finish.

Red shot straight up in bed. "Really?"

He kissed her hand, hoping she didn't notice how much he trembled. "We'll talk about it later. Right now I just want to lie here and hold you. Go back to sleep if you want."

"Sleep, now? I couldn't possibly!"

"Sshh. We'll talk about it later."

She finally lay back down and rolled over and he began to caress her back.

"Mm. Feels good."

It wasn't long until her breathing evened.

Chapter 31

Outside the judge's chambers, Gary Russo shook Sam's hand. The judge's decision signaled a new beginning. With guardianship over his father's affairs, he was finally free to do whatever he wished with the property.

A week had passed since the night at the Chehalem bed and breakfast, a glorious week in which Sam and Red spent every free moment together. In public, at Poppy's Café, the bar at his consortium, the Radish Rose, and in private in his modest bedroom, it didn't matter. There was no more hiding his feelings for Dr. Red McDonald.

Sam still harbored considerable anxiety. But while the house was still legally in limbo, he could ignore it.

But now, on the drive back to Clarkston, there was no more ignoring it. His anxiety grew and grew until he felt like it filled the whole van.

In a stab at normalcy, he called Keval to see how things were going at the consortium.

"Quiet," said Keval. "Now that the website's running smoothly, we're getting orders at a regular pace."

"I'm headed in soon," said Sam.

When he arrived, his pulse ratcheted sky-high when he found Red in the reception area talking to Keval, looking more beautiful than ever.

"Surprise!" she said, holding two brown bags aloft. "I brought us lunch."

He nodded. "C'mon back."

She followed him to his office, chattering nonstop about paint colors, furnishings and gardening ideas.

* * * *

Red had spent the past week telling anyone who would listen about the saltbox. She'd stocked up on glossy decorating magazines and begun feverishly pinning pictures to her house board on the internet. She couldn't wait to finally claim the house and start transforming it.

"No clients?" asked Sam.

Red deposited his brown bag in front of him and started unfolding the top of her own. "I had a cancellation, so I thought I'd get us some soup. Now, before you get too excited, it's not homemade," she said, carefully withdrawing a takeaway container and a spoon and setting it down on his desk in front of him. "But once I have my very own kitchen, look out, because I'm planning on cooking up a..."

Ignoring his bag, Sam picked up a pencil and beat out a staccato tempo on the desk.

"Sam? Is something wrong?"

He met her eyes for the first time since he'd arrived.

"Where were you this morning?" she asked, suspicion creeping into her voice.

* * * *

Sam's first instinct was to lie. It would be so easy. He was in and out of the consortium all the time. There was any number of places where he could have legitimately been. Crisscrossing the county, visiting his growers and vintners was part of his job.

But he didn't want to be the old Sam anymore, the Sam with dirty socks stuffing his chest cavity like bread in a Thanksgiving turkey.

"I just came from the courthouse."

Her face lit up with hope. "And? Did you get it? Did you get the power of attorney?"

He swallowed and scratched his ear, putting off the inevitable. Out in the reception area, Keval still answered tourists' phone calls. Annoying ads still popped up on his computer screen.

"I changed my mind about the house."

Red's mouth dropped open. "What do you mean, you changed your mind?"

"I can't sell it to you."

"Why not?"

"I made that offer to you in a moment of weakness."

She stared hard at him. "Is that what you call our beautiful night together? A moment of weakness?"

"No. You know what I mean. A moment of..." Desperately he sought the words that would make her understand. "Vulnerability. You made me feel vulnerable."

"How did I do that?"

"By being so, damn, *nice!*"

Pain filled her eyes.

"When you apologized for rushing me to talk about things. For using that stupid sex technique."

"So I'm not supposed to be nice to you?"

"Yes! No! I don't know."

"*Well*," she huffed, rising, her arms at her sides, "thanks for making that perfectly clear."

"I offered you the house in a moment of weakness, and it's been bothering me all week and I didn't say anything, thinking I'd figure out how to deal with it when the time came and not wanting to mess things up between us. And now I realize I can't do it. It's like I said back in the beginning. I hate it there. I don't want to back go there any more. And if you're there, I won't have any choice."

Red looked around the room. She opened her mouth to speak, then thought the better of it and closed it. Then she paced a few feet and stopped. "I don't know what to say, Sam. You got me so excited. I've told everybody. I'm going to feel like such a fool when I tell them it's not happening."

"I know. I'm sorry. I just . . . I'm sorry," he said, rubbing the back of his neck.

"What happened there that you can't get over? Whatever it is, it's in the past. We can talk it through. I'll help you. I'll help you get past it."

"It's my house," he said, his voice cracking like an adolescent choirboy's, "and I can do what I want with it. You want a relationship? This is the only way."

In a flat voice, she said, "I'll never understand you, Sam Owens."

Sam mitigated his guilt by snapping at her. "Get in line."

For a long moment, Red just stood there and stared at him, dry-eyed.

Then she threw up her hands. "You know what? This too hard. I'm through."

And with that, she turned and walked out of his office and out of his life, leaving behind nothing but two bowls of tomato soup.

Chapter 32

The morning after Red walked out on him, Sam picked up his phone, expecting it to be the Lafayette grower he was trying to persuade to join the consortium.

But instead, the display said Woodcrest.

Probably calling to tell him about the new diagnosis.

He put the phone on speaker and continued browsing his computer.

"Sam Owens."

"Mr. Owens? We're going to have to ask that you come and get your father."

His hands stilled on the keyboard. The Dad problem was over. He wasn't going backward now. Only forward.

He sat back. "What do you mean, come get him? It's taken care of. He has dementia. It's confirmed."

"I'm aware of that.'"

He felt his anger, always just under the surface, rising. "Then what's the problem?"

"I'm afraid your father has been harassing the other residents. There's been some unwelcome touching, even groping. Last night he accosted a woman in the elevator."

Sam sat up straight. When did players stop playing? At what age would the old goat finally call it quits?

"What do you mean, accosted?"

"Held Mrs. Piccolo against a wall and kissed her. The victim's husband has threatened to press assault charges. Ironically, the dementia diagnosis came just in time. Without that, his complaint might have had legs."

He grabbed his phone, taking it off speaker as he rose from his desk and went to the window. "I'll call my Dad and talk to him."

"That won't work. We had to confiscate his phone."

"What?"

"The fire department called and said Mr. Owens has been calling them repeatedly, complaining that he was being mistreated. The police, too. To be honest, that's nothing we haven't dealt with before. Nevertheless, you understand why we couldn't let it continue."

"It won't happen again."

"That's right, it won't, because he can't stay here."

Sam ran a hand through his hair.

He had to stay there. He couldn't possibly come home. If Sam followed through with the plan that was becoming rooted in his mind, there would be no more 'home."

"Look. I'm sure this is all a misunderstanding."

"It's beyond that. For the well-being of our other residents, I have no choice but to ask you to remove him."

"But there's no place else for him to go."

A heavy sigh in the phone. "I'm sorry, but you're going to have to locate something."

"This isn't right. You can't just kick him out. I'm going to talk to my attorney."

"That's fine. We'll need to hear back from you within twenty-four hours."

"Twenty-four hours? How do you expect me to find a place in that amount of time? You can't do that. There has to be a law."

"We're a private facility, Mr. Owens. The well-being of our residents and staff is our highest priority. Imagine if the situation was reversed. If it were someone else, harassing your father. How long would you tolerate that?"

"Can't you confine him to his room or something?"

"That's neither practical nor humane."

Of course it wasn't. What was wrong with him?

Sam hung up, mind racing. What did people do in these circumstances? He couldn't take Dad back to the saltbox. And the old consortium wasn't an option. It had only the one small bedroom. Besides, there was nothing for Dad to do there all day while Sam was at work. Somewhere there had to be another facility that would take him. But not with a mere twenty-four hours' notice.

Dad needed help.

What to do? He was supposed to be this master manipulator. But no amount of physical dangers, high-threat, clandestine meetings, or the psychological burdens of extreme loneliness and detachment had prepared him to take care of an aging parent.

He had never come up against anything like this. He spoke high school

Spanish, a little Russian, and was fluent in Arabic, but he couldn't speak medicalese. He needed someone who could. He needed professional help.

* * * *

When Red saw who was calling, she turned back to the medical history she was reviewing.

Sam could call her all he wanted. She wasn't going to respond.

When the call finally went to voice mail, she breathed a sigh of relief, shook her head, and went back to her chart.

Seconds later, it rang again.

"I'm not talking to you," she spat to the phone. She needed fewer problems in her life, not more.

She tried to concentrate on the referral on her computer screen. *Patient is a thirty-nine-year-old female with hypertension and hypercholesterolemia. She is not having any trouble with her medications.*

A thought needled her. What if something was really wrong?

The third time, she snatched it on the first ring.

"What part of we're through don't you understand?"

"You've got to help me, Doc. He's not going back to that house. I'm not taking him back. It's not an option."

She frowned. "What do you mean? I thought it was settled. He has dementia. He needs twenty-four hour supervision."

"kicked him out."

She clutched the phone while Sam explained the events that had transpired since George's diagnosis had been handed down.

"I don't know what you expect me to do. It's out of my hands. I have no pull at Woodcrest. I've only been there a short while."

"You can talk to them. You speak their language."

"Woodcrest is not the problem. The problem is your father."

"Talk to him, then. Try to talk some sense into him."

"It sounds as though it's too late for that. A decision has already been made."

"I can't go back to the way it used to be. Do you hear me?"

"You have to understand that Woodcrest has their reputation to safeguard. Word gets around that residents are being groped in the hallways and they're not doing anything about it, there's going to be a stink."

"Talk to him. Please. Go over and talk to Dad."

She snorted. "I have a full slate today. I can't just walk out on my patients."

"After work, then. Just talk to them, will you? Buy me some time. Talk to Dad. See if you can figure out what's going through the son of a bitch's head. If anyone can do it, you can."

She sighed.

"I'll see what I can do."

"Thanks, Doc." She could hear his relief through the phone.

"I'm not making any promises."

"I understand. Just let me know the minute you have news."

Chapter 33

Red walked her last patient to the door and checked her watch. As usual, her day was ending later than she'd planned.

Before leaving for Woodcrest to see what she could do about Sam's dad, she took a final glimpse at her planner.

Oh, no. She'd completely forgotten her appointment at Curl Up & Dye. She and Junie were getting their nails done, and Junie was doing a trial run of her wedding hair and wanted Red's opinion.

She sighed.

There was no getting around it. The wedding was mere days away.

She ought to call Sam, but she was already late. And frankly, she was still angry with him.

She pressed her fingertips into the nape of her aching neck. How long had she been holding herself tight as a drum?

Trying to reach between her shoulder blades by herself was useless. She propped her elbows on her desk and dropped her head into her hands. She felt pulled in all directions. Her patients, Sam, Junie… She felt compelled to solve all their problems.

Maybe she *was* a little too self-sacrificing.

She forced herself to breathe. At least she didn't need an appointment at Woodcrest, thanks to her professional status. She would just have to get there when she could get there.

She got up, gathered her things, and rushed down the street to meet Junie.

Her aesthetician was waiting at the reception desk. "There you are."

"Sorry I'm late. Is my friend Junie Hart here?"

"Is that the bride-to-be? She's back with Steph. She should be out soon. Want to get started?"

Red's hands were slathered in moisturizer and enclosed in plastic mitts when Jordan came over.

"And how is Dr. McDonald this evening?"

"Please, call me Red. Everyone else does. Last time I talked to Keval, you two were on your way to Portland. Did you have a good time?"

"A great time."

"So…" Dare she ask? "Did he invite you to the wedding?"

"He did."

Red felt her face light up. That was the best news she'd heard in a while. At least someone was happy. But how ironic. Now Keval had a date and she didn't.

"But I had to say no."

"Oh." Her face fell again.

"I forgot. I already had a thing."

Red's lips pressed together. "I see."

It seemed she and Keval were fated to go to that wedding together.

Junie came walking out from behind a partition, followed by her stylist.

"You like?" She struck a pose.

Junie's jaw dropped.

Where was Junie's braid? Her hair waved softly along her shoulders. And what was that on her face? Makeup?

"You look fantastic. Your skin…your eyes. That shadow makes them pop."

Junie grinned while her stylist held an errant strand in place and shellacked it with enough spray to hold it until Junie's first anniversary.

"Am I done?" Junie asked the stylist.

Having gotten permission, she plopped down next to Red.

"I'll be right back. Need some fresh towels," said the aesthetician.

"How was your day? How's Sam?"

"I'm not sure."

"What do you mean?"

"You know his dad's at Woodcrest."

"Manny told me. It's so sad."

"Well, it's not working out. Sam has to find another place for him, and he asked me to help. The thing is, he only has until tomorrow, and I'm not sure what I can do in that short a time."

"Sam could take him to his place."

"He could, as a last resort. You've been in the old consortium. It's not even conducive to Sam living there, let alone his elderly father. There's only one bedroom, and no real living room."

"What about his old house? The one in the country?"

Red sighed. "Sam is adamant that he can't go back there."

Junie nodded. "Manny said something about that, too. Something about how Sam wished he could burn it to the ground."

Red frowned. "What did you say?"

"Not really," she hastened to add. "It was right after his Dad's accident with the fireplace. He was frustrated. You know how people talk. Especially guys. Especially former, so-called badasses." She laughed to assuage Red's look of concern.

The manicurist dashed back into her seat across from Junie and began removing her old polish.

Stuck with her fingers and toes being worked on for the next hour, Red had plenty of time to think.

And to worry.

Chapter 34

Somehow, Sam made it through the work day. Finally, five o'clock came. He stayed at the office, tying up loose ends, trying not to watch the clock.

Six o'clock came.

His office had never looked neater. He was at a loss for what to do. He could eat, but he had no appetite.

Seven o'clock.

Seven-thirty.

At seven-forty-five, he broke down and tried to call Red.

When she didn't answer, he gazed unseeing out the window and cursed under his breath.

He had to face the fact that he'd have to go get his dad. He would find a new place for him, somehow. Woodcrest wasn't the only assisted living center in Oregon. But it wouldn't happen overnight.

The question was what to do with him in the meantime.

He grabbed his keys and headed out.

"Where are you off to in such a rush?" asked Keval.

"Something I got to do."

In the old consortium, he ran to his room, to ready it for Dad to use until he could find him something better.

He changed the sheets, emptied the top two drawers of the dresser of his clothes to make room for Dad's. He bent to straighten the throw rug, and when he did, the older of his two duffel bags under the bed caught his eye. He paused, then hoisted it out onto the blanket. The day he packed it came back to him. It was in the midst of a raging haboob, seven thousand miles away from the soft, moist air of the Pacific Northwest.

He was twenty-two and already a seasoned combat veteran, on his way home. He'd sworn he had vanquished his demons and was done with the

Army. Hatched a plan to finish school, start a business and a normal life.

But no sooner had he graduated than he found himself sitting for the Officer's Candidate School exam, to go back in as a lieutenant at age twenty-five.

Some people never learned. They just kept repeating the same mistakes.

He blew the dust off and undid the drawstring. He'd been required to turn in his service weapons, rifle-cleaning kit, hydration harness, and sniper mat, to be reassigned to the next guy. They let him keep his logbook, though. He cradled the spine and let it fall open at random to his KIAs. Like he needed reminding. One thing no marksman ever forgot was his number of kills.

He draped the patriotically striped ribbons across his palm and stared at the three Bronze Stars earned for displaying exceptional courage under fire and reducing risk of harm to coalition troops.

Inside, emotions bubbled and gurgled ominously, like an underground volcano.

He thumbed to his Evaluation and Counseling Record. Most of his marks were "average" and "above-average," except in the categories of Professional Knowledge and Quality of Work. In those, he was ranked "exceptional."

Time was running out.

He only had until tomorrow morning.

He knew his dad. He would insist on going back to the old house. But he couldn't be left alone. Sam would be forced to stay there with him, or hire someone who would, in which case he would still have to check in regularly to be sure he was being properly taken care of.

That is, unless there was no house left to go back to.

Chapter 35

Woodcrest's director agreed to talk with Red before she interviewed George.

"We always regret having to ask a resident to leave, but in George Owens's case, we have no choice. We can't jeopardize the safety and well-being of our other residents and staff. He's bothering women at dinner and during social functions. Pawing them, trying to kiss them. The elevator incident was the last straw. I can't even allow you to meet with him alone. I don't want the liability. I'm going to have one of our male associates accompany you."

Red called Sam as she slapped down the hall, still wearing her disposable salon flip-flops, toward the room where she counseled patients.

He picked up on the first ring.

"Are you still in your office?"

"Yeah."

His terse response was freighted with tension.

"I spoke with the director. But they won't budge on the issue of your dad leaving."

There was a brief pause while Sam came to grips with that fact. "What am I going to do, Red?"

It was the first time Sam had ever called her something other than the casual throw-away "Doc."

In spite of her anger, her heart went out to him. "There have to be other options. If we have to, we'll go to Portland."

From the elevator down the hall came George, accompanied by Judy and a man in scrubs.

"I'm at the consulting room now. Your dad's on his way. I gotta go."

There was no time for good-byes.

George and Dave, a male nurse, entered the consult room, followed by Red.

"Have fun with Randy Andy," Judy said out of the corner of her mouth.

After helping George take his seat, Dave took the chair behind him, discreetly tucked into a short hallway by the door.

The first words George said were, "Are you here to get me out of this place?"

"We'll talk about that in a minute. First, I need you to tell me what's up with you and the female residents. I'm hearing there's been some inappropriate behavior."

"What? I don't know what you're talking about."

"You haven't been saying things to the ladies here? Touching them?"

"I have a perfectly good wife and three kids back home. Luke, Cindy, and Sam."

Red made some notes.

"We talked a little before about the reason why you're here. Do you remember that, George?"

"My son told me we were going to McDonald's. Strangest McDonald's I ever seen. That was a long time ago. I'm ready to go home. Where'd he get to goddamn it?" Restless, he turned in his chair.

From his seat near the entrance, the nurse kept careful watch.

Red's head spun. *George couldn't stay here, but neither could he go back to the saltbox. Sam didn't want him there.*

"Where's my phone? I'm going to call him now. Tell him to come down here and bring his gun."

"Settle down. We're not through talking."

"Do you know my son?"

"As a matter of fact, I do."

"Crackerjack sniper. Three Bronze Stars for meritorious service in a combat zone. I raised him up." Talking about his son, George glowed with pride. "But it was the Army that gave him his mental stamina. Tempered him in fire till he was hard as flint."

In dementia, long-term, episodic memory often remained intact even while the hippocampus was damaged. There was an unmistakable ring of truth in the proliferation of details George gave.

"A sniper?"

Red fought to separate her emotions from her professionalism.

"Always was a helluva marksman."

She recalled Sam's habit of estimating distances down to the inch.

"Who do you think it was taught him to shoot?" He thumped his chest. "First gun I got him was an air gun. Next was a Winchester."

The long rifle hanging above the fireplace in the saltbox.

"Started out shooting squirrels and rabbits, same way my daddy taught me. Then one morning I caught that dog of his with another one of his mother's chickens in his mouth. Know what I did?"

She held her breath.

"Dug a hole under his bedroom window. Threw in the half-eaten bird. Then I marched right upstairs to the boy's room and shoved that Winchester in his hands. Threw up the sash and told him to call his dog. Dog come runnin' the minute he heard Sam's whistle.

"'Shoot him,' I said. Couldn't do it at first. Still had sleep in his eyes. 'Shoot him or I will.' I was doing him a favor.

He knew I wasn't half the shot he was and it might not be as clean. He shot him then. Dog fell right into the hole I dug for it. You look for it, you can still see the cross."

Behind George, the nurse's eyes were saucers.

Red leaped from her chair, grabbed her bag, and flew past George and the nurse and out the door.

No wonder Sam hated that house. Her hand shook as she jammed her key into the ignition. Abandoned there by his mother, brother, and sister… left to fend for himself with a quintessential psychopath…a man who was shallow, uncaring, and selfish.

She had to find him, before he spun out. Before he destroyed her dream house.

Chapter 36

Sam was probably watching his phone, waiting to hear from her. But there were some things that should be talked about in person.

She headed for his office.

During the tourist season, the consortium stayed open later Friday nights.

When she got there, she found a smiling Keval sitting at the bar with—Jordan Hasselbeck.

She allowed herself a brief moment of satisfaction. But there would be time to congratulate herself later.

She waved to Keval on her way back to Sam's office, as if she weren't falling apart inside.

"He's not back there," called Keval.

She stopped dead in her tracks. "Where is he?"

Keval shook his head. "He tore out of here about an hour ago. I asked him what his hurry was, and he said there was something he had to do."

Red got back in her car and headed west.

Now she knew what Sam meant about being a mess even before he'd joined the Army. That's why he felt like he had to protect everyone around him. No wonder he considered it his solemn duty to protect what he loved best. His country, his consortium members, and now, her. At a crucial age in his development, he hadn't been able to protect the only creature who loved him unconditionally: *Riggley.*

She got back in her car.

As she drove, she saw again in her mind's eye the images she had clung to for so long: the sweet bungalows with their distinctive windows, the colonials with their colorful front doors, the ornate Victorians, and last but not least, the saltbox. All this time she'd believed that the only way she'd ever be whole was to one day own one of them. But this time when she thought of them, she felt nothing. As usual, Grandma was right. It wasn't the house that was important. Humble trailer or grand estate, what mattered most in a home was who you shared it with.

A mile before she got to the house she saw the faint orange glow. As she navigated the rutted road, it grew brighter and brighter.

There was Sam's bike, parked safely back on the road.

And there was the saltbox—once, her dream house—engulfed in flames.

She parked and ran as close as she dared to where sparks danced in the billowing smoke, frantically scanning the grassy area lit up by the blaze.

"Sam!" she screamed.

But she couldn't see him through the smoke.

She ran around to the back of the house, oblivious to the thorns on a clump of bushes scratching her legs.

"Sam!"

She thought she saw movement up on the small hill. Blinking in the acrid smoke, she scrambled up it, stopping to peel off her sandals until she found him lying on his stomach on the rough ground.

"Get out of here!" Sam cried with a sweeping motion when he saw her coming.

He still had the Winchester pointed toward the house.

"I know everything."

"This is none of your business. Now get out of here! I don't want you anywhere near this place if the cops show up. Can't have you involved, do you hear me?"

At a loud pop and a flash from the depths of the house, Red cringed.

Sam leaped up, leaving his gun lying in the grass, and grabbed her by the arm. Standing before her wide-legged he thumped his chest and yelled, "My life. My house. My call. Now get out!" He pointed, straight-armed, toward the driveway.

Nothing in Red's training could have prepared her for this. She acted straight from the heart.

"I'm not going anywhere. I know about Riggley," she said, coughing. "Your dad told me."

"Riggley trusted me with his life, and what did I do? Destroyed him."

"It wasn't your fault! You were a child. A little kid! Your father made you do what you did."

His face distorted in agony. He covered his eyes with his hand and turned away.

"The only way I could erase that, become the kind of person who doesn't destroy his loved ones, was by destroying the place where it happened."

"Sam. Your father is so proud of you. He always was. He just didn't know how to show it. He doesn't have the skill set. To this very day, if anyone told him he had done wrong by you, he would deny it. He was raised the same way he raised you—perpetuating a vicious cycle of bad parenting. It happens all the time. It happened to me."

Red clutched his arm, turning him around, refusing to let him go through this alone.

He yanked away from her. "Why don't I see you burning down your past?"

"There was a time I would have said because I talked about it. But the truth is, I don't know. There are some things we just can't know. Not even us shrinks."

She reached for him again.

This time, he gave in, relaxing into her with a wail of pain.

She held him close, absorbing his heaving sobs into her body, making them her own. Shushing his cries on her shoulder, she gazed out at the inferno, watching the roof on her one-time dream house collapse, taking with it any remnants of attachment she'd once had for it.

Sam leaned on her with all the weight of his six foot, hundred sixty pound frame. She braced herself to keep from buckling, appreciating her strong body as never before, holding him tight as together, they watched his past go up in smoke.

Chapter 37

"I would like to start by saying what a pleasure it is to be best man at Manolo and Junie's wedding."

Sam paused his speech to look out at the guests assembled under the stars at Broken Hart Vineyards. There was Manolo's mother, her walker within easy reach, next to her chair.

His father, who had come to his senses and shown up for his only son's nuptials. Keval, with—*who was that tall dude with the biceps that threatened to burst through the sleeves of his suit jacket?*

"Marriage is going to be great for Manolo. It will teach him loyalty, compromise, and all those other qualities he wouldn't need if he had just stayed single."

Laughter rippled across the crowd.

"But I doubt that anything could ever teach Manolo to be humble. He has always been conscious of his good looks. In fact, just this morning he asked if there was anything I could do to not show him up at his wedding. I told him not much, short of wearing a bag over my head. And I'd rather not do that again."

He exchanged significant glances with the groom.

"Sorry. Private joke from our Army days. Lieutenant Santos is a living reminder of the values we share: loyalty, integrity, and personal courage. At different times throughout our lives he's been my brother-in-arms. My confidante…" He paused to clear his throat. "My conscience. Manny is the finest friend any man could ask for. Were it not for him, I wouldn't have this woman." Sam looked at Red. "The best thing in my life. The woman I'm proud to call my girlfriend. Red McDonald." He held his hand out to her.

From her nearby table, Red shook her head, but Sam was insistent, and so to cheers and applause, she finally got up and stepped under Sam's outstretched arm. There, in front of the whole town, Sam dipped her backward and kissed her.

After the main course, Pat Berg sidled up to Red at the crowded dessert buffet.

"How are you?" Red asked congenially.

"Three weeks, and no nightmares," Pat replied, holding up crossed fingers. "Who would have thought our minor marital spats would cause Cassadee so much worry? Then again, how were we supposed to know the parents of not one, but two, of her friends were divorcing?"

Red shrugged. "Never hurts to talk. Communication is everything."

"Speaking of communicating, how is Sam's 'little problem'?'" she said, making air quotes.

Red frowned. "Sam has a problem?"

"You know," Pat winked, "between the sheets?"

Over Pat's shoulder, Red saw Sam approaching, holding a small plate. She straightened up to her full five foot eight. "Thanks for your concern," she said. Then, enunciating each syllable loudly enough to be heard all the way over at the strawberry shortcake, "Sam Owens is a freaking stud. Nice talking with you."

Heads turned as Sam escorted Red back to their table.

"What do I owe you?" asked Sam, watching Pat scamper off to spread the word of his virility.

"A bite of your chocolate mousse," Red said, without missing a beat.

The patio had been cleared of furniture to make room for dancing. As Sam and Red left the floor after Michael's "The Girl is Mine," the tall man Sam had noticed during his speech tapped him on the shoulder.

"Excuse me. My name's GQ. Have we met?"

Sam's gaze traveled over his size forty-eight shoulders to his thirty-two waist. Coolly, he said, "You must have me mixed up with someone else."

Unconvinced, the man frowned. "I could have sworn—"

"Hear that?" Sam asked Red at the prelude to Stevie Wonder's "Signed, Sealed & Delivered." "Our song."

He grabbed Red's hand and pulled her back onto the patio. But instead of joining in with the other eager dancers, he dragged her across the patio to the abandoned tasting room.

Slipping in behind her, he wrapped her up in his arms and kissed her.

"Our song, huh?" she asked, puzzled yet smiling, when they came up for air.

"Mm," he said, smacking his lips, pulling her tight against him. Over her head he mumbled, "You taste good."

"Strawberry shortcake."

"Not bad."

"I thought you didn't like strawberries."

"I didn't used to. But I'm developing a taste for them. They make your kisses taste sweet."

She leaned back from the waist and straightened the knot in his tie. "Are my kisses as sweet as Manolo's?" she asked with a sparkle in her eye.

e held her at arm's length. "How long have you known?"

She threw her head back and laughed out loud.

"Manny told Junie the minute they got home."

Sam pulled her close again. "Damn. Don't those two have any secrets between them?"

"Why else do you think they're so happy together?"

As her words sank in, Sam took Red's hand and twirled her to the music playing outside.

"Here I am baby," he sang. "Signed, sealed, delivered, I'm yours."

Chapter 38

Two months later

Red was standing at the counter at Poppy's Café when Sam walked in and gave her a kiss.

"Hey," she said. "How was lunch with your dad today?"

George was living in a new home that specialized in memory care forty-five minutes away in Beaverton that Red had helped Sam find.

"He has moments when we're able to connect. We were talking about back when I was a kid."

"That's the thing about Alzheimer's. Though it's hard to remember what you did yesterday, sometimes you can call up things that happened a lifetime ago."

"He was telling me how hard it was to keep an eye on me, back when I was starting to walk."

Red laughed, because that's all you could do. "He can remember things you can't even remember."

"Ironic, isn't it?"

Red smiled with sympathy. "I'm just glad you two have had this chance to get reacquainted."

Sam nodded. "You almost ready? The Realtor's going to be waiting for us."

Sam still had a low tolerance for sappy.

"I'm ready." She patted her shoulder bag.

They got in Sam's van and headed west out Meadowlake Road, up a hill and across a stream. Ten minutes outside of Clarkston, they pulled into a paved driveway leading to a wood frame farmhouse surrounded by a fenced-in yard. On the southeast side was a large, well-tended vegetable garden. Ten-foot tall tripods served as supports for the pole beans that had been harvested earlier in the season. Now, pumpkins the size of basketballs lay scattered in one corner. Yellow sunflowers hung their heavy heads over the fence.

It was their second visit to the property. The realtor was already in the driveway, waiting for them.

"I'd like to go inside again," said Red.

"You two go ahead," he said. "Now, don't forget about the amenities. You've got ten private acres, hand-scraped hickory floors, and skylights."

Quivering, Red looked up at Sam. It wasn't the chill in the air. It was pure excitement.

He put his arm around her and gave a squeeze.

"Take your time," said the realtor. "I'll wait out here."

Red wandered through the spacious interior to the screened-in back porch.

Sam came up behind her and put his arm around her. Together they gazed out at the panorama of blue hills.

"What do you think?"

"I think I like it."

"What do you like about it?"

"The established garden, of course. It has a sense of permanence. It's just rural enough that I feel like I'm in the country, but not so far that Grandma is afraid to visit. What about you?"

"I like that you like it."

"That's all? You have to want it as much as I do, Sam. I can't afford a place like this on my own."

"Aren't I the one who suggested we take a closer look at it?"

"After I spotted it on the net. I thought it was just a dream—"

"A what? You thought it was a what?"

"A dream house."

He took her into his arms and nodded toward the mountains, long, tawny lashes like crescent moons above those shining eyes…eyes that seduced her without even trying.

"See that lone oak out there?"

She turned and looked out at the edge of the wild forest beyond the close-cropped yard.

"When we get tired of the bedroom, maybe we can scr—*make love* out there on my old blanket. That is, if you like."

He kissed her, his hands resting lightly on her waist. Red's arms extended straight across his shoulders, hands dangling limply from her wrists, her new diamond sparkling brilliantly in the autumn sunshine.

Tucked away in a garment bag in the spare room of Grandma's trailer, waiting for spring hung her strapless, sweetheart gown composed of layers upon layers of frothy tulle.

She'd placed an order at Newberg's finest bakery for a three-tiered cake trimmed with the palest lavender and peach roses and eucalyptus leaves to match her bouquet.

She may have lost her original dream house, but she'd got her dream man.

"I like," she breathed, matching him kiss for sweet kiss.

Love spending time in Oregon Wine Country?

Keep reading for excerpts from the first two books in the Oregon Wine Country series!

THE CRUSH and INTOXICATING

Available now from Lyrical Shine!

Don't miss Heather Heyford's Napa Wine Heiresses series

A TASTE OF CHARDONNAY
A TASTE OF MERLOT
A TASTE OF SAUVIGNON
A TASTE OF SAKE
Available now from Lyrical Shine!

And keep an eye out for THE SWEET SPOT

The first in Heather Heyford's Willamette Wine Romances
Coming soon from Lyrical Books

Wherever print and ebooks are sold!

THE CRUSH

A PERFECT PAIRING

Juniper Hart has her dream job—or rather, her dream job has her. Under Junie's management, the winery her late father started is finally getting noticed. But she's lonely, deep in debt, and overwhelmed with work. Even if she had time to date, the only men she meets are smug, stemware-breaking hotshots like Lieutenant Manolo Santos, whose good looks and smooth charm don't half make up for the sour taste he leaves on Junie's palate.

After years as an army engineer and a childhood in a restaurant kitchen, Manolo can see Junie's winery is about to go sideways—and he's bursting with ideas to help. Except Junie's far too magnetic for comfort. He left New Jersey to escape becoming one more Santos man shackled to a captivating woman and a failing family business. But in the misty hills of Oregon, with a sip of supple pinot on his tongue, pulling away is the last thing he wants to do . . .

Chapter 1

Rap rap rap!

Juniper Hart was agonizing over which of her wine business's creditors would luck out and get paid this month when she heard loud knocking at the door of her tasting room.

Her head shot up from her bills. She scrambled out from behind her desk, heedless of the papers she set sailing. Inches short of the threshold, she skidded to a stop to smooth down her faded T-shirt emblazoned with WE ARE PINOT NOIR. From the other side of the door, she heard a familiar voice.

"Last I knew, Lieutenant, you had women in, let's see—Fort Bliss, Fort Belvoir, and New York City. And that's just stateside."

Though the words meant nothing to her, Junie recognized the timbre of her old friend Sam Owens's voice. Sam had racked up numerous awards for his military service before moving back to his hometown. These days, he made a living ferrying tourists around in his Clarkston Wine Consortium van, introducing them to Willamette Valley wine. And now, from the sound of it, here he was, delivering eager wine enthusiasts right into the palm of Junie's hand.

She pasted on her best smile and threw wide the door. "Welcome to the pinot state!"

"Hey, Junie!" said Sam warmly. "Like the new greeting."

"Sounds way better than 'Welcome to Broken Hart Vineyards,'" deadpanned Keval, thumbing his cell phone without looking up.

Junie cringed at the innocuous-sounding nickname. Keval Patel might be the town of Clarkston's god of IT, but he could use some help in the tact department.

But wait—these weren't Junie's desperately needed new customers making a detour off the established wine trail. Despite their chins sporting some degree of hipster stubble, to her, these guys would always be the same fresh-faced, coltish boys they'd been back at Clarkston Middle School. Ever since her dad died and her brother left town, they were practically all the family she had left. All except the one with the Ivy League haircut, dressed more for a job interview at Brooks Brothers than a drive-in the wine country.

"Thought you said Oregon was the *Beaver* State?" the stranger asked Sam, eyeing Junie up and down. "Because, *damn…*"

Heath Sinclair's burst of laughter was cut short by Sam's swift elbow to his ribs.

"Why else would I leave a city where women outnumber men to fly all the way across the country?"

"Thought it was to do a brother a favor, Lieutenant." Sam raised a weary brow. "Sorry, Junie. We've done two tastings already, and some of these bozos forgot how to spit."

"I had all good intentions of expectorating when we started out." Heath straightened, still clutching his side. "But I'm a beer drinker. Beer drinkers swallow. It's what we do." Heath should know—he was the founder of Clarkston Craft Ales.

"Juniper Hart"—Sam stretched out an arm toward the stranger—"this is Lieutenant Manolo Santos."

The lieutenant nodded in curt, military fashion. "Pleasure."

"Manolo's a construction guy from back east. Came out to give me some expert advice on the new consortium building."

Junie examined Manolo dubiously. Tall and broad shouldered with a flat belly, it was easy to imagine him in a sweat-stained work shirt, hefting a load of two-by-fours. But the quick gleam in his eye, the pride in his bearing, and his impeccable grooming pegged him as more than just your typical manual laborer.

"Construction guy?"

"Construction engineer, technically," he replied.

"What exactly does a construction engineer do?"

"The official U.S. Army definition?" He flashed her a blindingly white grin. "Someone who works a twelve-hour day/night shift seven days a week on a rotational basis in a remote location."

Sam gripped Manolo's shoulder affectionately. "What the lieutenant here does is solve problems. Converts ideas into reality. Manny's helped design roads, schools, and hospitals from Arizona to Iraq."

"Is that so?"

Manolo shrugged off Sam's compliment like a too-tight shirt. "Think of me as kind of a combination Jason Bourne and Bob the Builder."

"You're forgetting horndog," added Sam, to backslaps and shrieks of mirth.

Junie dismissed Manolo and slanted her eyes at those she knew better. "You guys sure you can handle another one?"

They straightened their spines, trying their best to look contrite.

Keval tsked and gave her an incredulous look. "Are you *serious*?"

"C'mon, Junie. Let us in," pleaded Rory, whose family's apple orchard adjoined Junie's land.

"I'm designated driver." Sam jerked a thumb toward his log-splashed van parked out in the field, some distance away.

She propped her hand on her hip and pretended to consider her options. If not for Sam roping them in, no tourists would ever find their way off the main road to her boutique winery. Junie owed Sam big-time.

When she figured they'd suffered long enough, she broke out in a conciliatory smile. "C'mon," she said, stepping aside.

The men shuffled past Junie into the tasting room in single file, with Tall, Dark, and Sketchy bringing up the rear.

"After you, ma'am."

His baritone was soft and deep. Arrogant eyes the rich brown of espresso made the back of her neck prickle. *A man who seems too good to be true usually is.* She brushed off her warning instinct, slipped behind the counter, and dealt out five generic white coasters. Those would have to do until the day she could afford to have them done right, custom-printed with her name.

Lieutenant Santos's head swiveled on his neck, absorbing every detail of Junie's humble tasting room…the unfinished ceiling, the plywood walls, the makeshift bar cobbled together from cast-off parts. The closer he looked, the more inadequate she felt. So what if it wasn't the Taj Mahal? She was doing the best she could.

She kept half an eye on him as he wandered over to the opposite side of the room, where a picture window would be someday, if she was lucky. His every movement was a study in controlled power. Wherever he went, the others followed, drawn to him like bees to a hive. He said something Junie couldn't quite decipher. Whatever it was, her friends found it highly entertaining.

Daryl Decaprio, Clarkston High's most notorious flirt. The resemblance was uncanny.

When the laughter finally died down, Daryl's twin drifted over to watch her work. The temporary bar served only four without crowding. But there was an eighteen-foot slab of live-edge white oak out in the barn just waiting for the right time to be installed.

"You wouldn't happen to have anything to eat back there, would you?"

"This is a wine-tasting room. If you're hungry, there're some restaurants in town."

He raised a palm. "Fair enough. No harm in asking."

She launched into her rehearsed pitch. "So, where're you from?"

"Born and raised in Hoboken, New Jersey. But I left there a long time ago."

Junie busied herself opening a two-year-old vintage. She felt the heat of his gaze travel over her hands, up her arms to her chest, her neck, and finally her face.

"What's a beauty like you doing hidden away in a place like this?"

Her hands paused where they struggled against the stubborn cork. Beauty? *Her?* He didn't just look like Daryl; he laid it on thick like him, too.

Stick to your script, Junie. What had they said at that free class for entrepreneurs at the Yamhill County Extension? She was the one who should be asking the questions. Marketing 101.

She gave the screw a vicious twist. The cork came out with a muted pop, and she began to pour the one-ounce servings used for sampling.

"How long will you be in the Willamette Valley?"

"Not long. I'm a traveling man. Just passing through."

Lieutenant Manolo Santos was a walking, talking cliché, thanks to his good looks and bad lines.

Be nice to everyone, they said in the class. *You never know who might turn out to be an ally.* She clenched the bottle tighter in her moist palm, determined not to fumble under his penetrating glare, ally or not.

Sam hoisted his glass and the others followed suit. But before he could make a toast, the stranger beat him to it.

"To the Beaver State," he said, eyes sparkling with mischief.

That brought more cautious chuckles, as her friends weighed their loyalty to her against the novelty of the suave newcomer in their midst.

Sam swirled his wineglass at eye level, checking for all the signs: color, viscosity, legs.

Rory downed his glass like cider and followed it with a satisfied belch.

Junie's heart sank. Heath was a brewer and Sam was in the wine business, like Junie. Keval was industry, too, if doing IT for the consortium counted. Was it too much to ask for them to appreciate what she was trying to do here? They'd tried her wine before. They knew word of mouth was everything. That's where sales came from. But they couldn't pass the word on about how great her pinot was if they persisted in chugging it like marathoners on Gatorade. Maybe they couldn't handle three tastings in one day, after all.

"Yummy." Keval licked his lips and picked up a battered copy of *Wine Spectator* from the bar. "Just think, Juniper. Maybe you'll be in here someday."

Yeah, right. She couldn't even afford to renew her subscription.

At least Sam had the decency to give his wine time to wander around his palate, letting it speak to his taste buds. "Your wine sings, Junie."

Junie swelled with pride. High praise, coming from Sam. But even he couldn't seem to find her a distributor, though he'd been looking for the past couple of years.

True to his word, he spat into the receptacle provided. "Now, how about that rosé?"

Junie poised the new bottle to pour, but there were only four empty glasses on the counter. She skimmed the room for the fifth, spotting it in the hand of Mr. New Jersey.

Thick, workingman's fingers cradled her fragile stemware. Dense lashes brushed against carved cheekbones as he lowered them to gaze at the ruby liquid. Then he glanced up over the rim, catching Junie staring. "Young, bright appearance."

He lowered his Roman nose into the bowl and sniffed, then looked up, his eyes landing in the vicinity of her chest. "Juicy plums." He swirled and sniffed again. "And some other fruit I don't think I've had the pleasure of tasting."

Junie forgot about the bottle she held poised, and it sank to the bar under its own weight. "Lingonberry. It's native to the Pacific Northwest."

Manolo drank then. But all the while he worked her wine around in his mouth, he didn't take his eyes off her.

The tasting room grew uncomfortably warm, despite the chilly April air. Lieutenant Manolo Santos had a politician's command of the room. Even the guys quit horsing around in anticipation of what he would say next.

"Soft and supple, yet structurally complex. I like that."

The breath Junie didn't know she'd been holding whooshed out through her broad grin. This vintage was her most ambitious effort to date, and that was exactly the response she had been going for.

"It's good in a wine, too."

While the guys cracked up, Junie's smile ebbed and her cheeks burned even hotter.

Manolo raised his glass. "To—Junie, was it?"

She glared daggers at him. He may have played her once, but she wouldn't let it happen again. Thanks to her experience with Daryl, she knew better than to trust guys like him.

"Could we, ah…" Sam motioned to the still-empty quartet of glasses.

Only then did she remember the bottle of rosé she still clenched by the neck.

After she set them up again, her usually levelheaded, sweet friends surrounded Mr. Big Shot.

"To Junie!" he exclaimed, eyes aglow with a fire that disconcerted her, despite her resolve.

"To a promising future," said Sam, with a nod of appreciation for her skill as a winemaker.

The others echoed with woozy tributes of their own.

Testosterone-fueled shoulder bumps were followed by more enthusiastic clinks. "One more?" Heath asked, holding out his empty glass.

More laughter, more rowdy toasting.

Then Junie shrank at the sound of crystal shattering.

"I'll get the broom." She hurried back to her office, adding the cost of replacing the broken stemware to her long list of expenses.

Chapter 2

Manolo reached behind the tasting room door to relieve Junie of the broom handle she clutched. "I'll get that, ma'am."

"I've got it," Junie snapped. The flame in her eyes would melt steel.

Dammit, he was trying to be a gentleman. He meant well. His behavior leading up to this mess was just his way of warning an attractive woman that he wasn't cut out for the long haul.

His hands flew open to grant her wish, but she wasn't expecting it. The long handle teetered on its bristles, then toppled over in slow motion, drawing their eyes downward.

He caught it mid-fall. But not before he saw the crimson ink on the statements scattered beneath the scarred old desk. What's more, she saw him looking.

Back out in the tasting room, Manolo made short work of the broken glass. "Where's the trash?"

Mutely, Junie reached under the counter and held out the can. He dumped the shards, then snatched a length of paper toweling off the roll on the bar.

She leaned over the counter to see where he was wiping the last streaks of blood-red wine from the floor. "You don't have to—"

"Done."

"Sorry." Sam winced. "Can't take these guys anywhere."

"Yeah, sorry, Junie," aped Keval, looking genuinely remorseful.

"Having too much fun," added Rory.

"No," Manolo said, wondering how he was going to make up for his lousy first impression. *She must think I'm a complete assjack.* "This is my fault. I take full responsibility." He jutted his chin toward the others. "Pulling these guys out of work so I could do a little day drinking."

Sam slapped Rory on the back. "Just wanted Manny to get to know my homies, here."

The woman wiped her palms down the sides of her slim thighs and tightened her lips against a retort.

Manolo put the broom back in the office, then strode behind the bar, lathered up, and offered her his freshly washed hand. "Please accept my apology."

Junie hesitated. Even after she grudgingly took his hand, she kept inventing ways to avoid eye contact. She blew a loose strand out of hair out of her eyes and, when that didn't work, shook back her whole shaggy mane... chewed her lower lip...looked at anything and anyone but him. Finally, she lifted her pointed chin and glared at him defiantly, as if she saw straight through his pretext.

Blue eyes. No, blue-green, like the turquoise drops dangling from her ears. Thankfully, that earlier wildfire in them had simmered down to a slow burn. Below the plane of the bar, her hand felt capable and strong, pressed against his. He brushed his thumb lightly across the base of hers. While he drew lazy circles on Junie's skin, he recalled the phone conversation when Sam had first told him that the pool of local vintners he'd started was crowding him out of his own house. He needed a real building. Sam's news had only confirmed the buzz back east: that this corner of the Pacific Northwest was fast becoming America's new capital of pinot noir.

From inside the bubble Manolo imagined surrounding them, Junie used her left thumb and forefinger to methodically pry his digits off her right hand, one by one. Short of being under enemy fire, nothing got Manolo's blood pumping like actually having to fight for a female conquest. For the sake of cover, he kept up their light banter while drawing out their private little game of handsies as long as possible. She had succeeded in peeling his grip away once, only to have him immediately retake his lost territory. One honest tug was all it would take to free herself from his covert caresses, if she really wanted to.

"Apology accepted, on one condition. I asked you how long you were going to be wreaking havoc in our neck of the woods."

"Six months, max."

She smiled ruefully. "Looks like I'd better stock up on glassware."

She was a good sport, after all. "Shortest lease I could find," he said.

"That'll be September. The crush. All the festivities start on the ninth this year."

"That's the plan," said Sam. "We need to have the new consortium up and running by then for the onslaught of tourists. Manny took a place on Main Street above The Radish Rose."

"Clarkston's best restaurant." She lifted an approving brow.

Finally, he'd done something right. Truth was, Manolo never went anywhere without first scouting out the area's best places for food and wine. "Speaking of which, what are you doing for dinner?"

Junie's hand snapped back to her side, and the bubble popped. "Working."

He waited for her to explain.

"I wait tables at dinnertime during the week so I can be here afternoons and weekends for customers."

Customers? In the nick of time, he bit back a laugh. They hadn't seen another soul since Sam's van had left the main wine trail.

Sam stepped up to the bar. "Junie's got a lot on her plate, now that—"

"I can speak for myself, Sam." She picked up her bar rag with a flounce and vigorously wiped the counter. "Budbreak is a busy time of year. I have to finish weeding and mowing and paying the bills—" Her mouth snapped shut again at the mention of bills.

Well played, Santos. You've just been shot down—in front of four other men.

Manolo waved away his dinged pride. "Don't worry about it. Good meeting you, Junie." He reached for his wallet. "Before I go, here, take this for the wineglasses. And I'll take six bottles of that pinot. Once word gets out, it's not going to last long."

* * * *

Sam and Manolo lagged behind the others on their way back to the van.

"Don't take it personal, man." Sam always could read him like a book. But then, he'd been highly trained to spot people's vulnerabilities or, as they said in military jargon, "handle assets." "Junie keeps to herself. Ever since she got back from UC Davis, she's been working her ass off."

"The big winemaking school?"

Sam nodded. "Right after she graduated, her dad died. That left just Junie and her mom to run the place"—he glanced backward out of an abundance of caution—"by which I mean, just Junie."

"Shame."

Manolo's practiced eyes skimmed over the faded brown landscape, across a winding silver ribbon of water to the misty distant hills. Evaluating ground for its development potential came as second nature to him. "Hard to believe grapes'll grow here. Day's more than half gone and those hills are still shrouded in fog."

"That was the old way of thinking," said Sam. "Brendan Hart was one of the first to see climate change coming."

From where Manolo was standing, the Willamette Valley felt different from anywhere else he'd been—and he'd been to a lot of places in his thirty-four years. While the East Coast seemed suddenly tired...sedate, rural Oregon still epitomized the frontier spirit, fresh and thrumming with possibility, its people brassy and vibrant.

"Pinot noir's the polar bear of grapes. The wine gets flabby if it's too hot. People assume it's cold here because of the latitude, but the Willamette today is like Napa was ten years ago. Now Cali's fried, and we're more temperate, like the Med. These hills are ideal for pinot."

"So, what happened?"

Sam made a face. "Do I look like a climatologist?"

"Junie's dad, numb nuts."

They struck out again across the uneven landscape. "The Harts aren't originally from around here. Junie was in middle school when Brendan retired as an MP. He was still young, so he started a second career as a state trooper. First month on the job, he neutralized some wing nut with an AR-15 holding a farm family hostage. Overnight, Brendan Hart was a hero.

"But being a cop was never Hart's main ambition. He might have gotten an instant reputation as a badass, but in person he was kind of quiet, mild-mannered. He found this old farm where hazelnuts and filberts used to grow, and somehow convinced his wife that this was where they were going to settle down, plant their family."

"Family?"

"Junie and her brother, name of Storm. Soup sandwich, you ask me. You know the type. Always looking for a fast buck without paying his dues. Back when we were in school, you could always find him and Junie out here working alongside their dad. Once he graduated, though, it only took one crush for him to realize what the next fifty were going to look like. Got out while he still had a strong back."

Manolo winced. He knew what it felt like to be saddled with someone else's dream. Like you were slowly suffocating.

"Last I heard, Storm was making money hand over fist running one of those cannabis outfits in Colorado."

Asking would only dredge up pain. But a deep-seated guilt made him need to know. "How'd the old man take it, his only son taking off like that, reneging on his family duty?"

"On top of a decade of tending grapes by moonlight after pulling eight-hour shifts busting drug dealers? Massive coronary, that's how. Junie found him one morning lying right over there, where he'd gone out to graft rootstock the night before." Sam pointed between long rows of stakes to where a flock of robins pecked at the thawing earth. Their chirps filled the resulting silence.

Neither Sam nor Manolo were strangers to death. Right now, Sam was probably reliving his own horrors from his time in Iraq. But, as for Manolo, he was obsessing over wayward sons and how they broke their fathers' hearts.

"Maybe the brother'll man up, once he matures a little."

"Doubt it." Sam pulled a blade of wild garlic and stuck it between his teeth. "Some say Storm got his mom's good sense and Junie's a dreamer like her old man."

Some were probably right. "What about her mom?"

"She's originally from down south. It's a wonder Hart ever got her to move to Clarkston in the first place. She never really fit in." Then Sam's detail-obsessed nature asserted itself. "Check that. To be fair, she's a surgeon. Could be she just never had the time to get in good with the locals."

"A surgeon. Impressive."

Sam gestured broadly. "You think you could raise two kids, put one through college, and subsidize all this on a cop's salary? Everyone in Clarkston says it's only a matter of time before Jennifer Jepson-Hart gets tired of throwing good money after bad and talks her daughter into moving back to civilization."

"Sounds like Junie's inherited some good genes."

"What Junie's trying to do takes more than good genes. Running a vineyard *and* a winery is like operating three businesses at once."

"Growing grapes...making wine...what else?"

"Entertainment. Junie's one of the most gifted winemakers in the valley. Hart Vineyards is starting to get noticed. But that's not enough. People want to be *entertained* as part of the wine-buying experience. If she falls short anywhere, it's there. I can't seem to get that through her head. But then, speaking of gifted, you know about the seven intelligences."

"Say again? I know what kind of structure works best on any given site and how to throw together a decent marinara. You're the smart one. Enlighten me."

"You just nailed it without even trying. Seven intelligences theory says the average guy has two or three things out of a possible seven in his wheelhouse." He counted off on his fingers. "Math, verbal, spatial, musical, interpersonal, intrapersonal, kinesthetic.

"Take you, for example. You see a piece of ground and you instinctively know what kind of building will work best on it. That's spatial intelligence. Me? Back in OCS when they gave me the aptitude test, I scored high in intrapersonal—knowing myself—and interpersonal—knowing others. On the other hand, I don't know a noun from an adverb, and I have zero chance of being drafted by the Seahawks. Junie? She might have kick-ass winemaking chops, but it doesn't automatically follow that she knows how to sell what she makes."

Manolo nodded in assent. "That tasting room's a disaster. Best thing that could happen would be to gut it and start over."

"Hart didn't see the point of a fancy tasting room, either. He invested the bulk of his hard-earned cash in the actual winemaking equipment. I suspect Junie's still paying for those French oak barrels. Nothing's lacking down there in the cellar. But as far as marketing, Junie's got her work cut out for her. She's strong, though. Strong and proud."

The image of Junie's late notices strewn across the tasting room floor popped into Manolo's mind. But he made it a policy to steer clear of women's personal business. Getting too close only made it harder to pull up stakes when the time came to leave.

He tipped back his head, inhaling the sharp tang of wood smoke and manure. *Ahh, the smell of springtime in the country.* That wasn't what Hoboken smelled like. The fresh air cleared his head, bringing him back to less disconcerting problems. Problems that could be solved using inductive reasoning and logic.

"That's some great pinot she's got. You're right, though. This property needs a major overhaul if she wants to turn it into a point of destination. For instance..." Manolo jabbed his bag of wine toward a slope just south of the tasting room. "Over there." He backtracked several steps. "That grade is just begging to be terraced." In an instant, the development crystallized in his imagination. "Maybe a pergola there, some tables *there*. Optimize the view while people are sampling the wine. Put them in the mood to buy."

Sam followed him a few steps to humor him. "It's not me you have to convince."

But Manolo wasn't listening. His head was exploding with ideas. He turned on his axis, pausing when the dove-gray siding and cheery yellow door of the main dwelling came back into view. "The house looks solid enough, except for that skeleton of two-by-fours on the north end. Is that an addition?"

"Junie hired some fly-by-night to start the side porch over a year ago, to be true to her dad's original plan. The guy promised her the moon, stayed a couple weeks, then disappeared with her partial payment in his pocket."

"That's the kind of jerk that gives my profession a bad name. Not good for the frame lumber to be exposed that long, especially in this climate. The wood's susceptible to mold."

Sam shook his head. "That's all Junie needs, to have to start the porch over on top of everything else."

"Nice-size house. Junie live there all by herself?"

Sam headed back to the path. "She's still got her mom."

There was a flash of wings as a hawk zoomed down on an unsuspecting robin.

"Kestrel," said Sam, as they watched the raptor fly away with his prey. He turned to Manolo. "Let's get something straight. We pushed the envelope today. No real harm done other than a few broken glasses. I'll take the blame for not stopping after two wineries—I like giving Junie business when I can. Just don't go getting any half-assed ideas. Junie's not hookup material."

Manolo almost ran into him. *"Hookup material?"*

"You know. 'Hit it and quit it.' You don't need to add Junie to your list of Tinderellas. And don't think I won't hear about it if you try to sneak in under the radar. Clarkston's a small town. We all look out for Junie. Same way her dad looked out for us."

They walked on. Behind Sam, Manolo grinned. "Now, that's going to sting for a while. I'm more highly evolved than that. Don't you know? I actually think of myself as a feminist."

"Hah!" Sam huffed without turning around. "I must've missed the memo."

"In fact—no disrespect, Cap'n—but I'm thinking maybe you got a bad case of the hots for Juniper Hart, yourself."

"Negative, Lieutenant," Sam replied without missing a beat.

A rush of relief surged through Manolo, surprising him.

"I blew my chances with Junie Hart a long time ago."

Now this was interesting. "Out with it. You can't leave me hanging after a line like that."

"If you got to know. Ninth grade, spring dance. You remember ninth grade. Hormones raging? Junie was still new, didn't have many friends yet. On top of that, she was kind of quiet. When it came down to time for the dance, I still hadn't gotten around to asking anybody, and she was one of the last ones left."

"So you asked her."

Sam nodded. "Strictly platonic. We danced, some with each other and a little with other people. I left the gym to get a Coke or something, and that's when I got kidnapped by Mona Cruz."

"Ah." Manolo nodded. "No mother should ever name her daughter Mona. That's just asking for it."

"Roger that. Mona was a sophomore, but she should've been a junior. A silver ring in her bellybutton, jeans so tight you could see the outline of her new permit in her back pocket. She'd been giving me signs all year, but I was too dumb to do anything. Finally she saw her chance, and dragged me around the corner and down the hall. I was supposed to fight that off?"

"A man's gotta do what a man's gotta do, even if he's only in ninth grade."

"Next thing I know, Mona's got her tongue down my throat, I'm copping my first feel—and Junie comes walking around the corner. Woody melted like a popsicle in an oven."

"Christ." Torn between Sam's predicament and Junie's hurt, Manolo's face twisted in a half grin, half grimace. "At least you *went* to your ninth grade dance."

"What?" asked Sam. "You couldn't get a date?"

If only Manolo could put a humorous spin on his own freshman dance. But even after all these years, there was nothing remotely funny about missing out on the cardinal event of his high school career to do what he did every Friday night, which was work. Even worse was when clusters of his classmates clamored into his family's restaurant after the dance ended. If he lived to be a hundred, he would never be able to un-see all the other guys and their cute dates, un-hear their exclusive laughter over all the fun that he'd missed. Scribbling down their food orders, scurrying to fill them, he had never felt so left out, before or since.

"I don't think I had a single date all through high school. My old man was unrelenting. All we ever did was work. My sisters didn't date, either. Two of my sisters ended up marrying the first guys that came along after graduation, for better or worse. I hightailed it in the opposite direction."

"You more than made up for lost time," Sam joked.

"You could say that." Manolo grinned unapologetically.

"Anyway, now I hear Mona's got kids by two different baby daddies," said Sam, going back to his story. "And I got my sights set on a full-bodied red with legs that'd make you cry."

Well now. This is *a good sign.* Manolo had been concerned that the only people Sam trusted anymore were the ones he'd served with. Covert assignments that ran a couple years over time tended to mess with a man's head like that. He slung an arm over his compatriot's shoulders. "Why, Samuel, you old rascal, you." Maybe Sam's invisible wounds were finally starting to heal.

Sam grinned, glued his eyes to his feet, and endured Manolo's brusque, one-armed squeeze.

"But I meant what I said earlier," he added earnestly. "Bad as we pissed Junie off today, we take care of our own around here. You two would never work. She's got enough aggravation."

"That big-brother act wouldn't have anything to do with old ninth-grade guilt, would it?"

"Maybe it does and maybe it doesn't. And, Lieutenant?"
At the look on Sam's face, Manolo's smile faded.
"That's an order."

Chapter 3

Junie tucked Manolo's bills into her metal cash box, pleased at the way they filled up the empty slots. Manolo Santos had presence. And Junie wasn't the only one who'd been affected. He'd had her guy friends eating out of his hand on his first day in town.

She tossed her head, hoping to shake him out, but all that did was register that he had really asked her out to dinner! And, genius that she was, she'd turned him down, pleading too many chores. Weeding and mowing? *At night?*

But getting involved with an admitted drifter was the last thing she needed.

She had just dived under the desk to retrieve her late notices when she heard the tasting room door open again. One of the guys must have left something behind.

"Junie?"

"Mom?" *What is she doing home already?* "I'm in here."

From the floor where she knelt, Junie saw a pair of Velcro-strapped Mary Janes coming toward her. Next, Mom's pink face came into view, the blood having rushed to her head when she bent over. "What are you doing under there?"

"I dropped something." She backed out on her hands and knees and slid the late notices to the bottom of the paper pile.

When Dad died, his life insurance had erased what was left of the mortgage, but his capital investment in the winery had left her with substantial debt. Storm had already moved to Colorado. Mom wanted to immediately put the house and vineyard on the market and pretend Dad's dream—Mom's nightmare—had never existed. But Junie, with the blind enthusiasm of a new college grad and no clue of the long, hard road ahead, had been adamant that she could make it on her own. If Mom found out she was now having money problems—

"A better question is what are *you* doing here?" Even when Mom was at home, she rarely ventured out to the big outbuilding containing the tasting room, press, and cellar.

"It's Friday, remember? I don't schedule appointments Friday afternoons."

"It doesn't usually work out that way, though, does it?" Even when Mom did manage to quit working at a decent hour, she usually stayed in the city with colleagues to take advantage of its superior restaurants.

"I made it a point to get home early today. I am tapped *out*." She looked around for a place to sit, but the only chair was the one behind the desk.

Junie studied her mother's face. If she had something important to talk about, why now, when they had all weekend?

Mom smiled cryptically. "How about you? When was the last time you ate anything? Something good for you."

Junie stuffed the late notices into a drawer. She tried to recall her last meal, but came up empty.

"That's what I thought. Want to go out and grab a quick bite before you have to get ready for work? There's nothing in the fridge. As usual."

Junie stiffened. Mom was always on her to eat better. Most nights, Junie mechanically wolfed down whatever was on special after her shift at Casey's Roadhouse. She knew she should make more of an effort. But food was way down on her list of priorities. Nothing ever seemed to really satisfy her hunger, anyway. Maybe working at mediocre restaurants for the past nine years had dulled her appetite.

"How about Poppy's?"

Poppy's, whose menu was stuffed full of the kind of sugary, highly glutenous confections that tempted even Junie's palate? Something was definitely up. Normally, Mom would have suggested a salad from Demeter or at least The Radish Rose, whose menu had lots of choices.

"Sure." As long as Mom was paying.

Chapter 4

"Poppy!"

Poppy Springer's looks were as startling today as they had been back when she and Junie were lifeguards at the Clarkston Community Pool. Junie jumped up from her booth to give her a hug.

"What are you doing home?"

"Busman's holiday. Mom and Pop took the motor home up to Whistler for a few weeks. Their annual vacation just happened to fall when I was between jobs. I'm holding down the fort. I left you a message."

"I know...." Junie slid back onto her vinyl seat. "Sorry I haven't gotten back to you. It's just that I've been so busy with work..."

Poppy set down their water glasses, eyes lowered.

"Join the club. She doesn't return her own mother's calls," Mom said.

Junie knew her excuses were getting old, but what could she do?

"How are you, Dr. Hart?"

"I'm fine, thank you very much. Nice to you again so soon, Poppy."

Poppy turned to Junie with a patient smile. "Your mom and I ran into each other at the place in the city where I'm hostessing part time."

"Really?" Junie frowned. Mom hadn't mentioned that.

"I'm not blowing you off, Poppy. I promise."

"Stop!" That was Poppy for you, swallowing her own disappointment so that Junie wouldn't feel bad. "I know you have your hands full out there. Now, what can I get you two? The sticky buns are hot out of the oven." She beamed at Junie. "Guaranteed to spike your blood sugar."

"I'll just have green tea. Decaf," said Mom.

Junie skimmed the menu for something her mother would approve of.

The bell above the door jangled, and two couples, the women in expensive linen and the men in cargo shorts, a camera with a telescopic lens swinging around one of their necks, entered the café.

"Do you need a few minutes?" To the untrained eye, Poppy appeared unaffected. But Junie knew she had alerted like a bloodhound on a kilo of heroin. In a town like Clarkston, catering to tourists was how restaurants survived.

Junie bit her lip. Those sticky buns sounded awfully good.... "Okay." Junie slapped her menu down on the Formica. "I'm in. A bun and coffee."

Poppy swept away their menus. "Coming right up."

"I'll be good tomorrow," Junie muttered.

"I'm not judging you. But it is worth remembering that excess sugar consumption causes diabetes."

Thank you, Doctor Mom.

Now that they'd ordered, Junie waited for her to come out with whatever it was she'd brought her here to talk about.

"Poppy's doing well," Mom remarked with mild surprise. "Did you hear about her new job offer?"

"Yeah. I'm really happy for her."

Poppy had left Clarkston right out of school to stock wine in a dusty little shop on a Portland side street. When the manager quit three years later, the owner had tagged Poppy to replace him, even though she was still a month shy of being able to take her first legal drink. From there, she'd started hostessing. Now, she'd been offered a plum position as wine steward at one of Portland's hippest restaurants.

"She's had luck on her side. Somehow she managed to find a great niche. Who knew female sommeliers would be the next big thing?"

"Or it could've been her strong work ethic and her natural way with people. Plus, she has a great memory. Have you noticed? She never writes down an order."

Mom folded her arms on the table. "If Poppy can make it in Portland, anyone can."

"Meaning?"

"Now, don't you get all defensive on me. You know as well as I do that nobody ever had any great expectations of Miss Poppy Springer. She got good genes, I grant you that," she said, in an obvious reference to Poppy's classic good looks. "But she has the cranial bandwidth of an amoeba. And without a degree..."

"Newsflash, Mom. College isn't for everyone."

A graciously smiling Poppy approached the table. Mom sat back to make room for her to set down her steaming tea. When she left, Mom went on. "I'm not here to argue about Poppy or extoll the virtues of college. Junie, you're my only daughter. I love you very much. And it's about time you got a real job."

"Mom." Junie closed her eyes, struggling to remain calm. "We're not doing this again. I already *have* a real job. Do you still think enology is some passing fancy?"

At their table nearby, the tourists turned and stared.

"Keep it down," said Mom. "And you've got circles under your eyes. You look exhausted. Have you lost weight?"

"Haven't checked lately." She hadn't weighed herself in months. The workweek flashed through Junie's mind like clips from a movie. Monday, the concerned look on the face of the volunteer from the co-op after examining her financials. Tuesday and Wednesday, trudging miles through rows of vines to tweak the pruning, racing to tie cordons to the top wires to keep the flower buds off the ground in case of a late frost. Her jeans did feel looser, come to think of it. Trust Mom to notice.

"*And* your freckles are coming out already, and it's only April. Aren't you wearing sunscreen? Juniper, darling, I know much you loved your father—we *all* did—but don't you think that vineyard has cost this family enough? It's been five long years. When I think of all the money sunk into this venture... and then losing Storm so he didn't have to see the disappointment in his father's face every time he looked at him—"

"Storm didn't *have* to move to Colorado."

"You saw what farming did to your father in the end." Mom knew how to angle the knife for maximum damage. "If not for Brendan chasing that pipe dream, he would still be alive today."

Junie frowned. "I can't believe we're having this conversation again, after all the times I've tried to explain it to you. Weren't you even listening?"

Mom appraised her with a cool eye. She wasn't used to being told no. When she walked down the halls of the hospital, the nurses snapped to, and in the ER she had absolute control over her staff. "You're a bright girl, Junie, a hardworking girl," she said in the detached tone used for stubborn patients. "I have connections. I could find you something Monday if you'd only let me. Stefon's partner is the people champion over at—"

"Who's Stefon?" Junie asked, exasperated. "And what's a 'people champion'?"

"*Stefon.* One of my surgical techs. People champion...what did they used to call them? Human resource managers? Whatever. Maybe you could even find something in the wine field that doesn't put your health at risk."

"Mom." Junie framed her words with her hands, homing in on her as if she were the parent and her mother, the child. "For the hundredth time. It's not Dad's dream anymore. It's mine. I'm the third generation of Harts to raise grapes. And it's only a matter of time before I start to break even." She took a meager salary, and she'd been doing all she could to keep up with her credit line and meet expenses. "All I need is a distributor. Sam says the market for Willamette pinot is growing so fast it can't keep up with the supply. It's just that I'm still new, I have a small yield, and my advertising budget's close to zilch."

"Tom Alexander gave me a call yesterday."

Junie cradled her forehead. "Why does he call you? Why doesn't he just call me? I'm twenty-eight years old. I don't need my mother to speak for me."

"Tom and I are colleagues as well as friends. We can communicate—unlike my own daughter and me."

Dr. Alexander probably owned tons of pretty coffee table books about grape growing and winemaking, but he'd never sifted the Willamette's ancient marine sediments through his long, elegant fingers. He hired other people to do the dirty work.

"Let me guess. He's worried about me."

"He asked how you were, that's all."

"He's trying to wheedle out of you whether he's going to be able get his hands on half my yield again this fall."

Last crush, Junie had had no choice but to sell some of her grapes to Dr. Alexander. Hand selling bottles out of her tasting room hadn't covered the payment on her line of credit, and coincidentally, Alexander had been scrounging for every bushel of grapes within a thousand acres of Clarkston.

Mom's eyes widened. "Honey. What's wrong with that? He's a shrewd businessman as well as an excellent physician."

Nothing was wrong with that. But Junie poured her heart and soul into her wine, while people like Tom Alexander used the interest off his investments to fund what was for him merely a prestigious hobby.

"He saved Storm's life."

Junie sighed. "That was a long time ago, and Storm's completely recovered."

"I'll never be able to repay him for that."

"None of us will, Mom. But that was then. Now, Tom Alexander just wants to buy up as many Clarkston area grapes as he can so his wine qualifies for the AVA stamp."

"AVA, XYZ. It's beyond me, the finer points of the wine business."

"Wine begins in the vineyard. You heard Dad say that a hundred times."

"About as many times as I heard him say, 'You can make a small fortune in the wine business, provided you start out with a large one.'"

"It's simply supply and demand. When the local vintners realized they were sitting on the mother lode of American pinot noir, they got together and lobbied for legal designation for six distinct viticultural areas. That changed everything. It painted a clear picture that wine from grapes grown on one side of the road tastes different from the other side, everything else being equal."

"You told me Tom's generosity was the only thing that got you by, these past few months."

"Generosity? Hah. Yes, he bought some of my grapes. But now he's having them made into a wine that will compete directly against mine."

"You'll both benefit. What's wrong with that?"

How could Junie make Mom understand her grapes were her children? Selling to Tom Alexander had broken open old wounds. It had made her mourn Dad all over again. Shock, denial, anger—the whole cycle. She'd promised herself: *Never again.*

"I'm sorry I brought it up," her mother said.

"That's not what you left work early to talk to me about?"

Her mom looked genuinely puzzled. "No, not at all."

Good Lord. "Then what?"

"I bought myself a townhouse."

"What?" Junie blurted.

"If you'd listened to my messages, you would know. I have asked you and asked you to go house hunting with me. You never wanted to come. You know how bad traffic's getting, thanks to the tourists and all the new development. And that was a close call I had last winter on the ice during the cold snap. Besides, it doesn't make financial sense for me to waste two hours a day commuting when I could be operating."

Junie's head swam. *First Storm, then Dad.* Mom had been threatening to move to Portland ever since Dad died, but Junie hadn't wanted to believe she really would. "You're moving out of the farmhouse?" The house Dad had built for them with his own two hands? The only house Junie had ever lived in that wasn't on some military base?

"It's sweet that you're nostalgic about the house. But be practical. This starry-eyed vision of living off the land never came true for your grandfather. You saw how your dad lived growing up—practically in squalor. And, Junie, as I live and breathe, it's not going to work for you. I've tried to be patient. But you've been chasing your tail for five years, and where has it got you?"

"There's a saying: 'Do what you love and the money will follow.' Most small businesses don't show a profit in their early years. Wineries need even longer to get in the black."

Mom shook her head. "I wish I could convince you to get out now, while you're still young. Like Storm did."

Junie worked like a demon between waiting tables and managing the vineyard without any real help. Now her deep-rooted anxiety bubbled up to the surface. Was she doomed, like Granddad and then Dad? Tears stung the back of her eyes. Was Mom right?

"The townhouse is in The Pearl. It's brand new, which means I can move in right away. It has three bedrooms, plus plenty of storage, and a cute balcony overlooking the shops and restaurants."

Junie envisioned The Pearl's crowded sidewalks, heard the cacophony of the late-night partiers when the bars let out.

Mom laid her hand on Junie's. There was a plea in her voice when she said, "Come to Portland with me. There're jobs, great food, culture, men...."

"One thing about being a server, I'll never starve. And there are plenty of men in Clarkston...."

The bell on the door signaled the arrival of a quartet of bearded lumbersexuals wearing colorful plaid shirts and skinny jeans. Bringing up the rear was an out-of-place, clean-shaven Hercules whose deltoids strained at the seams of his neatly pressed oxford shirt. He'd lost the navy blazer somewhere along the way, but Junie would have recognized him anywhere. When Manolo spotted her, he broke out in a spontaneous grin and scrubbed the top of his head, leaving his layered hair endearingly spiked. He angled his body in her direction.

Her heart stopped.

Then something spooked him, gave him pause. Maybe it was Sam and Heath's polite but guarded waves. The next thing she knew, Poppy had lassoed Manolo in with the others and led them toward a table on the other side of the café.

Only Keval peeled off from the group. But then, Keval had always been a maverick. In the words of Red McDonald, voted Clarkston's Best Therapist three years in a row, poor Keval had been "born without the ability to ascertain the emotional temperature of a room."

"Hello, ladies! Sam thought we could use some coffee—considering he got us all day drunk. Didn't expect to see you again so soon, Junie. And Dr. Hart! Don't you look precious? *Love* those glasses with your face shape."

"Hi, Kev." Junie sighed with a combination of relief and disappointment that he had been the one to come over instead of Manolo.

"Thank you, Keval. But now, if you'll excuse us, Junie and I are in the midst of an important discussion."

"Oops!" Keval's fingertips flew to his lips. "Sorry! Didn't mean to interrupt," he whispered loudly, tiptoeing backward. "Pretend I wasn't even here!"

"I meant *eligible* men," Mom said when Keval was out of hearing range.

Unlike Keval, Junie was apparently cursed with an *over*developed emotional barometer. The electricity that had been arcing between her and Manolo from the moment he'd entered her tasting room was stronger than ever, making the hair on her arms stand on end. It took all she had not to look over at him, to stay focused on the conversation at hand.

"Mom. I know what cities are like. When I was at college, I hung out in San Francisco more weekends than I can count."

"Even if we put the house and vineyard on the market right away, it will take awhile to sell. But, Junie, the movers will be here first thing tomorrow morning for my things. I could ask them to take yours while they're there."

"*Mom!* I've moved seven times in my life—eleven, if you count each year of college! I'm sick of moving. I want Clarkston to be my forever home. Wait—*tomorrow?*"

Across the room, five heads jerked up in unison. Manolo caught her eye over the top of his menu. His face remained carefully blank.

Mom putting a date on her move somehow made it real. Junie felt her face threaten to crumble. She swallowed the hard lump in her throat. "I'm meeting a guy about the porch at noon. Besides, tomorrow's Saturday. A good day for tourists."

Her mom sank back in her chair with a pitying look. Then she drained her teacup and intoned, "There's something else."

Now what?

"I've met someone, Junie."

Another one?

Just then, Poppy brought the check. She glanced at Junie's gaping mouth and the half-eaten sticky, sitting forlornly on her plate. "Chin up, sweetie," she whispered, bending down to give her a tight squeeze. "I'll call you."

INTOXICATING

In the second book of Heather Heyford's series, set in Oregon's wine country, having a crush takes on a whole new meaning when a lady sommelier teams up with the hottie from her high school days . . .

The Girl Most Likely

. . . to be a waitress at her hometown café. That's what Clarkston's high school yearbook said about Poppy Springer ten years ago and that's where the beauty queen is today. But that's about to change now that Poppy has been offered a position as a lady sommelier at a cutting-edge new restaurant. Only Poppy has an embarrassing secret that could keep her from landing her dream job. A secret her high school crush seems determined to help her with . . .

The Man Most Wanted

In high school, Heath Sinclair may have been voted most likely to blow something up, but these days the sexy science prodigy is a self-made success story with his popular microbrewery and chiseled good looks. So why is Clarkston's most-eligible man so hell-bent on helping Poppy prove that she is more than her reputation? Could it be the enigmatic bachelor has a hankering for the girl who got away?

Chapter 1

"Thanks for coming! Good seeing you again."

Poppy Springer scooped the coins left on the crumb-littered table into her pocket as she watched Sandy and Kyle Houser wheel their stroller out into the September afternoon.

Behind them, a stiff gust of wind sent the bell above the door clanging like a fire alarm. A page torn from a coloring book soared off the table and landed at Poppy's feet, only to skitter out of reach when she bent to pick it up.

Outside the café window, the couple didn't get far before Sandy paused the stroller to pull up the hood on her toddler's jacket.

Must be a storm brewing.

Poppy remembered the day that Kyle had balked at holding Sandy's hand in line at Clarkston Elementary. Now those two were expecting their second baby in May—though just this morning they had come to a mutual decision to wait a bit before telling anyone.

Poppy couldn't help but feel like the residents of Clarkston had become blind to her existence, discussing personal matters between bites of toast while she stood inches away, denying her the small courtesy of looking up when she topped off their coffees.

Poppy gave Sandy and Kyle the benefit of the doubt. They weren't rude, just preoccupied with their full lives. Besides, hadn't her father, known as Big Pop, always called her his human barometer—his teasing way of saying she was too sensitive to others' moods and emotions?

She slid the highchair out of the way, squatting to scrape up the congealing yolk of a dippy egg, and strode to the other side of the café to pick up the cartoon picture of a princess whose face was scribbled almost beyond recognition.

She was still gazing at it when the doorbell jangled again, and she looked up to see Heath Sinclair, Junie Hart, Keval Patel, and Dr. Red McDonald bluster in. The humble café her parents had named after her was the unofficial center of the tight-knit farming community, and Poppy had been a fixture there since birth. Along the way, she'd accumulated more friends than she could count, but she was particularly close with this diverse group, and her insides warmed like one of those rare autumn days when the sun filtered through the Oregon mist onto the vineyards and the pickers' carelessly discarded jackets were bright spots of color on the ground between the rows.

* * * *

Ten minutes later, Poppy rested her tray on the table edge and began distributing drinks and sandwiches. She felt the strain in her back and arms more than usual today, thanks to a late night of studying. For Poppy, book learning had never come easy.

Heath snapped shut the large hardbound volume he'd been leafing through and shoved it in his backpack.

"Red, here's your spicy Italian wrap. Junie, sticky bun. Keval, are you sure all you want is spring water?"

Keval sighed. "I'm on a cleanse."

"Heath—turkey BLT and lemonade." Her eyes flickered to his, then back to the food she handed him.

Poppy had known Heath forever. But since she'd come back to work at the café, the air between them had somehow changed. Maybe Big Pop was right. Maybe she *was* oversensitive.

"Thanks," he murmured, cramming his backpack onto the seat behind him.

Poppy was much better at reading faces than pages, but anyone could see that Heath was hiding something.

"How do you do that?" asked Junie Hart as Poppy deposited the empty tray on an adjacent table. "Always remember everyone's order without writing it down?"

Poppy just smiled and slid into the vinyl booth next to Red, who often stopped by between patients at her counseling practice a few doors down.

"Poppy has a great memory," said Heath.

She flushed with pleasure. She was used to getting compliments on her looks, never her intellect. Heath wasn't a man of many words. If he made the effort to say something nice, you could bet it was sincere.

She sought out Heath's hazel eyes to make clear her appreciation, for once not caring if it made him uncomfortable. *"Thank you,"* she said with emphasis.

But he was already intent on deciding on the best angle from which to attack his BLT.

At twenty-eight, Heath's angular face was still boyish. He had a naturally trim build beneath his fitted plaid shirt, and wavy hair the golden brown of the filberts that used to be ubiquitous to the Willamette Valley—until the Pinot boom came along and farmers uprooted the nut trees and replaced them with wine grapes.

Poppy folded her arms on the table and observed her companions as they ate and drank. Who would have believed that the brewery Heath had started in his basement would become so successful? And that Red, whose real name was Sophia, would one day be voted Clarkston's Best Therapist? Keval did I.T. for the local wine consortium, plus a few select clients on the side. Junie had taken the reins of her faltering family vineyard, and her work was paying off in increased sales.

All of them had made impressive strides over the past decade. All except Poppy. How did she even get to sit at the same table with the likes of them? With every step forward, she took two steps back.

She sighed. A few months ago, the little wine shop in Portland that she managed was sold, drying up her main source of income. She couldn't help but think that maybe the prediction written about her at graduation was destined to come true.

"I saw Big Pop at the vet this morning," said Keval. "He told me your news. Exciting!"

"What news?" asked Red.

Poppy hesitated. She hadn't decided how much to tell her friends about her long shot for the future, in case it didn't pan out.

At first when Cory Anthony—*the* Cory Anthony, one of Portland's top chefs—mentioned he might be able to put her knowledge of wine to good use at the new place he was opening up, she'd been ecstatic.

Then, during the formal interview, Chef told her the elaborate renovations were going to take longer than originally thought. The target opening date had been pushed back until the end of the year.

But the real clincher was that though he said he was impressed by Poppy having taught herself about wine, his job offer was contingent on her becoming official—earning her sommelier certificate.

Her elation had given way to panic. She was a terrible test taker. To this day, she still had nightmares about school.

"First I have to pass that exam," she told her friends.

"You'll pass. You've got a great bedside manner," said Keval. "Besides, it doesn't hurt that you look like that classic painting of Venus on the half-shell."

"Thanks—I think." Another well-meaning comment equating her worth with her appearance. "And it's called table service. The parts of the test are wine theory, tasting, and table service."

"Excuse me," said Keval, waving his fork in the air. "Do I know all those fancy wine terms? Promise me one thing. Once you're a famous lady somm with your face plastered all over, you won't forget your roots."

She chuckled. "I can safely say that's not something you'll ever have to worry about."

"You've heard, right?" exclaimed Keval to the others. "Poppy's been, quote unquote, discovered by a talent scout who happened to be having dinner where she used to hostess part-time. Not only is she going to be a wine steward at Cory Anthony's latest place, she's been tagged to be the new face of Palette Cosmetics!"

"Easy," said Junie, dodging Keval's utensil. "Here, Keval, eat part of this sticky bun. I can't finish it. Poppy, what's he ranting about?"

But Keval couldn't seem to help himself in his frenzy to be the one to spill the beans. "Am I making this up? Her father told me himself. He was leaving the vet's office with Jackson, and Miss Sweetie and I were on our way in. Miss Sweetie adores Jackson. Anyhoo, between the fabulous new restaurant, the modeling, the private parties, and the jetting off to who knows where—well, I'm just saying. Take a good hard look at her. We might as well say good-bye right now to the Poppy we know and love."

Heath's face paled to the color of the milk in the small pitcher sitting between them.

I'm going to kill my father first, and then Keval, thought Poppy.

"But I was just getting used to having you back," Junie pouted.

She and Junie had been spending more time together since Manolo, the itinerant engineer who'd created Junie's tasting room during last fall's crush, disappeared as mysteriously as he'd arrived.

"We've all missed her," said Keval hurriedly. "But what kind of friends would we be if we stood in the way of what she really wants?"

Red chimed in. "Details, please?"

Keval started to say more, but Red cut him off. "From Poppy, if you don't mind."

Poppy clenched her hands in her lap, her excitement tinged with nerves. "Well, it's far from a sure thing. The Palette people liked my test shots, but they're waiting to see if I pass the test and get the wine steward position. Everything hinges on that. So, I guess we'll just have to wait and see."

"It's a thing now for companies to use a so-called real person with an authentic career in their ads instead of a full-time model," added Keval, stuffing the wad of cinnamon-encrusted dough Junie had given him into his mouth. "What's hotter than a lady somm?" he asked around his mouthful. "Everybody either wants one or wants to be one."

Keval had a way of putting a dramatic spin on things, yet he was right about one thing. The day would come when a somm was a somm. But for now, flaunting women sommeliers was a way for restaurants to get buzz.

Red squealed and hugged Poppy as best she could in the narrow space between the table and the booth. "That's fabulous!"

"Go Poppy!" said Junie from her seat by the window, raising her mug in a salute.

All these premature congratulations made Poppy anxious. She looped her ponytail around her hand again and again until she noticed the right angles poking against the canvas of Heath's backpack. She pounced on the chance to change the subject.

"What's that?" she asked playfully, craning her neck.

"What?" replied Heath.

"That book."

"Nothing. Just a book." He drained his lemonade and wiped his mouth with his napkin.

"Our old high school yearbook," said Red.

Poppy's smile dissolved. "That's ancient history." She had long since thrown her copy in the Dumpster out in the alley behind the café. But not before the senior superlative that yearbook editor Demi Barnes had managed to sneak by the advisor had become fixed in her mind.

After all these years, it still hurt.

Anyone else would have been content to stick with the traditional lines: Best Dressed, Most Likely to Become President, and so forth. Not Demi. She'd had it in for Poppy since seventh grade, when she found out Daryl Decaprio, the guy she had a crush on, was playing Poppy sappy love songs over the phone at night.

In a small town, your senior superlative defined you like an epitaph carved in stone. Except unlike an epitaph, you weren't dead when you got it—you had to live with it for the rest of your life. Demi had used her creative writing skills to create the ultimate parting gibe.

"What made you haul that out of storage now?"

Junie said, "You know Heath. He doesn't like letting go of things."

Heath gave Junie a look, causing her to blush, while Keval fidgeted with his spoon.

"You were saying?" prompted Red, smoothing over Junie's gaffe.

Cautiously, Junie continued. "Our tenth class reunion's coming up. Didn't you get the invitation?"

"I haven't checked e-mail for the past couple days," said Poppy. Lately she'd been spending every free minute studying.

"Well, anyway, Heath and I thought it'd be fun to look at faces. You know, jog our memories. Guess who'll show and who won't."

Heath pulled out his phone, tapped something in, and handed it to Poppy. "Here. Read this."

Instantly, Poppy stiffened. Heath knew her trademark fault better than anyone. How could he put her on the spot like this? Surely everyone around the table could see the signs of rising panic: her shallow breathing, the pink climbing up her neck to her cheeks. She had trouble with the simplest things. Texting. Making grocery lists. Reading instructions. People said, "practice." What they didn't get was, even a word she had read a hundred times could look different the next time.

She swallowed and slid her damp palms down her thighs. *You're not stupid*, she told herself firmly. But her shame at being dyslexic was still paralyzing sometimes, especially when she had to read out loud, in public. And not being able to control her shame made her feel guilty. Inadequacy, shame, guilt—a vicious cycle.

Heath held her gaze. "Go ahead," he said evenly. "You've got this."

She felt his strength seep into her. Haltingly, she reached for the phone and bowed her head over the screen. The letters of the alphabet swam and shifted before coalescing into a pattern of rune-like shapes.

"Deep breath," said Red gently.

Dutifully, she inhaled and attempted to decipher the words. "Clarkston High School Ten-Year Reunion," she read haltingly. "The Radish Rose. Dinner and dancing. RSVP to Demi Barnes, Reunion Committee Chairman."

"First Saturday in December. So, who's in?" asked Red, clasping her hands atop the table.

"I am," sang Keval with a wave of his fingers.

Of course Keval would go to the reunion. Reunions were made for people like him. Following four years of exceptionally awkward adolescence, Keval was a walking "it gets better" ad.

"It'll be good for business," said Junie. "I don't get out enough as it is, what with running both the vineyard and the winery."

Red looked at Poppy. "What about you?"

"Think I'll pass." She handed Heath's phone back and attempted to bolt, but Red stopped her with a hand on her forearm.

"Aw, come on. It'll be fun! Dancing, seeing people you haven't seen in forever..."

"That's after Poppy's test. She might be living in some Portland penthouse overlooking the river by then," said Keval.

Maybe not a penthouse. But she'd better have some place in her sights. If not, that would mean she had flunked the test, failed to get the sommelier position, and was doomed to keep living at home with her parents. And also that Demi had been right about her all along.

"She can come back for it," said Red. "It's only an hour's drive."

That might be true, but learning two new, high-powered jobs and all that went with that was going to require all Poppy's time and energy. It wouldn't be like before, when she could hop in her Mini Coupé and run back to Clarkston on a whim. That made this endeavor all the more nerve-racking—finally leaving her friends and parents behind to really strike out on her own.

Still perched on the edge of the booth, Poppy ventured to ask Heath, "Are you going?"

He shrugged. "Don't know."

Heath had come a long way since his own senior superlative: Most Likely to Blow Something Up. He'd been on the watch list of the Clarkston F.D. since sixth grade, when his attempt to build a geyser with a pack of Mentos, a liter of soda, and duct tape worked a little too well.

Poppy smiled to herself, forgetting her own problems for a moment. Heath had always been somewhat of an enigma. Their teachers used to murmur behind their hands that he was a science prodigy. Who could forget his Edible Skin Layers Cake made from Fruit Roll-Ups (epidermis), Jell-O (dermis), and mini marshmallows (hypodermis)? Rumor was, he'd aced his college boards. Yet he'd tossed out all those scholarship letters without opening them, and now beer drinkers all over the Pacific Northwest couldn't get enough of his ales with names like Newberg Neutral and Ribbon Ridge Red.

When it came to social skills, there was a sweet innocence about Heath that made him hard to get close to.

Given Heath's case of arrested development, Junie didn't waste her breath pressuring him. Everyone knew he'd rather face an angry rattlesnake than make chitchat at a party. Instead she focused on Poppy. "Don't you want to see all the people we went to school with?"

"I've never stopped seeing most of them," replied Poppy. Even during the four years she worked in Portland, she still lived at home. "For everyone else, there's Facebook."

"A lot has happened over the last decade. Some people went away, some got married, had kids, got divorced, won and lost jobs . . ." mused Red. "People change."

"Exactly. That part of my life is behind me. I don't feel the need to see how I'm measuring up."

"But how can it hurt?" pleaded Keval. "Come on, Poppykins. It won't be any fun without you."

She set her jaw. Finally, she said to Heath, "Hand me that yearbook."

Outside, rain pelted the windows, and there was the rumble of distant thunder.

Poppy thumbed through the pages until she found what she was looking for. She laid the open book in the middle of the table and pressed her index finger to the passage that still haunted her.

Red, Junie, and Keval tipped their heads and read silently, while Heath's eyes skittered restlessly around the room like he'd rather be anywhere else but there.

Most likely to still be a Clarkston waitress at our tenth class reunion: Poppy Springer. Poppy's most endearing talent is writing her name backward. She is a true golden retriever at heart, as evidenced by her blond mane and a mind refreshingly free of deep thoughts. Poppy's hobbies are organizing individually wrapped tea bags and leaving a trail of smiling faces wherever she goes.

Following a brief pause, everyone started talking at once.

"Are you serious?"

"Who cares about an old senior superlative?"

"That doesn't define you."

"Who's going to remember that? It was the freaking Stone Age."

Lightning flashed. The café door opened and a tall woman in a silk blouse and pencil skirt blew in, shaking the rain off her umbrella.

Demi Barnes had started out as an assistant at the statehouse down in Salem and worked her way up the ladder. Recently she'd nabbed the job of running their state senator's newly opened Willamette Valley satellite office—quite the achievement.

She paused inside the entrance, combing her fingers through her windblown hair.

Poppy was the only server working until the dinner shift came in at three. It was her job to greet Demi. Yet somehow, she found that her butt was glued to her seat.

When Demi spotted Poppy she started toward her, heels clicking ominously with every step.

From the corner of her eye Poppy saw Heath slam the yearbook shut and slip it into his bag.

"Well, look who." Demi stared down at the splashy orange flower on

Poppy's uniform. "Back working at your parents' café?"

"For now," she replied. The crack in her voice betrayed the scars from Demi's subtle yet razor-sharp bullying, back when they were in school.

"Things didn't work out in Portland?"

Why does Demi always make me feel so inferior? It was her own fault for letting Demi get to her. Inadequacy, shame, guilt.

Somehow, she managed to mask her inner turmoil. "Things worked out fine. I'm just...back home temporarily, until my new job starts."

"Oh, really? What job is that?"

There was a roaring in Poppy's ears, and before she knew it she was back in second grade reading circle at Clarkston Elementary and Demi was laughing at Poppy's stab at reading about Danny O'Dare, the dancin' bear. To this day, though blessed in many ways, on some level she still felt like everyone was always waiting for her to mess up yet again. She looked around the table to see five sets of eyes on her, reflecting every emotion from encouragement to empathy to—in Demi's case—disdain.

Defiance welled up in her. She was tired of being talked down to. Underestimated.

She squared her shoulders and lifted her chin. "I'm going to be a sommelier at Cory Anthony's new restaurant."

Her heart pounded. *What am I saying?*

Demi's jaw dropped. She was speechless.

And Poppy was loving it!

Keval caught Poppy's momentum. A haughty grin spread across his face. "*And* a model. *Boom.*" He punctuated the syllable with his fork.

Demi's eyes swung back to Poppy's, seeking clarification.

"You've heard of Palette Cosmetics?" Poppy tossed her ponytail and stared straight into Demi's treacherous green depths.

I'm already in way over my head. Might as well go all the way.

"They've hired me to be their spokesperson."

What alien being has taken over my body?

As swiftly as Demi had been caught off guard, she recovered. "Isn't that special? You'll definitely have to come to the big class reunion, then! I'm sure everyone will be fascinated when they find out we have a sommelier *and* model in our class. In fact, spreading the word ahead of time might get more people to come."

The faces around the table froze.

Demi sensed weakness like a shark smelled blood. "That is...unless it's not a done deal?"

Keval said, "Oh, it's a done deal. Done as a dog's dinner. Tell anyone you want. Tell the world! Poppy Springer has evolved. Our golden retriever's going to compete at Westminster. Instead of sorting tea bags, she'll be sorting French chardonnay. In place of smiley faces, she'll be the face of—"

"Poppy's going to be a great somm." Compared with Keval's rising hysteria, Heath's voice sounded rock solid.

Poppy wanted to kiss him—even if it did make him squirm.

Red took advantage of the uncomfortable lull to start gathering up her belongings. "Nice to see you, Demi. Poppy, could I scoot out and pay? My next client's coming at two."

"I should get going, too," said Junie, reaching for her own bag.

Poppy let Junie out and remembered that for the time being, her job was pouring nothing stronger than Stumptown's Hairbender. She offered Demi a nearby table.

"Actually, I'm not as hungry as I thought," Demi said. "I've got an idea. We were going to have our reunion meetings at The Radish Rose, but I think this would be a better spot. The next one's scheduled for Tuesday evening. I'm going to go contact the committee. I'm sure they'll all want to hear all the details about your new job."

"I'll look forward to it," said Poppy, her smile feeling as phony as a three-dollar bill.

"Oh, and Heath? I just thought of something else. Get your dad to loan us some potted trees from his nursery. The theme this year is Bacchanalia, and some greenery will be just the thing for that Roman garden look I'm going for. Now, I've got some calls to make."

They watched Demi walk briskly out the door and down the sidewalk, umbrella in one hand, phone in the other.

Poppy's heart sank. If only she had kept her mouth shut! There had never been any expectations of her. She could have gone on working at her parents' café forever, and no one would have thought the less of her.

But now, if her fabulous new life didn't happen, she was going to be the laughingstock of Clarkston.

Chapter 2

"Ow," hissed Keval, rubbing his shin.

"I barely tapped you," replied Heath.

"Next time, try using your words."

"Next time, try not saying every word that comes into your head."

"Can you believe Demi Barnes walked in here just when we were reading Poppy's yearbook superlative?"

"After what she wrote, she's got nerve setting foot in here at all," muttered Heath.

"Nerve is something Demi has in spades. Did you hear her? 'Heath, get your dad to loan us some potted trees,'" Keval mocked. "How'd she ever get that job in Senator Hollin's office, with that kind of diplomacy? That's what I'd like to know." He shuddered. "What are we going to do?"

"Do?"

"About Poppy. You know how she is. She'll never pass a written test without some major academic intervention."

Secretly, Heath hadn't exactly been devastated when he found out Poppy had lost her job at the wine shop. Not that he didn't want her to be happy, but the idea of having her back at the café on a regular basis warmed him inside. No one else made his turkey BLT quite like she did: bacon fried crisp, light on the mayo. He had already started getting excited at the idea of her being present at all the town's big annual events—the post–Memorial Day Hike, the Clarkston Splash in July, and the fall crush celebrations, just like back in the good old days—when Keval broke the news of her plans to leave again in three short months.

He looked up from where he'd been staring into his empty glass. "A waitress at rest tends to stay at rest unless an external force is applied to her. Newton's First Law of Motion."

"That is so nerd."

"Nerd has such a negative connotation. I prefer intellectual badass."

Keval rolled his eyes and glanced over at where Poppy waited on another table. He inclined his head toward Heath's. "You know what I mean."

Heath did know. If not for that hotshot restaurateur who had set his sights on his Poppy, right now the world would be falling back into apple-pie order. But he couldn't exactly share that with Keval. Or with anyone, for that matter.

"Don't make me say it," Keval whispered.

"Say what?" Heath was lost in his fantasy of seeing Poppy's friendly countenance every day again, instead of only glimpses now and then. Not that he couldn't have found her if he'd needed to over the past few years. Her parents' house was right down the road from his. At least there'd been that.

"I love Poppy to pieces. Who doesn't? But let's be real. The eel-whay's inning-spay, but the amster-hay's ead-day."

"Pig Latin. Brilliant. Shoulda been a spy, like Sam."

Keval's eyes grew round. "Is it true what they say? Was Sam really a spy?"

Heath slapped his forehead. "And you think *Poppy* has a short attention span?"

Right before Sam Owens started the consortium, he'd been awarded a chest full of medals for his military service. When asked about he details, he was infuriatingly closemouthed. His reticence had turned speculation about his past into one of the town's favorite ongoing pastimes.

"Why are you asking me?"

Keval sat back and folded his arms. "Heath Sinclair, that is a hedge if I ever heard one. You're one of Sam's best friends. I knew it. I always said—"

"Forget Sam. Back to Poppy. You're right about her."

"Then you admit it—she's in way over her head."

"No." Heath instinctively rushed to Poppy's defense. Fate had first thrown them together when they were barely tall enough for the carnival rides at the Yamhill County Fair. Over time, they'd grown as thick as the tangled roots on one of his dad's overgrown perennials, and just as hard to separate. He knew her limitations better than anybody.

On the other hand, he couldn't deny that Keval had a point. "Maybe. Poppy might not be well-read, but she's not dumb. What I meant was, I agree she's going to need help."

He stopped short of volunteering himself. The truth was, he didn't want Poppy to pass that test. He wanted her to stay right there in Clarkston.

Keval, on the other hand, was plenty smart, but he didn't have the patience to spend hours tutoring Poppy. Heath felt safe bouncing the ball back to him. He gave Keval a penetrating look.

Keval glanced over his shoulder. "Are you looking at me?"

"Why not? Aren't you the cybermayor of Clarkston?"

"Just because I do promo for a wine consortium doesn't mean I know diddly-squat about wine. You were the one who held her hand all through school. With all due respect, if not for you, Poppy still wouldn't have graduated. And now you're in the beverage business. You're a shoo-in."

"I'm a brewer, not a winemaker." Heath's highly tuned olfactory senses worked as well for wine as for beer. But Keval didn't have to know that.

"Shhh—here she comes."

Poppy approached sporting her usual winning smile despite the incident with Demi minutes earlier.

Heath braced himself for her unique blend of orange blossom, jasmine, and sandalwood—a blend that never failed to stimulate a rush of cortisol and adrenaline in his blood.

"Anything else, guys? More water? Lemonade?"

"Aren't you upset?" Keval blurted. "I can't believe you just told Cruella de Clarkston that you already got the sommelier and the modeling jobs. What are you going to do if you don't pass your test?"

So much for zipping it, thought Heath. "No one would know anything about this if you had so much as an atom of self-control."

Keval's mouth crinkled into a suitably sheepish expression. "The news was bound to come out sooner or later."

Heath sighed and scrubbed a hand over his face.

"I'll think of something," Poppy replied. Her smile remained steadfast though her eyes sparkled wetly. Then her lips quivered as she gulped unshed tears. "Somehow."

Chapter 3

"Hey, boss."

Heath's marketing manager, John, stuck his head in Heath's office on his way back from lunch.

"I'm free to fill you in on yesterday's Brewer's Guild meeting whenever you are."

Heath looked up from the spreadsheet he'd been studying, rocked back in his chair, and locked his fingers behind his head. "How'd it go?"

"Same as last month. It was all about brewpubs again. That's all anyone wanted to talk about."

Heath sighed. "Sounds like a song on repeat."

For months, John had been trying to convince Heath to open a bar in the front of the brewery where they could serve their own brands on tap. And he wasn't the only one. Sam Owens had been hammering him, too.

Across from Heath's desk, John perched on the arm of a chair. "Think of the bucks we're missing out on. We can charge more per pint in our own bar than we can sell it at through our distributor. Not only that, in case you didn't notice, you're becoming a one-man cult. Your customers want to meet the brewer. They want to know *you*."

"*We're* becoming a cult," Heath corrected him, scooting his chair back in. "We, not me. I didn't build this business by myself. And I didn't start out brewing beer for the notoriety. I like to keep a low profile."

He bowed his head over his spreadsheet again, signaling the conversation was over.

John pressed his lips together. "Ironically, the fact that you've always flown under the radar has made you in even bigger demand. Like it or not, you've become a recognized brand. We should have a point of destination where people can sample everything on the line."

"We're doing fine without a bar," said Heath, without looking up.

"We could do even better. When's the last time you went on a good pub crawl?"

In the early years of setting up his business, Heath had been in countless ale houses. But these days, Clarkston Craft Ales's phenomenal rise had him spending more time crunching numbers and plotting the next big idea with his brew team.

"What say you drive over to the city with me for the next guild meeting. We can spend the afternoon checking out the competition."

"That's what I got you for."

Wearily, John got up and turned to leave, but lingered in the doorway.

Heath looked up. "That it?"

John gave the wall a resigned slap. "That's it."

When the sound of John's steps faded away, Heath sat back and scratched his head.

Both John and Sam had excellent business sense, and they weren't the only ones raving about brewpubs. He might not travel much, but he kept his subscriptions to the industry journals up to date.

But the thought of his own bar—schmoozing and posing for strangers' selfies—made him wince. His comfort zone was right here, behind the scenes.

Besides, what with checking on his dad every day, he had a full plate.

John was right about one thing, though. It wouldn't hurt to drag himself out of his lair and take a trip up to the PDX soon. It was long overdue.

* * * *

A warm front had swept in on the heels of yesterday's storm, leaving the autumn air feeling almost balmy.

Fifteen feet up, in the wide-reaching arms of an oak, Heath flipped on the string of white lights hanging along the roofline of the tree house he'd started hammering together when he was eight years old, after his world fell apart.

He stood back, imagining how this place would look today through Poppy's eyes.

When Keval wussed out at the café, there had been nothing else to do but step up to the plate. No way could he resist those tears that Poppy tried to hide.

Still, this wasn't going to be easy.

He ran some water into a plastic cup with the name of one of his best-selling ales emblazoned on the side and watered the ivy hanging from a macramé cord.

Heath didn't deal well with change. Not even good change.

The success of his brewery operation had been completely unexpected. He had never set out to be named one of the most successful craft brewers under thirty in the Pacific Northwest. At least once a week, someone asked him what he was still doing in tiny Clarkston, why he didn't move to the city. It was a logical question. Portland was the home of more breweries than any other city on earth. The consensus was that he ought to take his rightful place.

But Heath didn't want to move to Portland. He didn't want to move anywhere. All he wanted to do was experiment with his kettles and hydrometers and quietly run his business.

Anyway, to his way of thinking, being the only beer producer in a wine town was an advantage, not a handicap.

First thing he'd done when he could afford it was put away enough for Dad to live on when he finally retired from his tree nursery.

Next, he started building himself a *real* house on the land he'd been trespassing on since he was a kid.

The thought of Poppy coming up here tonight weirded him out. He'd had a few guys here, back in the days of skinned knees and hide-and-seek. But it had been a long, long time since anyone other than himself had stepped across the threshold.

But what else could he do? Poppy needed help. And they had an unspoken arrangement that stretched back years.

A fat yellow feline twined through his legs. She'd been a starving kitten when Heath first heard pathetic cries coming from the weeds along the edge of the Albertson's parking lot in McMinnville on a sweltering July day. After unloading the week's worth of food for him and his dad that he'd been carrying into his car, he'd gone back to investigate and found two terrified gray eyes staring up at him through the grate of a storm drain. He'd endured her wailing for two hours until someone from the county public works with the right tools finally came out and took the grate off. The loss of the meat and ice cream sitting in his hot car all that time had been worth it.

He named the kitten Vienna, after a trip he'd taken to learn about Austrian beer. That's where he saw an orphanage with a revolving crib built into its wall. Back in medieval times, when an abandoned baby was placed in the outside half of the crib and a bell rang, the monks inside would go retrieve it.

That's also what had given him the idea to cut a garage-sized hole in the wall of his tree house so that he could roll his double bed in and out, as weather permitted.

It was already October. There wouldn't be many more nights as warm as this one. It'd be a shame to stay inside. He rolled the bed out onto the porch then stood back looking at it, frowning. The tree house wasn't designed with company in mind.

Why was he obsessing? It was only Poppy.

The purple comforter looked wrinkled. He whipped it off, shook it a few times, and spread it carefully back on the bed.

There. That looked better.

Heath bent to stroke Vienna's soft fur, and she shut her eyes, bowed her head, and purred her appreciation. "That's all this is tonight, Vienna. A mercy mission."

He could still remember the first time Poppy had come to his rescue. Sam Owens's seventh birthday party. Heath's dad had to promise him yet another trip to the Museum of Science and Industry just to get him in the car. Even then, he'd sat with his arms folded tightly across his chest the whole way over to Sam's house.

Once Dad pulled away from the curb, Heath hid behind the sycamore tree in Sam's front yard, stealing an occasional peek toward the jungle gym where all the other kids clamored and shouted.

Outside, Guinness and Amber started barking, shaking Heath out of his reverie.

"Heath?" called Poppy, her voice carrying up from the wooded path, bringing him fully back to the present.

He held back the beaded curtain and peered down to see his pit bull mutts blocking the path. Beyond the dogs, in a swirl of fallen leaves, stood a vision in a jeans jacket over a long white dress. A slouchy patchwork bag was slung over her shoulder. The setting sun filtered through her skirt, outlining the shape of her legs, triggering an inappropriate tug of desire he pretended not to notice.

"Amber. Guinness. Come."

Tongues lolling happily, the dogs turned tail and galloped up the steep ramp Heath had built for him, first Amber and then Guinness on his three good legs. Both looked like completely different animals from the trembling, sad-eyed mutts Heath had found cowering at the shelter.

Poppy nodded toward the glass-and-steel structure up on the hill that was partially visible through the trees, now that the leaves had started to fall. "How's the new place? Did you move in yet?"

"Couple months ago."

"How's your dad doing since you moved out?"

For the past nineteen years, it had been just Heath and his dad in the old house, a stone's throw away. It looked exactly the same today as when Mom left. Heath had offered to take him shopping to buy some new things, but

Dad wasn't interested in making any changes. Heath felt guilty leaving, but he was tired of living in a shrine. Besides, a man needed his own place.

"Helps that I'm right next door."

"I'll bet." Her candy-pink lips widened into a complicit grin. "Remember that time Old Man Waters chased us out of here?"

"Summer between tenth and eleventh." How could he forget? He had snitched four beers from the fridge, lodging two among the rocks in the creek to keep them cold. He and Poppy were sitting on a felled log dangling bare toes in the water, feeling very grown-up holding their beers when Mr. Waters had come stumbling down the bank with a raised fist, yelling for them to get off his property. They had hightailed it out of there in a hurry, sloshing beer in their wake, laughing so hard they doubled over, panting with relief by the time they reached Heath's property and safety. Was it their fault the finest swimming hole on the creek happened to be on private property?

Since then, Heath had bought out Waters for a fair price and had his ramshackle old house bulldozed. Now this entire hillside belonged to him.

Poppy stood at the base of the tree, looking around at the rope hammocks slung between branches, the fire ring Heath had built from fieldstone, and the brightly colored Adirondack chairs. "It looks way different than it did back then."

"I've fixed it up over the years. Guess you could call it a hobby. Come on up."

She climbed the boards nailed to the tree and emerged through the curtain, sending a thousand beads clacking.

He sniffed the air for her intoxicating scent.

Tonight, the citrus topnote was diluted by the breeze, leaving him wanting more.

Poppy took a step in the direction of the opening in the wall and peered out toward the green Chehalem. "Is the rope we used to swing on still down there?"

"Still there. Been, what—twenty years? Don't know if I'd trust it. Probably pretty deteriorated."

Poppy's leg nudged the bed, inadvertently causing it to roll an inch.

"It's on wheels!"

"Casters." He demonstrated by rolling it back and forth a little. "I made it mobile, so you can fall asleep looking at the stars." No sooner had the words left his mouth than his face grew hot with their implied meaning. "Not *you*—"

Poppy smiled softly and turned her attention to the tree house's interior. That was one of the things that made Poppy so great. She pretended not to notice when he stuck his foot in his mouth, which he tended to do every other sentence.

"If it looks like rain, I roll the bed inside and close the shutters."

"You've got a little galley kitchen and everything."

Heath pushed a button on a remote and the small screen hung high in a corner flickered on. He turned that off, pushed another switch, and music filled the tree house.

"Sweet," breathed Poppy, nodding with appreciation as she continued to look around.

Heath kept his expression neutral, but deep inside, he glowed at her approval.

Amber loped back down the ramp. Poppy bent to pet Guinness, curled up on the rug. "This would be a great place for a party!"

"You know how I am at parties."

Their eyes met, recalling as one the day when she had noticed him standing alone under that sycamore tree at Sam's birthday party, taken him by the hand, and led him over to where the others played.

Even in second grade, Poppy had never had to think twice about what to do, what to say, or how to act around people. It was her gift, just like Heath was driven to understand how things like temperature and pressure and the other forces of nature acted on matter, the stuff of the universe.

"This is my getaway. It's where I go when things get crazy."

She nodded in understanding.

Even when they were kids, she had accepted without judging that he was better one-on-one than in big groups.

"Look," she said, backtracking toward the curtain, sidestepping Guinness's bulk, "I appreciate you asking me here. But you're really busy, what with building a new house and running your business. We don't have to do this...."

"If I didn't want to, I wouldn't have offered."

"Are you sure?"

He lowered himself onto the bed and swatted the mattress. "Sit down. Show me what you got. I mean, your stuff. Er, you know what I mean."

Her childlike enthusiasm returning, she hopped up across from him, crossed her long legs in front of her, and pulled some folders from her bag.

"First, here's the multiple-choice exam I already passed."

Heath's eyes zoomed in on her grade, circled in red.

"Sixty-six?" he exclaimed, the words slipping out before he could catch them. "What's passing?"

"Sixty. I didn't say I aced it, I said I passed."

Barely.

"Okay. What's next?"

"Sitting for my Certified Sommelier Exam, the test I need to get my new job. If I don't take it within three years of passing the first one, I have to start all over."

"It all sounds very professional."

"It's pretty intense."

"But didn't you say the restaurant's opening in three months?"

"Now you get why I'm so stressed. Here, look."

He read aloud from the page she gave him. "'Part One. Table Service. Recommend, select, prepare, and serve wine in the appropriate glassware with skill and diplomacy.'"

"Diplomacy? You've got that nailed." Poppy was at ease around all types of people.

She shrugged. "I've been waiting on customers my whole life. But I need more practice popping champagne corks without putting someone's eye out and pouring the bottle evenly on my first trip around the table. The biggest assortment of wines in town is at the consortium. I told Sam I'd foot the bill if he agreed to proctor some mock tastings. Will you be one of my pretend customers?"

That sounded simple enough. "Tell me what to do."

"I'll recruit enough people to fill up the table and hand out information about all the wines ahead of time. All you have to do is act like finicky diners. Challenge me to figure out which wine you want by asking probing questions, and I'll try to guess what it is and serve it."

"Could probably get Holly and Junie to come. They know a lot about wine."

"Great idea. So, we're good on table service. Keep reading."

"'Part Two, Practical Tasting. Identify six different wines, tasted blind.' How are you on that?"

"It's a matter of naming three whites and three reds in twenty-five minutes. I just need someone to pick and pour the wines so that I can't see the labels, and then I'll try to determine what they are."

"I've done that. It's the same as tasting ales."

"Then comes Part Three, the part I'm nervous about. I have to write about the classic regions, grapes, and terms."

This was where things got tricky, thought Heath. "You must have learned a lot working in the wine shop or you wouldn't have started down this road."

"I memorized pictures and terms from studying labels. Having visuals to go with the words really helps. But there was no pressure. I could take my time. And I didn't have to write anything."

Heath recalled a game they used to play in Mr. Lu's class. One student left the room. Another hid. Then the first student came back and had to guess who had hidden.

"You always killed in that Who's Missing game."

"Training myself to be good at memorization was the only way I managed to get through school. But you know that."

Heath did know. He'd tutored her on and off for years in exchange for her smoothing the way for him at school and parties. If not for her, his social life would be as empty as his home life.

He leafed through the rest of the folder. "You'd think they would come up with a way for people to take the wine steward test orally."

"This isn't public school. The governing body for sommeliers might allow that, eventually. But I don't have time to wait. It's on me to adapt, or else it's back to the café. Back to square one."

"'Part Three, Theory, examines comprehensive knowledge of wines and wine production. Candidates are given one hour to complete a written exam.'"

"Here's a sample question," said Poppy, pulling a paper from the sheaf.

"'Define and compare the following viticulture practices: sustainable, organic, and biodynamic.'" Lowering the paper, he frowned. Poppy knew her limitations, otherwise she wouldn't be here, asking for help. Still, he was a realist. "Writing aside, can you talk about this stuff?"

She chuckled. "All day long. It's reading the questions and writing the answers in the time allotted that gives me a problem."

"Obviously you're going to memorize the sample questions. What do you want me to do?"

"I'll dig up material that I think will be on the test. You make up questions based on that and quiz me orally. I'm not nervous around you. I'll be able to take my time coming up with answers. I'll write everything down as I go and then read back over it on my own until I have it down cold."

More than once, Heath had seen Poppy break down in tears over the most basic written assignment. He skimmed over the rest of the questions with growing doubt. This exam was no walk in the park, even for someone without dyslexia. He could feel her eyes on him, waiting for a response.

"Well? What do you think?" she pressed, looking worried.

"I don't know..."

He felt the mattress shift as she sat back, discouraged. "You think I've bitten off more than I can chew."

Now was his golden opportunity. Without realizing it, Poppy had just dangled the key to his future within his grasp. All he had to do was reach out and take it.

She couldn't pass this test without his help. If he refused, she wouldn't be going anywhere. He'd have her right there where he wanted her. Thanks to all they'd been through together, she trusted him implicitly. Whatever came out of his mouth next she would do, without question.

He'd be a fool to throw this chance away.

Tasting victory, he plunged ahead before his conscience could intervene. "Look . . . you're right. This is a bad time. Building the house has already taken me away from the creative side of the brewery for too long. I need to catch up. Plus, I've got development targets, marketing goals . . ." He pushed back the lock of hair that was always falling into his eyes, tempering his rejection with a wry grin. "Can't even find time for a haircut."

"I understand," she said with a quiet resignation that nearly ripped a hole in his heart.

She began gathering her scattered papers into a pile as he tried to quell the rising panic inside him.

No. He couldn't do this. She had just arrived at his tree house, and now she was leaving. He had to drag this out until he came up with a better solution.

"What's wrong with Clarkston?" he asked, provoking an argument. Anything to make her stay.

She stopped what she was doing. "Nothing's wrong, it's just that I need to move on."

"Why? Because of some dumb thing someone put in the yearbook?"

She turned on him, red-faced. "It's not just 'some dumb thing'! It's me. Or what people think of me, anyway. 'Stupid Poppy.'"

Exasperated, she began cramming her messy pile into her bag.

"Have you thought about looking for another hostess job or a wine steward position that'll take you on the basis of the test you already passed?"

She shook her head as she yanked her overstuffed bag, papers peeking out of it, onto her shoulder. "That's okay. I'll figure it out."

"If it's just about being in Portland, you could find work as a server tomorrow, even without your certification."

She avoided meeting his eyes. "I'd be working at least forty hours per week, with no prospects for advancement. I'm better off working thirty at the café, studying in my off hours, and saving money by living at home. Besides—" She stooped to retrieve a paper that had slipped onto the plank floor.

"What?"

"I promised Red I'd model in her fashion show."

Something in her tone caught his attention.

"Fashion show?"

Cautiously, her eyes met his. "It's a benefit. You know, for people going through hard times. And people who are sick."

They shared a look full of meaning. Heath knew all about hard times... serious illness.

She hiked up the strap on her bag that was slipping down her arm. "There was no reason to bring it up before. No sense in dredging up bad memories."

Hayden. He'd died years ago. But it hadn't ended there. The death of his twin had shattered the family to pieces. When no one else could—or would—look out for Heath, the Springers had stepped up to the plate without a second thought. And now Poppy was *still* protecting him.

And here he was, making her believe she was incapable of reaching her dream so that he wouldn't have to face her leaving. Who was the *real* loser?

"Anyway, I promised. Figured it'd make me feel useful while I'm stuck here, studying for my exam."

She unfolded her fawnlike legs and set one foot on the floor.

"Wait."

She stopped in the midst of hoisting her body off the bed and looked up at him.

"I'll coach you."

"Really?" Slowly, she sank back down.

If she failed, he would have himself to blame. That only added to the cost. But if life had doled him out his share of tragedy, it had also given him broad shoulders. And the hope in her eyes was worth missing a few meetings. Even having to face a life without her, if that's what it took to make her happy.

"It would mean so much to me, Heath."

"I'm not gonna lie. It's going to be tough."

Poppy threw her arms around him, catching him off guard.

Behind her, his hands hovered inches over her back while his preganglionic sympathetic nerves released acetylcholine, speeding up his heart rate, stirring stagnant blood, and tightening his muscles in the textbook "fight or flight" response.

"Stay and love" had never been one of the options.

Tentatively, his palms came down on her silky hair. Her sweet, tart scent filled his senses...her body was warm and lithe, pressed up against his.

It wasn't the raw, sensual attraction itself that terrified him. He might be a klutz at cocktail parties, but he didn't need the lights on to find his way around the bedroom.

It was that these were *Poppy's* arms gripping him in a stranglehold...little Poppy, who had talked his ear off after school at her parents' café until his dad got home from work.

Poppy, whose incessant chatter at the science club meetings his dad insisted they invite her to in return made everyone lose track of their experiments.

She pulled back until her hands rested on his shoulders.

"How soon can you do a mock tasting?"

It took him a second to remember what they were there for.

"What about that reunion meeting next week? You told Demi you already got the job. How are you going to fix that?"

Poppy's hands slid into her lap, leaving him feeling relieved and at the same time, robbed of something priceless.

"I got a little carried away there, didn't I?" She laughed drily. "I figure the best thing to do is dial it back a bit—admit to Demi the fact that I have to take a little test as a requirement for the new job. I don't have to add that I happen to be scared out of my mind about it."

"Watch out. Demi Barnes is a ballbuster."

But Poppy was already on her feet, her usual, sunny grin restored. "Thankfully, most people aren't like Demi. I'm hoping there'll be some friendly faces on the reunion committee."

Heath wasn't nearly as optimistic as she was. But then, who was? "Just saying. Be careful, and don't let anything Demi says bother you. You're smarter than you think."

She put one foot below the other as she climbed down the ladder with the burden of her satchel. Despite her disability, she was so bold, so brave.

"Careful," he called, wishing he could wrap her in a cocoon of protection wherever she went.

Watching her shoes stir up the new-fallen leaves as she made her way back up the path, his heart squeezed. Poppy had always been there for him. He would do whatever he could to help her pass this test, even if it meant losing the best friend he'd ever had.

A TASTE OF CHARDONNAY

Join author Heather Heyford as she uncorks a sparkling new series following the St. Pierre sisters, heiresses to a Napa wine fortune who are toasting the good life and are thirsty for love...

Chardonnay St. Pierre's father is as infamous for his scandals as he is famous for his wine, and it's up to Char to restore the family name. The Challenge, an elite charity competition held in Napa, seems like the perfect opportunity for the socialite to cement her image as a philanthropist. But all eyes—including Char's—are on the Hollywood heartthrob who's also entered the race...

Long before his face was splashed across the gossip magazines, Ryder McBride grew up in a working-class family in Napa. He knows all about the St. Pierre sisters and their notorious father, and when he learns he'll be up against Char in The Challenge, he assumes the grape doesn't fall far from the vine. But the more they get to know one another, the more they begin to realize that nothing pairs better with a heated rivalry than a healthy pour of flirtation...

A TASTE OF MERLOT

Raise your glass and join Heather Heyford as she pours a second serving in her series following these headstrong wine heiresses in their quest to strike out on their own...

Merlot St. Pierre is struggling to break free from her family name. Her college classmates whisper behind her back that her passion for jewelry design is little more than a hobby, since she'll always have her father's fortune. But Meri is determined to prove them wrong, and with the help of a handsome jewelry buyer, she just may taste her first sip of success—as long as she can hide who she really is...

Mark Newman's family owns a chain of high-end jewelry stores, and he's working hard to get out from under his aunt's thumb and prove he has a good eye *and* a head for business. He's certain Meri's designs could be the next big thing, but he'll have to convince her that she can use her famous last name to her advantage. As their business partnership takes root, an attraction begins to flourish—but they'll both find that love, like wine, takes time to perfect...

A TASTE OF SAUVIGNON

Join Heather Heyford as she returns to Napa for a third taste in her series following three wine heiresses, each as vibrant and unique as the grapes for which they were named...

Sauvignon St. Pierre has always been fiercely ambitious. She easily could've cashed in on her family's fortune, but instead she struck out on her own, breezed through law school, and landed a job at a small firm in Napa. Savvy's life is as tidy and straightforward as her sizable collection of little black dresses, and she likes it that way—but every now and then, she can't help but long for her first sip of love...

After a chance encounter with Esteban Morales, the *caliente* son of Papa St. Pierre's long-time rival, something inside Savvy wakes up. It could be that Esteban's interest in cultivating lavender appeals to her passion for perfumery. But there's something else about the charming but down-to-earth farmer that she simply can't resist. They both know their families are an unlikely pairing, but together, Savvy and Esteban just may be the ideal varietals for a perfect blend...

A TASTE OF SAKE

As author Heather Heyford pours a final glass in her series following three Napa wine heiresses, a newcomer must work her way into a tightly-knit family whose bond has been fermenting for years...

Though they each have their own ambitions and are known to be competitive—even with one another—the St. Pierre sisters are fiercely loyal. Chardonnay and Merlot are thrilled about Sauvignon's wedding day, and it's slated to be the soirée of the decade among Napa's most elite residents. Given the family's notoriety, it almost stands to reason that their eccentric father, Xavier, would arrive by helicopter. But no one could have anticipated the wedding surprise he'd brought along with him...

The product of one of Xavier's many affairs, Sake is introduced as the half-Japanese sister the St. Pierre girls never knew they had. She struggles to break into clique-ish Napa society—and getting in with her sisters is proving more difficult than nabbing a '74 Cabernet. It seems only high-end realtor Bill Diamond can tell there's more to Sake than meets the eye. Afraid of repeating her mother's mistakes, Sake just hopes that getting drunk on love won't leave her with a hangover of rejection...

Meet the Author

Heather Heyford learned to walk and talk in Texas, then moved to England. *("Y'all want some scones?")* While in Europe, Heather was forced by her cruel parents to spend Saturdays in the leopard vinyl back seat of their Peugeot, motoring from one medieval pile to the next for the lame purpose of "learning something." What she soon learned was how to allay the boredom by stashing a *Cosmo* under the seat. Now a recovering teacher, Heather writes romance novels set in the wine country. She is represented by the Nancy Yost Literary Agency.